PRAISE FOR

Allergic to Death

"[A] delicious, de-liteful debut. Gigi is a heartfelt protagonist with calories to spare. Tasty food, a titillating story, and a spicy town and theater, rife with dramatic pause. Add a dash of romance, and you have the recipe for a successful series."

—Avery Aames, Agatha Award–winning
author of the Cheese Shop Mysteries

"Full of colorful characters, delicious diet foods, a rescued dog, and an intriguing mystery, *Allergic to Death* is tasty entertainment."

—Melinda Wells, author of the Della Cooks Mysteries

"The meals that Gigi Fitzgerald makes may be low in calories, but author Peg Cochran serves up a full meal in her debut book."

—Sheila Connolly, *New York Times* bestselling
author of the Orchard Mysteries

"A delicious amateur-sleuth tale . . . Culinary cozy fans will take De-Lite with Peg Cochran's first recipe."

—*Genre Go Round Reviews*

Steamed to Death

Peg Cochran

BERKLEY PRIME CRIME, NEW YORK

THE BERKLEY PUBLISHING GROUP
Published by the Penguin Group
Penguin Group (USA) Inc.
375 Hudson Street, New York, New York 10014, USA

USA | Canada | UK | Ireland | Australia | New Zealand | India | South Africa | China

Penguin Books Ltd., Registered Offices: 80 Strand, London WC2R 0RL, England
For more information about the Penguin Group, visit penguin.com.

STEAMED TO DEATH

A Berkley Prime Crime Book / published by arrangement with the author

Berkley Prime Crime Books are published by The Berkley Publishing Group.
BERKLEY® PRIME CRIME and the PRIME CRIME logo are trademarks
of Penguin Group (USA) Inc.

For information, address: The Berkley Publishing Group,
a division of Penguin Group (USA) Inc.,
375 Hudson Street, New York, New York 10014.

ISBN: 978-0-425-25220-8

PUBLISHING HISTORY
Berkley Prime Crime mass-market edition / June 2013

PRINTED IN THE UNITED STATES OF AMERICA

10 9 8 7 6 5 4 3 2 1

Cover illustration by Teresa Fasolino.
Cover design by Sarah Oberrender.

ALWAYS LEARNING   PEARSON

To my readers who took a chance on a new writer and purchased my first book. I hope you will enjoy this one as well.

Acknowledgments

First, I want to thank my editor, Faith Black, and my agent, Jessica Faust, for all their help in launching my writing career.

I'd like to thank my writing buds—Avery Aames, Laura Alden, Janet Bolin, Krista Davis, Kaye George and Marilyn Levinson—for their brainstorming, hand-holding, plot ideas, encouragement, support and stories that made me laugh.

And, of course, my family for their support and patience through the sometimes difficult process of producing a manuscript!

Chapter 1

Giovanna "Gigi" Fitzgerald was relishing the bite of her newly sharpened chef's knife in the plump, ripe neck of the zucchini lying on her cutting board when she noticed an ominous sign. A very ominous sign.

Water was puddling on the floor by her feet, and the miniature lake was spreading by the second. Within moments it was lapping at the toes of Gigi's sneakers.

The water was coming from the cupboard under the sink. She opened the door cautiously and bolted backward as water sprayed out, soaking the legs of her jeans and enlarging the creeping flood on her floor.

Her cottage was old but in decent shape. Gigi had spent several hundred dollars on an inspection before signing the papers that put the charming, hundred-year-old house in her name. Not that the inspection really made any difference. She'd been determined to have the cottage no matter what—it was the first place she'd felt at home in many years.

She knelt down and, shielding her eyes from the spritzing water, examined the pipe. It was caked with rust and looked to be original to the house. Maybe if she'd paid the inspector more he would have taken the trouble to bend down and examine the plumbing under the sink?

Gigi sighed. The timing couldn't be worse. She was in the midst of preparing some test recipes for Branston Foods. They were interested in producing a line of Gigi's Gourmet De-Lite Dinners, and she had to create a number of dishes that would translate well to being flash frozen and stuffed into a cardboard container.

And she had all the hors d'oeuvres to create for Felicity Davenport's upcoming party to celebrate the fact that her soap opera, *For Better or For Worse*, had won the newly created Merrill Award. Felicity had originally hired Gigi to help her lose weight. Felicity had joined the cast of the soap in her twenties and had quickly become the star, but now, in her forties, she'd found that creeping middle-aged weight gain was not making her any more attractive to the camera.

Felicity had also hired Gigi's best friend, Sienna Paisley, to organize her comeback campaign, which would launch when Felicity was ready to emerge, like a butterfly from its chrysalis, having lost twenty pounds and been made over from head to toe. Sienna had given up a six-figure income as a publicist to move to Woodstone, Connecticut, to run the Book Nook and hopefully, start a family. Her husband Oliver's new law practice had been slow to take off, and they needed the income.

Gigi supposed she ought to turn the water off at the source. She remembered that there was a valve of some sort in the basement. She dried her hands on her jeans and headed down the dark, winding staircase.

Gigi found the control after several false starts. The knob

was covered with cobwebs, and she shuddered as the thin strands tickled the backs of her hands.

There. The water was off. That would at least stop the lake that was slowly forming on her kitchen floor.

Gigi climbed the stairs back to the kitchen, swiping at the insistent cobwebs still clinging to her hair. She retrieved the phone book from her desk drawer and ran her finger down the listing marked "Plumbers."

There were two. No one answered at the first location. Gigi listened to the brief message before clicking off. She glanced at the phone book again. It looked like it would have to be Hector's Plumbing and Heating.

"Pipe's sprung a leak," Jackson, or at least that was the name embroidered above the pocket on his shirt, said, rising from his knees.

Gigi bit back a sharp retort. "Really?" she said with only a hint of sarcasm.

Jackson nodded his head. "Yup. Big leak. The pipe's all rusted out." He knelt down again, his knees giving a creak that sounded like a gunshot. He opened the cupboard door and stuck his index finger through a hole in the pipe. "You need a new pipe," he concluded.

"Can you replace it for me?"

"Gotta order it first."

"How long will that take?" Gigi twirled a strand of auburn hair around her finger—something she always did when she was stressed.

"Dunno. A couple of days maybe."

Gigi groaned. "But I can't wait that long. Isn't there something you could do temporarily?"

"Like what?"

I don't know, you're the plumber, Gigi wanted to say, but she bit her tongue again. "Like maybe a patch or something?"

"Wouldn't hold."

Gigi felt like stamping her foot. There had to be something that could be done!

Jackson took a dog-eared pad from his back pocket. "Do you want me to order the pipe for you?"

"Yes," Gigi all but screamed. "Obviously there's no alternative."

Jackson looked confused.

Gigi gestured toward the paper in his hand. "Yes," she repeated. "Please order the pipe for me."

Jackson licked the end of his pencil and laboriously penned a note.

"Want me to call you when it comes in?"

"Of course."

"It's just a leak. Nothing to get all worked up about," Jackson said, replacing the notepad and pencil in his pocket. "We'll have it fixed for you in no time," he called over his shoulder as he left.

No time! Gigi thought. She wondered what sort of eternity *no time* amounted to. She paced the kitchen, furiously darting evil glances at the offending pipe. She had to have her kitchen back. There was only so much she could do without water. Correction. She couldn't do anything without water. She felt panic rising in her throat like a tidal wave. She stared at the vegetables spread out across her worktable. They all needed to be washed before she could do anything with them. Fortunately, Felicity was her only client at the moment. She'd offered a sum handsome enough for Gigi to take a break from providing meals for upward of a dozen people at a time. And she'd asked Gigi to prepare light and tasty hors d'oeuvres for the huge bash she was planning. The entire local "A" list had been invited along with a smattering of New York people plus Felicity's manager, leading man, and costar. Woodstone had been buzzing about the event for weeks. Gigi had enlisted Alice, who worked part-time at the police department, to help.

The phone rang, and for one delusional minute Gigi thought it might be Jackson calling to say the new piece of pipe had arrived, and he'd be right over to install it. Of course, in reality, Jackson was probably still in her driveway trying to fit his key into the lock of his truck door.

Gigi grabbed the receiver. "Hello?"

"Gigi? It's Felicity." Gigi recognized the actress's fruity tones and well-practiced modulation even without the introduction.

Gigi groaned. What was she going to say if Felicity asked her how things were going? She'd always been taught that honesty was the best policy, but more than once that had landed her in hot water.

"Actually, Felicity, I'm in a bit of a bind. My kitchen pipe sprang a leak, and the plumber won't be able to fix it for several days."

Felicity made a sound that Gigi took to mean she was sorry to hear that, but then Felicity quickly plowed ahead with what she had planned to say herself. "Listen, some of our guests for the party are arriving early, and a few may be spending a day or two with us afterward. It's turning into something of a house party since we're all currently on hiatus from the show. Our housekeeper normally does the cooking for me and Jack, and it's perfectly fine, but I'd like to offer my friends something a notch above. Is there any chance you'll consider acting as chef for a few days?"

"Ah . . . ah . . . sure," Gigi stuttered.

"It would probably be easiest if you just moved in temporarily. My kitchen is state-of-the-art, and I have a very comfortable spare bedroom you should find suitable."

"I don't know . . . I can't leave Reg—he's my dog—alone—"

"Bring him," Felicity said in a voice that clearly brooked no opposition. "We've a golden, and she's pining for some canine companionship."

That was that, then, Gigi thought as she stuffed some clothes into an overnight bag. Reg, her West Highland white terrier, hovered around her legs, weaving in and out and making the process take twice as long as necessary. "Don't worry, you're going, too." Gigi bent down to scratch his ears. "Felicity is a big dog lover and insisted you come along."

Reg watched as Gigi shoved a worn pair of jeans into the suitcase. He tilted his head to one side and fixed her with a beady stare.

To Gigi it looked as if he were saying, *Why are you bringing those old things with you?* If she hadn't sunk all her money into the purchase of the cottage, perhaps she could update her wardrobe. She drooled every time she went past the window of Abigail's on High Street. But she didn't regret her decision—not for a minute. And with the deal with Branston Foods actually looking as if it would go through, she'd soon have a bit more leeway when it came to spending money.

Gigi heaved her weekend bag into the trunk of her bright red MINI Cooper and settled Reggie in the front seat. He immediately stuck his head out the partially opened window, but then pulled it back when he discovered there wasn't any breeze.

Gigi gave a last backward glance at her cottage. She'd watered the asters in the planter, swept the steps and put out the fat pumpkin she'd purchased at the local farmer's market. She hated leaving her cozy little home, but there was no help for it. Without water, she was up a creek. Although perhaps that wasn't the most apt analogy!

Gigi glanced at the front windows of the Book Nook as she drove down High Street. She knew Sienna wasn't there—Felicity had given her a small office on the third floor of her house to work in. Sienna had rather reluctantly left the reins of the shop in the hands of Madison Frost, the sullen twenty-something who had been helping Sienna for several years. People had become used to seeing her behind the counter of the Book Nook, and the subject of her nose ring was no longer a topic for conversation around town.

Gigi passed Abigail's where something pink, fluffy and very feminine was hanging in the window. She noticed Reg's head swivel toward the garment as they drove by. "Someday, boy, I'm going to buy stuff like that. You wait."

Gigi instinctively slowed as she passed the police station, although she was already slightly under the speed limit. It would be too embarrassing to be picked up for speeding and possibly have Detective Mertz come out of the building. Gigi found him infuriating and attractive in equal measures. She was almost sure he was interested in her, but then, he still hadn't asked her out although they'd known each other for several months.

The green and white striped awning that had shaded the front of Al Forno, an Italian restaurant, had been replaced with a red one with *Declan's Grille* written on it in white letters. Gigi felt a pang every time she went past. Life in

Woodstone wouldn't be the same without Emilio and Carlo. She felt her face get warm at the thought of Carlo and pushed the gas pedal a little harder. Declan's retreated in her rear-view mirror, and Gigi tried to turn her thoughts toward Felicity's upcoming party and the menu she was planning.

Gigi came to the end of the High Street shopping area and turned right. The road wound away from town past several old churches and cemeteries with crumbling head-stones, clumps of trees and finally open fields. About a mile down the road, she began looking for the fence that heralded the beginning of Felicity's property.

She caught sight of it at the last minute and came to a screeching halt, grateful that no one was behind her. She backed up carefully and turned down the long drive that zigzagged through a copse of trees. They were so dense that Gigi reached to turn on her headlights, but right before she did, she exited the trees and was out in the open again with the sun peeking through her window.

Felicity's house, a southern-style colonial, stood on a slight rise and was flanked by weeping willow trees whose leaves were starting to turn yellow. The house was over one hundred years old but had been meticulously restored. Of course, it was only one of Felicity's many residences—there was also the Manhattan apartment with spectacular views of Central Park and the Palm Beach condo that was right on the beach. Felicity's salary for acting in *For Better or For Worse* had plenty of zeroes after the initial figure, but her husband, Jack Winchel, really raked in the money as the manager of a large hedge fund.

Gigi passed the house and pulled her car up to the curb just beyond. She supposed Felicity would tell her where she wanted her to park.

Reg dogged Gigi's heels as she retrieved her overnight

bag from the trunk of the car, along with several grocery bags, and mounted the wide brick steps to the house. She wondered if she was expected to go around to the servant's entrance. Every great house such as Felicity's had one of those, along with a set of back stairs and a rabbitlike warren of rooms on the top floor meant for staff.

She hesitated for another moment and then rather timidly smacked the door knocker against its post. It didn't seem to have made much noise, but the door was thrown open almost immediately by a young man who would have been very handsome if it hadn't been for his rather weak and petulant-looking chin.

"Can I help you?" he asked in a voice that matched the plummy tones of Felicity and other actors Gigi had known. She recognized him as Felicity's leading man in *For Better or For Worse*.

Right behind him was a large, eager golden retriever.

"I'm Gigi." She stuck out her hand. Reg stood stiffly at her side, gazing at the other dog as if taking its measure.

The fellow enveloped Gigi's hand in both of his own. "I'm Alex Goulet." He gestured toward the football-field-size foyer. "Welcome to the madhouse."

Gigi hesitantly stepped over the threshold and looked around. Each time, she couldn't help being struck by the grandeur of Felicity's home. A huge staircase spiraled up toward a second-floor landing, and a living room and dining room yawned open on either side of the foyer, framed by carved, white columns.

"I think Felicity's in the kitchen."

Gigi followed Alex as he led the way toward the back of the house. Reg trotted at her side with the golden close behind, its nose perilously close to Reg's hindquarters.

The foyer ended in a small round room whose ceiling

and walls were draped in fabric. An elegant, antique-looking desk stood dead center. They rounded a corner and went down a long hall that opened into an enormous kitchen, at the far end of which was a large bay window. An island dominated the center of the room, and all the countertops were granite. Gigi glanced around in awe—the appliances were state-of-the-art, commercial grade. Cooking in this space was going to be a real luxury.

The room was empty.

"I can't imagine where Felicity has gotten to," Alex said. He looked around as if he were expecting Felicity to pop out of a cabinet at any minute. "I'll go see if I can find out where she's gone."

Before Gigi could say a word, he was gone, too, leaving behind only a wisp of fragrance from his aftershave.

Gigi heaved the two laden grocery bags she was carrying onto the counter and sorted through the contents. She opened the refrigerator and began organizing her supplies on the sparkling glass shelves.

Reggie found a quiet spot under the wood refectory table and lay panting, his pink tongue bobbing up and down. The golden crawled underneath and took up residence right next to him, its bright red tongue lolling from the side of its mouth.

"He's done it again. After I told him absolutely not to." Felicity burst into the room, her long red hair flying around her shoulders. She was wearing a hot pink velour tracksuit with a very chichi brand name scrawled across her rear in fancy black script. She gripped a purse by one handle, the bag yawning open and threatening to eject its contents all over the kitchen floor.

She stopped short when she saw Gigi. "Oh, so sorry. I

didn't realize you were here." She made a dramatic gesture that Gigi recognized from episodes of *For Better or For Worse*. "Derek's been in my purse again."

For a moment Gigi had a vision of someone named Derek scrounging in Felicity's purse for her lipstick or powder compact.

Felicity dumped her handbag on the table and yanked her wallet from its depths. She fanned open the billfold and waved it toward Gigi. "Empty! Completely empty! And I went to the ATM yesterday. That boy is going to be the death of me." She blew back a piece of hair that had fallen onto her forehead.

Gigi must have looked as confused as she felt because Felicity went on to explain.

"Derek is my stepson. He's in the habit of going through my purse and helping himself to money whenever he runs short. His father gives him more than enough for his allowance. I can't imagine what he spends it on. We provide virtually everything he needs, and he has charge accounts in every store on High Street."

Must be nice, Gigi thought. She wondered how old the thieving Derek was.

A young man strode into the room, stopping short at the sight of Felicity and her open purse. He was tall and thin, with dark hair that fell across his forehead and flopped over the collar of his shirt. Gigi judged him to be in his midtwenties.

"Derek," Felicity declared with a broad sweep of her arm. "You've been in my purse again."

The young man gave a snort of disgust, grabbed an apple out of the basket on the counter and bit into it decisively. "Don't look at me. I didn't do it. It must be that new maid you've hired."

"Anja has impeccable references," Felicity called after his retreating back.

"As I said, welcome to the madhouse." Gigi turned around to find that Alex was standing behind her.

"I gather you two have met." Felicity indicated Alex with a wave. She opened the refrigerator, gazed at the contents for a moment and then shut the door resolutely.

"I've already lost ten pounds," she announced to Gigi triumphantly.

Gigi felt the glow of satisfaction she always did when one of her clients succeeded. Sometimes she thought she was even more excited than they were.

"Let me know if there's anything you need." Felicity tapped Gigi on the shoulder before whirling around and disappearing out the door, leaving a cloud of expensive perfume in her wake.

Gigi set to work cutting radishes into decorative flower shapes to garnish the hors d'oeuvre serving platters. They would keep in a bowl of water in the refrigerator overnight, and she wouldn't have to fuss with them the day of the party. They were easy to prepare and always made a spectacular presentation. Gigi firmly believed that everything tasted better when arranged attractively. It was one of the tips she regularly gave her clients—put your food on a pretty plate, use a linen napkin and sit down and savor each bite. She dropped the radishes into a bowl of ice water as she finished carving.

She was carrying the bowl to the refrigerator when Sienna popped her head around the corner to say hello.

"Welcome to the madhouse," Sienna said, echoing Alex's earlier statement. She had just come in from outside, and her cheeks were blushed with color from the crisp air. Her long, strawberry blond hair was twisted into a precarious knot on top of her head, and she had a newspaper tucked under her arm. Gigi noticed that her stomach now protruded through the opening of her jacket.

Sienna must have seen her glance. She patted her belly happily. "The little bugger has been unbelievably active today. Oliver thinks he's going to be a soccer player."

Gigi smiled. "What if it turns out to be a she?"

Sienna laughed. "Please, don't tell Oliver that! He's convinced it's going to be a boy." She was quiet for a moment. "Either way, we're going to love it. We're both so happy."

Gigi smiled at her friend. It was good to see Sienna so happy. She and Oliver had weathered some major storms, but it looked as if they'd finally sailed into calm waters.

Sienna tilted her head toward the ceiling. "I'm going to go upstairs and get some work done. You've done wonders with Felicity," she said, rubbing her belly again. "She said she's already lost ten pounds, although frankly, I think it's closer to five."

"At least she's going in the right direction."

"We've planned a complete makeover," Sienna confided, "new hairdo, new wardrobe, the works. Then we're going to unveil the new Felicity Davenport at the Crystal Awards in Las Vegas. I'm confident that she's going to make a smashing comeback."

"I've got complete faith in you," Gigi said.

A furrow creased Sienna's brow.

"Don't worry," Gigi interjected. "I'll be sure to keep her on track as far as her diet's concerned."

Sienna's shoulders slumped with relief. "Thanks. That's been a huge worry, but if anyone can do it, you can."

Sienna disappeared around the corner to begin the long climb to the third floor.

Gigi scraped the bits and pieces of radish carvings into the sink and turned on the disposal. Her thoughts turned somber. She'd hoped that she and Ted would have been in the same position as Sienna and Oliver by now. But Ted had left her for another woman—an older woman; Gigi cringed every time she thought of it. Right now the only child in her future was Sienna's baby, for whom she was going to be the godmother.

She caught sight of Reg under the table, his bright pink tongue sticking out of the side of his mouth. She smiled. Right now, Reg was her baby, and she was more than happy to have him.

Gigi dumped a bunch of veggies from her bag into a colander and ran cold water over them. She realized, as she ran her fingers through the icy stream, that she'd spent her life taking water for granted. She gave the strainer a vigorous shake and set it on the counter. She was reaching for some paper towels when she heard a noise that sent her swiveling toward the door.

Raised voices echoed from one of the rooms overhead. Gigi paused momentarily trying to identify the two feminine voices. She was shocked when she realized that one of them sounded like it belonged to Sienna. And the other? She cocked her head to one side, straining as hard as possible to hear. She realized, with a start, that the other voice belonged to Felicity.

Gigi couldn't hear exactly what they were saying, but anger clearly crackled from Sienna's tone. Felicity? She sounded more amused.

Finally, silence descended, and Gigi breathed a sigh of relief. She put the freshly washed vegetables in a ziplock bag and tucked them into the produce drawer in the refrigerator. They were ready for the crudités platter she would put together tomorrow right before the party.

The silence was suddenly broken by a sound that Gigi identified as that of someone stamping their foot. That was followed by an outburst that clearly came from Sienna.

"I swear, someday I'm going to kill that woman!"

Chapter 2

Gigi had her hands full prepping for the upcoming party as well as preparing a light dinner for the guests already assembled at Felicity's house. By the time she got upstairs to check on Sienna, her office was dark and empty.

The guest room Felicity had prepared for Gigi was on the third floor, down the hall from the room she'd turned into a working space for Sienna. Twin four-poster beds covered in fluffy comforters were nestled beneath two dormer windows, and there was a small bathroom en suite. While Gigi hated to be away from her own tidy little cottage, the room was certainly charming.

"Which bed do you want?" she asked Reggie as she hauled her suitcase onto the luggage rack and flung it open. Felicity had insisted Gigi join them for dinner, and she desperately needed to change from her flour-dusted jeans and T-shirt.

Reggie cocked his head and gave her a curious expression.

"I know, boy." She bent down and scratched behind his ear. "We always share a bed, don't we?" Gigi often awoke during the night to find herself curled into a tight ball while Reggie sprawled on his back, limbs spread wide.

Gigi scrounged through her suitcase, although she already knew exactly what was in it. She settled on a pair of black trousers and an emerald green silk blouse that set off the color of her auburn hair.

She gave her face a quick splash and scooted, with Reggie close on her heels, back down the stairs to the kitchen. Lights were on in the paneled library, and as Gigi got closer, she could hear the rise and fall of voices and the clink of ice against glasses. She glanced into the room as she passed and noticed the golden, whose name she'd been told was Tabitha, stretched out in the center of the Oriental carpet, surrounded by a small group of people.

Gigi didn't linger but scurried into the kitchen, wrapped a clean chef's apron around her waist and grabbed a silver tray from the cupboard. She'd created some light appetizers for Felicity and her dinner guests—stalks of endive tipped with a scant spoonful of goat cheese and bejeweled with several grains of caviar, a yogurt-based dip for ice cold crudités and shrimp salad on cucumber slices. She arranged everything on the tray, garnished it with a few of the radish flowers and headed toward the library.

Felicity met her at the door with outstretched arms. "Do put the tray down, dear Gigi, and join us." She made a sweeping gesture toward the room.

Gigi felt herself shrinking inside. She wasn't particularly shy, but she liked keeping a barrier between herself and her clients. Especially when her client was someone as famous as Felicity Davenport.

But Felicity insisted. Gigi perched on the edge of a

leather-covered club chair and quickly untied her apron. She balled it up and stuffed it behind her.

"Name your poison." Alex swept a hand over a drinks tray laden with top-shelf liquors and cut crystal decanters.

Gigi spied an open bottle of Merlot. "A glass of red wine, please."

"Red wine it shall be."

While Alex poured the ruby red liquid into a delicate stemmed wineglass, Gigi looked around the room.

Felicity must have noticed her glance. "So sorry. You don't exactly know everyone, do you?" She smiled apologetically. "You've met Alex, of course. And Derek." She scowled at the young man in jeans and a stretched-out sweater who was lounging in a velvet-covered wing chair with his legs slung over the arm. "Derek, please do not sit like that."

Derek glanced toward a tall man with a head of thick gray hair who was nursing a cut crystal tumbler of amber liquid. He shrugged, and Derek reluctantly swung his legs off the chair's arm and stuck them straight out, sliding down to sit on his tailbone.

"My husband, Jack Winchel." Felicity blew a kiss toward the gray-haired man.

"My manager, Don Bartholomew." She indicated a slightly plump, dark-haired man who was chewing on the end of an unlit cigar. He nodded briefly at Gigi.

"I'm Vanessa Huff." A tall, curvy blonde leaned toward Gigi and tapped her on the knee. She had the face of an angel with large blue eyes and long, dark lashes, but Gigi suspected she was anything but.

Gigi took a few polite sips of her wine and glanced at her watch. According to Felicity, her Finnish housekeeper, Anja, would be back from her day off in time to serve the dinner, but Gigi wanted to be there to supervise. Besides, she still had to grill the salmon with teriyaki glaze that was the centerpiece of the main course.

When Felicity and Don became engaged in a heated argument over Felicity's newest contract renewal with the television network, the others looked on with bored expressions.

Gigi sat quietly as the conversation flowed around her. Everyone seemed to have forgotten her, but she didn't mind. It felt good to be off her feet. She sipped her wine and relaxed, leaning back with her head against the chair. A quick glance at her watch, however, told her that it was now time to return to the kitchen.

Gigi excused herself and hurried down the hall. A woman with white blond hair was in the kitchen putting dishes into the warming oven. Gigi supposed this was the housekeeper Felicity had mentioned. She was wearing black pants and a white shirt and had a clean apron wrapped around her waist.

She turned when she heard Gigi's footsteps.

She was apple-cheeked with deep blue eyes. She smiled shyly at Gigi.

"Hi," Gigi said, putting out a hand. "I'm Gigi."

"Anja," the woman replied, ducking her head. "I am sorry. My English is sometimes not so good. I hope you will forgive me."

"Of course." Gigi smiled reassuringly.

"I will be serving the dinner so you can go sit if you would like."

"I still need to cook the salmon," Gigi said, opening the refrigerator and pulling out the beautiful piece of coho salmon she'd scored at the fishmonger's. Gigi always had a basic menu plan in mind when she went shopping, but she was flexible and willing to change it according to what was best and freshest in the market. When she saw the salmon, she knew it would be perfect for Felicity and her guests.

Anja pointed at the salmon. "Lovely. In my country we prepare it with fresh dill and a little cream."

"I'll have to try that someday," Gigi said, and Anja looked pleased.

Gigi got to work spreading teriyaki glaze on the fish. She reheated the vegetables she'd prepared previously and arranged them in serving dishes. The timer on the oven pinged, and she removed the fish, placing it on a long, white platter with scalloped edges.

There wasn't any more to be done at the moment. With a sense of relief she untied her apron, threw it across a chair and retreated to the dining room. There was an empty seat next to Alex, and Gigi slid into it. Vanessa and Don were across the table from her. Their chairs were pulled closer together than any of the others.

Anja placed the vegetable serving dishes on the table and went around to each guest with the platter of salmon. Gigi helped herself to a small piece, pleased to note that it was cooked to perfection. She glanced around the table and was relieved to see that everyone seemed to be enjoying their food.

The dozen white votives scattered around the dining table and on the sideboard flickered softly, sending shadows dancing on the walls. A low buzz of conversation floated about the room, punctuated by the gentle clink of silverware against china as the guests savored their meal.

Anja was serving the apple galette Gigi had prepared for dessert when Alex leaned toward her. "I noticed you glancing at our fellow guests earlier." He nodded his head toward Vanessa and Don.

Gigi felt her face flame. Had it been that obvious?

"I'm sure you're wondering, like the rest of us, what gives." Alex stirred a spoonful of sugar into his coffee cup.

Gigi opened her mouth but didn't know what to say.

"I'm not one for gossip, but I think the beautiful Vanessa is trying to get a leg up, so to speak, in the television business. I think she's tired of playing second fiddle to Felicity and wants to advance her career." The way he said it put quote marks around the word *advance*.

Gigi still didn't know what to say. Especially since she'd been thinking the exact same thing herself.

"And, although Vanessa has been staying at one end of the second-floor hallway, and Don the other, I've heard plenty of scurrying at night, and it's not mice afoot." Alex played with his teaspoon, turning it over and over. "It's worse than one of those English drawing room comedies." He scrunched the last bite of his galette between the tines of his fork and licked it off. "Don has been Felicity's agent for years, and she wasn't at all pleased when he signed Vanessa *and* got her a part on *For Better or For Worse.*"

Gigi made a vow to tune into the soap the next opportunity she got. She'd watched it once or twice when she was sick in bed, but she certainly hadn't seen it since Vanessa joined the cast.

"And," Alex said breathlessly, his eyes open wide, his gaze pinning Gigi's, "Don used to be Felicity's exclusive property, *if you know what I mean*. And you don't take from Felicity what is Felicity's. At least not without suffering the consequences."

Gigi couldn't help it. Her head swiveled toward Felicity's husband, who was at the head of the table, his plate pushed to one side and his cell phone pressed to his ear.

Alex waved a hand. "Jack and Felicity have what could be called an *open* relationship. She doesn't question him, and, in turn, he lets her go her own way."

It was all too much for Gigi. She excused herself quickly and beat a retreat to the kitchen to help Anja with the dishes.

* * *

The next day, Gigi was already showered, dressed and up to her elbows in flour when Alice Slocum arrived to help. Alice worked part-time at the police station and was one of Gigi's most successful clients. She'd started Gigi's meal plan several months before the wedding of her daughter, Stacy, and by the time the big day rolled around, was fitting into a very nice size ten.

"It's going to rain," Alice said ominously as she shed her knitted jacket and ran a hand through her silver curls, removing a dried red leaf that had blown into her hair. "How is it going?"

Gigi looked up from the pastry crust she was rolling out. "So far, I'm on schedule." She brushed at the flour that clung to her forearms.

"How is Woodstone's very own diva?" Alice picked up the apron Gigi had set out for her and tied it around her now slim waist.

"Felicity? About what you'd expect. Half-nervous, half-excited. Fortunately she's been staying out of the kitchen." Gigi picked up her rolling pin and dusted off the excess flour. She glanced at Alice out of the corner of her eye and noticed that Alice's normally cheerful face was anything but. Was something wrong?

"Okay, boss, what do you want me to do first?" Alice smiled, but Gigi noticed the smile didn't reach her eyes.

"I'm going to need at least two cups of chopped onions, so maybe you can start on those."

"Right-o." Alice tore open the netted bag of yellow onions, took a handful to the sink and began peeling them. She flushed the peels down the disposal and began cutting the onions into quarters.

Gigi noticed her dash a hand across her eyes.

"They say if you run some cold water, it will keep your eyes from tearing."

"Thanks."

Alice's voice sounded funny. As if she really *was* crying. Gigi turned around.

"Hey, what gives? I don't think it's that onion making you cry."

Alice shook her head.

"Want to tell me what's wrong?" Gigi went over to Alice and put a hand on her arm.

Alice gave a loud sniff and laid down her knife. She reached into the pocket of her skirt, pulled out a tissue and blew her nose. "It's Stacy," she mumbled around the tissue.

"Is she okay? Is something wrong?" Gigi went back to the pastry she was fitting into a tart pan.

Alice nodded. "She's fine. Physically, anyway."

Gigi waited. She knew Alice would tell her in her own time, in her own way.

Alice chopped one of the onions and swept the pieces into a bowl. "I don't know what it is with young people these days." She gave another loud sniff. "They expect everything to be easy. Marriage isn't always easy."

Gigi's ears perked up. Alice's daughter had been married only a few months. Was trouble afoot already?

"Are they not getting along?"

"No, according to Stacy, it's not that. She feels like the magic has gone out of the relationship. I told her you can't expect the honeymoon to last forever."

That's for sure, Gigi thought. She and Ted had lasted almost eight years. Gigi had thought they were happy—she had been at least, but apparently Ted hadn't felt the same way. No use thinking about that now.

"But surely, it's just talk. Maybe Stacy and Joe had an argument."

Alice shook her head so vehemently her gray curls bobbed up and down. "No. I wish that were the case. But Stacy mentioned"—she gulped and tears sprang into her eyes—"the *d* word."

"Oh no." Gigi didn't know what to say. "Is there someone else?" she asked tentatively.

Alice shook her head. "I don't think so." She slid her knife through a new onion. "I think she's looking for that courtship-and-honeymoon excitement. That's not what marriage is all about."

"Hopefully these feelings will pass, and she'll settle happily into married life."

Alice looked doubtful. "I hope so. I'm afraid Stacy is still a bit immature. Maybe she should have waited till she was a bit older—you know, after she saw a bit more of life—to get married."

Lunchtime came and went, and Gigi was still working hard. Alice had already left for her part-time job at the police station. Gigi glanced at the clock. It was after two, and her stomach was reminding her that she hadn't eaten anything since a boiled egg and a cup of coffee early that morning. She found some bread in the refrigerator and a jar of peanut butter in the pantry and slapped together a hasty sandwich. The old proverb about the shoemaker's children going barefoot popped into her head as she munched and cooked.

By three o'clock Gigi had things well enough under control that she felt she could afford to take a break. She whistled for Reggie, who was asleep under the kitchen table, and together they climbed the back stairs to the third floor.

Sienna's makeshift office was at the top of the stairs, and Gigi realized she hadn't seen her since the day before.

Gigi stuck her head around the door of Sienna's office. It was empty. It didn't look as if Sienna had been in at all—the desk chair with the special backrest Sienna had ordered was pushed in tidily. The top of the desk was clear of papers, and the trash can was empty. Gigi put her hand on the green-shaded banker's lamp, and it was cool. That was odd. Perhaps Sienna had had to go into New York for the day?

Gigi turned around and was about to leave when she noticed a folded newspaper on top of the filing cabinet. Perhaps she would take it to read while she took her break. She tucked it under her arm, shooed Reggie out from under the desk where he was busy spelunking and went down the hall toward her room.

Gigi collapsed on the bed and leaned against the pillows, Reggie stretched out next to her sighing deeply, as if to say *It's about time*. Never mind that he'd already spent the whole morning sleeping in one area of the kitchen or another.

Gigi unfurled the paper, glanced at the seventy-two-point-type headline and began to read. Her eyes were starting to droop, and she was about to put down the paper when something on the *New York Post*'s infamous "Page Six" caught her eye.

"No!" She sat bolt upright.

The grainy black-and-white photograph explained everything. No wonder Sienna had threatened to murder Felicity!

Chapter 3

Gigi read the bold, dark headline. "Felicity Davenport Holed Up in Her Connecticut Home with New Man." The black-and-white photograph accompanying the article was slightly blurry, but there was no mistaking the handsome, shirtless man. It was Sienna's husband, Oliver.

No wonder Sienna had been so furious with Felicity! Was this some sort of publicity stunt on Felicity's part? She doubted that this was Sienna's idea of a comeback plan. Gigi examined the photo more closely. It looked as if it was taken in Sienna and Oliver's backyard, which was adjacent to Felicity's property. The carriage house that they lived in had once been a part of the estate that Felicity now owned.

She was tempted to call Sienna—she must be very upset—but a glance at her watch told her she didn't have time. Gigi scurried down to the kitchen, Reg at her heels, and donned a fresh apron. Her plan called for having every-thing ready so that Anja and the other servers could keep the hors d'oeuvres warm and ready to circulate. Felicity had insisted on Gigi attending the party, and Gigi had dug one of her little black dresses out of the closet—something she used to wear with far more frequency when she was married to Ted and living and working in the city. She planned to slip into it at the last minute.

Gigi grabbed a saucepan from the pot rack and put it on the stove. Her hands shook slightly as she adjusted the gas burners on the Aga. What a luxury it was working in such a well-appointed kitchen. Her worries about Sienna increased as the water came to a simmer and finally a full boil. Would the shock of seeing that picture in the paper harm Sienna's baby? Maybe she'd already gone into premature labor?

Gigi could no longer tolerate the thoughts circulating in an endless pattern through her mind. She dug out her cell and punched in Sienna's number. She waited until Sienna's voice mail kicked in.

Gigi turned back to the stove and dropped a bagful of miniature red potatoes into the pot of boiling water. She would partially hollow them out and fill them with a dollop of low-fat sour cream. Some would be topped with a sprinkle of red caviar; others would get a dash of chopped, fresh chives. Potatoes were great for soaking up liquor at a cocktail party. She'd passed the library earlier where two young men in short white jackets were setting up the bar with bottles of every liquor imaginable, dozens of crystal glasses and cocktail napkins festooned with a large, flamboyant *F*.

Gigi was using a demitasse spoon to remove the insides of the potatoes when Anja bustled into the room. Her blond hair was swept into a low ponytail, and she had a knitted poncho over her shoulders.

"I must be going out for something."

"What do you need? I might have—"

But Anja was already shaking her head. "No, I am afraid you won't have what I need. I am getting Miss Felicity some of the herb tea that they blend especially for her at Bon Appétit. She takes it every morning to help with the . . . how do you say it"—she made a sweeping motion down the length of her body—"getting rid of the water." She looked at Gigi and smiled. "We are out, and she will need it tomorrow."

Gigi nodded, understanding. It must be Evelyn Fishko's famous diuretic tea, Gigi thought. A combination of dandelion, cucumber and burdock that flushed excess water from the body. Evelyn was the owner of Bon Appétit and something of an amateur herbalist. Gigi knew that people from towns all over Connecticut came to her for her special blends thought to cure everything from edema to arthritis.

"I must be going, then." Anja tossed her scarf over her shoulder and started toward the door.

She was stopped by an abrupt cry coming from the corridor. Both she and Gigi spun around.

"Help. Oh, help. Someone, I need help."

Before either of them could move, Felicity burst into the kitchen. "Oh, help, someone," she repeated. She was wearing a strapless, form-fitting, tiered fuchsia cocktail dress and was reaching behind her with both arms. "Help," she repeated, dancing around the room, trying to reach in back of her.

"What is the matter?" Anja put down her handbag and regarded her employer curiously.

"I can't get the zipper up," Felicity fretted. "I knew I shouldn't have had that extra glass of wine last night. I'm retaining water," she finished on a wailing note.

"You must take a sauna," Anja said. "It will get rid of the water, poof, like that." She made an expressive gesture with her hands.

"You're right." Felicity gifted Anja with a broad smile. "Of course! Why didn't I think of that?" She threw her arms around the housekeeper. "You take such good care of me, Anja. I don't know what I would do without you."

Anja smiled shyly, ducking her head at the compliment. "You go upstairs and take your sauna, and I will go and get your special tea. You can have a cup as soon as I get back." She took a step toward the door. "Between them, you will fit into your dress perfectly."

Gigi breathed a sigh of relief as Anja headed out the back door and Felicity went upstairs to her bedroom suite. Gigi was slicing a baguette when Alice arrived.

"The wind is picking up, and I think it wants to rain," Alice announced as she whipped off her raincoat and hung it from a hook next to the pantry. She was going to help serve and was dressed accordingly in a slim black skirt and plain white blouse.

Gigi got out the bowl of ice water from the refrigerator where she'd been keeping the carrots, cauliflower and other vegetables she'd lightly blanched the day before. She cut the vegetables into bite-size pieces and dropped them back into the ice water to keep them crisp. She was making a tangy yogurt and spinach dip to go with them. She was cutting the last carrot when Vanessa Huff drifted into the room.

Alice's head swiveled around, and her mouth opened in a small *o*. Alice, Gigi knew, was a fan of *For Better or For Worse* and watched the show regularly.

Vanessa was wearing what Gigi had heard called a "bandage" dress because it wrapped so tightly around the wearer. It was bright red and strapless, and Vanessa's famous assets nearly spilled out the top. Up close, she looked younger than on television, and Gigi noticed that a blemish was forming to the right of her mouth. Her blond hair was softly curled and hung past her shoulders.

"Is Anja here?"

Gigi was about to answer when Don stuck his head around the door. His white dress shirt was open, and the ends of an untied bow tie dangled from his neck.

"Vanessa, be a doll and help me with this, would you?" He brandished the ends of the tie.

"Can I get you anything?" Gigi asked, but Vanessa shook her head and followed Don out of the kitchen.

Gigi breathed a sigh of relief. She had plenty to do as it was. She wondered if Sienna and Oliver would be at the party or if Sienna would even continue as Felicity's publicist under the circumstances. Gigi didn't think for a moment that Oliver and Felicity were really having an affair. The very idea was ridiculous. Oliver was head over heels in love with Sienna and completely focused on the upcoming birth of their baby.

Gigi took the satay sauce out of the refrigerator to come to room temperature. It was a mixture of various Asian spices along with soy sauce, sesame oil, chopped peanuts and spicy hot red chili paste. She would serve it with tiny bamboo skewers of grilled chicken. It was very tasty and relatively low fat. Of course, she was assuming that Felicity's guests would nibble their way to a full meal at her party, although Gigi was not so naïve that she didn't think there were some who would go out for a late, full dinner afterward.

Gigi glanced at her watch and felt a small bubble of panic rise in her throat. She had to finish soon and get upstairs to freshen up and slip into her dress. She'd thought about trying to do something with her hair—other than her usual style of letting it curl every which way around her face—but it didn't look as if she would have time. She envied women who could, with a couple of twists and a bobby pin, create a charming up-do. Sienna was like that—she could plop her hair on top of her head without even looking and have it appear as if the best New York hairdresser had worked on it for hours.

Suddenly the door to the butler's pantry swung open and both Gigi and Alice jumped.

"Is Felicity here?" Winchel demanded. He was already dressed in his dinner jacket, and a scowl marred his handsome face.

"Uh, nnnno," Gigi stammered.

"Damn woman would be late for her own funeral," he said before letting the door slam to in back of him.

Gigi and Alice exchanged a glance, and Alice raised one eyebrow.

"Captain of industry," Gigi said succinctly and smiled.

"Indeed," Alice concurred. "I'm so glad my Tom was a simple salesman, may he rest in peace." Alice looked up at Gigi. "Tom and I were so happy, you know. Did the honeymoon last forever? No, not exactly. But we were happy. Long term, we were perfectly happy. I don't understand my daughter." She wiped at a tear that was threatening to spill over her lid and down her cheek.

Alice wasn't the type who sought overt sympathy, so Gigi looked away and allowed her a moment to get herself together.

She was untying her apron when Derek slunk into the room. He was wearing a blazer with patched sleeves, dark velvet jeans and a sulky expression. "Is there anything to eat?" he asked petulantly.

Gigi was at a loss. There would be plenty of things to eat in an hour. Did he expect her to fix something especially for him?

"Here," Alice said in experienced parental tones as she pushed a bowl of fruit toward him. "Have a banana or an apple."

"I thought there were going to be hors d'oeuvres." His lips turned down in an exaggerated pout.

"There will be," Alice said firmly. "But you'll have to wait for those."

Derek rolled his eyes and sidled toward the door. "Have you seen Felicity?" he mumbled in Gigi's direction.

Before she could shake her head, he had backed through the door, and they heard the crunch as he bit into the apple he'd palmed from the fruit bowl on his way out.

"Shouldn't Felicity be down here by now?" Alice pushed up the sleeve of her blouse and checked her watch. "Her guests will be arriving soon."

Gigi was about to answer when Anja burst into the room. Moisture clung to her blond hair, and her cheeks had a blush of color from the cold air. She was carrying a small white plastic bag with *Bon Appétit* written on it in script. She pulled out the container of special tea Felicity liked and stuffed the bag in a sleeve that hung from the pantry door.

"I have to start getting the hors d'oeuvres plated," Gigi said as she watched Anja swing a teakettle under the faucet. "Can you show me where the serving platters are?"

Anja pursed her lips. "First, I must get Madam's tea, okay?"

"I'll do that." Alice put out a hand for the kettle. "You help Gigi with the hors d'oeuvres."

For a moment Anja looked doubtful, but then she gave a curt nod. "Use one heaping spoon of tea," she admonished over her shoulder as she began opening cupboards and drawers.

Alice took a delicate bone china cup and saucer from the

glass-fronted cupboard, spooned in the correct amount of tea and as soon as the water had boiled, poured it over the loose tea leaves. She wrinkled her nose. "It smells like someone's front lawn."

"But it is good for the water," Anja reassured her.

"Maybe I'll try it," Alice said as she placed the tea on a small silver tray. "Felicity's room is . . .?"

"Second floor, end of the hallway," Anja said.

Gigi had filled several small crystal bowls with spiced nuts to sustain Felicity's houseguests until the other guests arrived. She carried one in each hand toward the living room.

The living room ran the length of the house and had large windows at either end. An enormous marble fireplace dominated one wall, and a fire had been laid in the grate in preparation for the party. Flowers were everywhere—large arrangements on the occasional tables, small ones on the coffee tables. Candles were placed strategically around the room waiting to be lit. Gigi paused for a moment and took it all in. It was like something out of one of those fancy decorating magazines. Even the air smelled good, perfumed by bowls of expensive potpourri, the subtle aroma of furniture polish and the scent of the bouquets.

She put the nuts out on the coffee tables. Reggie and Tabitha had been secured in the kitchen so there was no worry of their disturbing the food or annoying the guests. Gigi had secured two juicy bones from the butcher to mollify them in their exile.

Gigi was heading toward the kitchen when she heard a strange, high-pitched noise coming from upstairs. She turned and moved swiftly toward the enormous sweeping staircase that rose from the foyer to the second-floor landing. The unidentifiable noise grew louder until it slowly resolved itself into a scream. A very high-pitched, feminine scream.

Before Gigi could mount the first step, Alice came bar-reling down the staircase, her blue eyes as bulging as a spooked horse's, her mouth still stretched wide in a scream. She collided with Gigi, uttering a loud *ouf*. Her scream tapered off, and she started sobbing hysterically.

"Alice, what is it? What's wrong?" Gigi put her hands on Alice's shoulders and tried to steady her.

Alice took a huge shuddering breath and made an almost superhuman effort to control herself. "It's Felicity," she panted.

"What about her?" By this time Anja had come out of the kitchen and stood staring at Alice.

"It's terrible," Alice gasped, still trying to catch her breath.

"You must tell us what has happened," Anja demanded.

Gigi put her arm around Alice protectively. She felt Alice sag against her.

"I think," Alice began, "I think, Felicity is . . . dead."

Chapter 4

Gigi's knees turned to rubber, but she took a deep breath to steady herself. "Alice"—she gave the woman a quick hug—"are you sure? Maybe she only looked—"

Alice was already shaking her head, her gray curls bobbing around her face, her eyes still bulging in terror.

"What's going on?" Winchel came out of his study, his cell phone in one hand, an unlit Cuban cigar in the other.

"Apparently, something has .... happened . . . to Felicity," Gigi said, not wanting to alarm everyone until she knew the full scope of what was going on.

"Better check it out now." Winchel stuck the cigar in his mouth and bit down. "I've got important guests expected shortly."

Gigi raised her eyebrows at Alice, but Alice shook her head.

"No thanks. I don't want to go up there again."

Alice sat down on the bottom step as the rest of them

began mounting the staircase. They had reached the second-floor landing when Vanessa drifted out of her room. "What's this? A parade?" She nibbled at the edge of a fingernail. Gigi noticed that they were all bitten to the quick.

As they passed the open door to Vanessa's room, Gigi saw someone moving about within. She didn't see who it was, but she caught a glimpse of a dark jacket.

"Felicity?" Winchel bellowed as they neared the end of the hall and the yawning door of the master bedroom.

"I don't think you want to—" Gigi began, but he ignored her and barged into the room.

The king-size bed was already turned down for the night, and light from a crystal lamp glowed on the bedside table where a book and a pair of reading glasses were laid out. The room, however, was empty.

Winchel strode toward an open door at the other end of the room and stuck his head around the edge. "Felicity, for heaven's sake, what is the—" He stopped abruptly and pulled his head back as quickly as a turtle retreating from an enemy.

"Oh my God." He backed up until he was sitting on the edge of the satin-covered bed.

Gigi didn't want to look, but someone had to do something. She peeked around the edge of the door into the lavish master bathroom. The room was stiflingly hot and at first appeared empty. White marble gleamed under the recessed lights, and there were double sinks and a spa bathtub large enough for two people. Built into one wall was a sauna.

The door was open, and Felicity was toppled half in and half out of the small, heated enclosure. She was the color of a boiled lobster and appeared to be quite dead.

Gigi stuffed her fist into her mouth to stop the scream that rose in her throat. Vanessa and Anja had piled in behind her, and she heard Vanessa make a noise like a wounded kitten. Anja was quietly stoic, her face set in grave tones, her thin lips clenched tight.

"Is she dead? Should we call nine-one-one?" Vanessa backed away from the sight on the bathroom floor.

Gigi shook her head. "I don't know. Someone needs to check for a pulse."

"I will do it." Anja stepped forward calmly, knelt beside Felicity and placed her fingers against her employer's neck.

A moment later she stood and shook her head. "I am afraid she is gone."

They had to get the police, Gigi thought. Detective Bill Mertz came to mind, and the idea of his strong, solid presence made her feel considerably calmer. Mertz would take care of things. Gigi scrambled for the cordless phone on one of the bedside tables and punched in 9-1-1.

They were about to leave the room when Don and Alex burst in. "What's going on? What's happened?" they chorused.

"It's Madam." Anja stepped forward and blocked their entrance to the bathroom. "She has taken ill, and we are calling for the ambulance."

Don stuck his head around the corner of the bathroom. "Oh my God," he burst out, much as Winchel had earlier.

Alex looked too stricken to speak.

"Maybe we should all go downstairs," Gigi said, anxious to get away from the scene in the bathroom.

The peal of the front doorbell sounded throughout the house, and they all looked at each other with expressions of horror.

"The guests!" Gigi groaned.

Fortunately it was only Sienna standing on the doorstep when Gigi flung open the front door. Gigi was surprised to see her given how angry she had been with Felicity yesterday.

"What's wrong?" Sienna asked as she stepped into the foyer. She put a hand on either of Gigi's shoulders. "Have you had some sort of culinary disaster?"

Gigi shook her head mutely.

Sienna smiled. "I didn't think so. You're too much of an expert to let that happen." She glanced at Gigi's face again. "But something's wrong."

Gigi found her tongue. "It's Felicity. She's . . . she's dead."

"Dead?" Sienna repeated, her face going white. "What happened?"

"I don't know. We're waiting for the police to arrive."

"The police?" Sienna looked alarmed. "Why? Does it look like—" She sank down onto the bottom step of the sweeping staircase.

"I don't know," Gigi repeated. "I guess whenever death is sudden . . ."

Gigi brushed ineffectually at her flour-bedecked jeans and T-shirt, sorry she hadn't had the opportunity to change into her black dress.

Sienna was outfitted for the party in a flowing caftan embellished with beads, sequins and tiny mirrored disks. The fabric puddled around her ankles as she sat huddled on the stairs. Her long blond hair was down and flowed around her shoulders.

"Where's Oliver?" Gigi asked.

A strange look crossed Sienna's face. "He'll be here . . . later."

Gigi started to open her mouth then realized this was no time to bring up the newspaper and the picture of Oliver. She would have to ask Sienna about it later.

Before they could move away from the door, it opened again and several more people spilled in. Anja rushed forward and began collecting coats. Gigi noticed they were flecked with water. The rain, which had been threatening all day, must have started. Gigi recognized one of the guests as Hunter Pierce, director of the Woodstone Players. More people followed until the living room was filled with chattering voices.

It looked as if Felicity was going to have her party after all.

Gigi hurried into the kitchen where Alice sat in a chair nursing a cup of tea. Her hand shook as she raised it to her lips.

Gigi looked at her in concern. "Are you okay?"

Alice nodded. "I heard the door. Are the police here?"

Gigi opened the refrigerator and pulled out a bowl of ice cold crudités. "No, but some of the guests are. Winchel sent Derek out to warn the others away, but I've got to feed the ones who are already here."

"I'll help you." Alice rose from her chair decisively. "I'll feel better if I keep busy. I keep seeing that poor woman . . ." She shook her head and started separating lace doilies for the silver serving trays.

Gigi had managed to dash upstairs to change into her dress and was circulating among the handful of guests with the tray of stuffed potatoes when the police arrived. A uniformed patrolman was first on the scene, but Mertz wasn't far behind. Derek dragged in right after them, looking damp and sulky, his long hair plastered to his head.

Gigi bolted for the kitchen to grab a fresh tray of hors d'oeuvres. When she arrived back to the assembled guests,

Mertz was standing in the foyer speaking with Winchel. Winchel looked annoyed and kept gesturing toward the living room. Gigi noticed two men in the corner nursing tumblers of whiskey. They wore dark suits and serious expressions. Gigi supposed they were Winchel's important guests from New York. Mertz looked equally annoyed and frustrated. He kept gesturing toward the crowd of people and running his hands through his short, dark blond hair.

Don was deep in conversation with Hunter Pierce. The recessed lighting glanced off Pierce's head, his scalp shining through the thin, black strands. As usual, he was wearing a tweed jacket with suede elbow patches. As Gigi drew closer, she heard Felicity's name. She hovered nearby, pretending to rearrange the black bread with salmon slices on her tray.

"I am devastated," she heard Pierce say. "Felicity would have brought positively hordes of people out to the playhouse."

Gigi leaned closer. The Woodstone Theater had recently undergone a complete renovation. It had started life as a working barn and, sometime during the sixties, had been converted into a theater by an enterprising actor from New York City. Recently, a developer had erected an enclosed mall on the weedy fields that had once surrounded it. The theater itself had been gutted and rebuilt. Gigi hadn't realized that Felicity had been planning on performing there during her self-imposed Connecticut exile.

Sienna was sitting on the sofa with a plump, older woman Gigi recognized as the wife of the mayor of Woodstone. Sienna stifled a yawn as she nodded encouragingly at the older woman.

Gigi motioned to her subtly, and Sienna excused herself and rose from the sofa.

"Oh, thank goodness," she said as she joined Gigi on the fringe of the crowd. "That woman is very nice but a terrible bore. I was wondering when I'd be able to make good my escape. I'd just wanted to sit for a moment; my ankles are beginning to swell." She made a face and gestured toward her feet. She lifted the edge of her caftan, and Gigi saw she was wearing a pair of rubber-soled flats.

"Heinous, aren't they?" Sienna let her dress drop back into place. "But they're the only pair I can get on at the moment."

Gigi put her tray down on the nearest table.

"I just heard that Felicity was planning on appearing at the Woodstone Theater. Hunter Pierce was talking to Don Bartholomew about it."

Sienna gave a small smile that disappeared almost immediately. "Investigating already, are you?"

Gigi started to protest, but Sienna put a hand on her arm. "Don convinced Felicity to agree to a small run in their next production. They often have actors out from New York or even traveling companies. He thought it would be good for her." Sienna played with one of the mirrored disks on her dress. "At least it would have kept her mind off of food. The network powers-that-be were really beginning to grumble about Felicity's weight gain. They wanted to move toward a younger image for the show. Don had a hell of a time negotiating her latest contract."

"Sounds like this could be a wonderful opportunity for our resident ingénue, Vanessa."

Sienna snorted. "Indeed. Vanessa is doing everything she should to score a bigger part on the show—and lots of things she shouldn't."

"Alex did drop a few hints along those lines." She wondered if this was a good opportunity to bring up the newspaper and Oliver's picture. "I saw the *New York Post*," Gigi began.

Sienna shook her head tersely. "That ridiculous thing! Felicity wasn't content to leave the publicity campaign in my hands but decided to come up with that absurd story to get her name back in the gossip columns." Sienna smiled sadly. "Silly woman."

"Where is Oliver?"

"Oh, Gigi." Sienna looked at her with wide eyes. "You don't think for a minute that I believed that stupid story, do you? Oliver is absolutely furious with Felicity. At first he refused to come to the party tonight, but I convinced him that would only stir up more rumors. I guess when he ran to the Shop and Save to pick up some milk for me, people were staring at him and pointing. He was mortified."

Sienna ran a hand over her belly. "But I told him he can't bury his head in the sand. He should be along shortly, although I doubt the police will let him in."

Gigi glanced at the foyer out of the corner of her eye. Mertz was still speaking with Winchel, whose posture was getting stiffer by the minute. Even from a distance, she could sense his impatience at being told what to do when he was usually the one doing the telling.

"I'm going to sneak off to the kitchen and put my feet up," Sienna whispered to Gigi.

"Go ahead. There's a pitcher of iced tea in the refrigerator. Help yourself."

Gigi was turning around when Alex came up behind her.

"Mind if I sneak one of those?" He reached out and snatched one of the salmon hors d'oeuvres off the tray Gigi had set on the table. He inclined his head toward the foyer. "I don't know why the police don't ring for the ambulance to come get the body and let the rest of us go about our business."

"I guess when a death is even remotely suspicious—"

Alex's laugh cut her off. "I think the police have been watching too many television shows. I'm sure it was just a sad, sad accident." He was thoughtful for a moment. "Do you suppose they'll question us? Ask us where we were this afternoon and all that?"

He laughed, but Gigi had the distinct feeling that he was nervous. And that he very much didn't want the police asking any questions.

A flash of bright red caught Gigi's eye. Vanessa was deep in conversation with Don. Gigi picked up the tray and used it as an excuse to sidle closer.

She caught the word *policy* before Vanessa whirled around.

"Hors d'oeuvres! I'm starved!" Vanessa smiled, but her eyes were shadowed.

Vanessa helped herself and began nibbling at the bread like a rabbit. Don waved the tray away with a pained look. He reached into his pocket and pulled out a pack of antacids. He popped one into his mouth, hesitated, then popped in another.

Gigi's tray was almost empty. She made her way through the crowd toward the foyer. She noticed that Winchel had joined his important New York visitors, but she didn't see Detective Mertz anywhere. A patrolman was standing at the door, shoulders back, spine straight. Gigi shivered. She supposed he'd been stationed there to keep them from leaving.

Alice was in the kitchen arranging a new tray of hors d'oeuvres. She was subdued, but Gigi was glad to see that some of her usual ruddy color had returned.

"Here you go." She handed Gigi the tray.

"I'm going to sit for a minute." Gigi pulled out a chair opposite Sienna, plopped into it and stretched out her legs.

"Want me to take this around?" Alice brandished the canapés.

Gigi shook her head. "I think everyone has had enough for now."

Gigi turned to Sienna. "Any news from Oliver?"

"He texted me that the police wouldn't let him in." She was silent for a moment. "This is all so odd." She inclined her head in the direction of the living room. "Everyone eating and drinking as if this were a real party, as if Felicity wasn't upstairs . . . dead."

"I do wish the ambulance would get here," Alice said. "It seems wrong leaving her there like that."

"I suppose the police need to be certain there's nothing suspicious about the death." Sienna plucked a canapé from Gigi's newly refilled tray and popped it into her mouth.

"Speaking of the police, where are they?" Alice wiped her hands on her apron.

"I think they're still upstairs poking around." Sienna dabbed at her lips with a cocktail napkin.

"And one of them is posted at the front door," Gigi added.

Alice nodded. "That whiny young man, what's his name?"

"Derek?" Gigi supplied.

"Derek. He came through a couple of minutes ago and said they were doing all sorts of things in Felicity's bedroom." Alice shivered.

Just so they stayed upstairs, Gigi thought.

"Time I took that tray around." Alice said, pointing at the loaded platter that still sat on the table.

"You're right; we should get back out there." Gigi began to struggle to her feet.

"You sit for a bit. I don't mind," Alice said. "I'm curious to see what the crowd looks like."

"Then be my guest."

Sienna struggled up from her seat. "I'm going to the ladies' room. Again." She sighed.

Gigi sank back into the chair. She glanced at Reggie and Tabitha, who were napping under the table. She could do with a nap herself. She'd been working hard, and she was exhausted. She let her eyes drift closed. Just for a moment, she promised herself.

When she opened them, Detective Mertz was standing in front of her, the suggestion of a smile hovering around his mouth.

Chapter 5

Gigi jumped to her feet so suddenly she barked her elbow against the table edge. It hurt like the dickens, but she didn't want to look stupid in front of Mertz, so she gritted her teeth and plastered a smile on her face. She stuck her hand behind her back so she wouldn't be tempted to grab at her smarting joint.

She and Mertz had had a run-in several months ago when he all but accused her of poisoning her client with peanut oil. Gigi found him annoying, overbearing and unbelievably attractive in equal measures.

Tonight was no exception.

"I was, er, resting for a moment." Gigi immediately put the width of the kitchen island between them.

"There's no crime in that, as far as I know." This time Mertz actually did smile. It softened the hard planes of his face and put some light in his ice blue eyes.

Gigi smiled back. "No, I guess not." She tried to relax,

but there was an attraction between them that always made her nervous and awkward. If Mertz ever got around to asking her out, she was pretty sure she would say yes with indecent haste.

"I'm hoping you can fill me in on some details."

"Certainly." Gigi stood up straighter and matched his formal tones.

"Was Mrs. Winchel in the habit of taking saunas?"

For a moment Gigi couldn't think who on earth he was talking about, but then she realized that Felicity was, in her private life, Mrs. Winchel.

"I honestly don't know. I suppose she must have been."

"So presumably Mrs. Winchel knew how the apparatus works."

Gigi nodded. "I would guess so."

"Had any of the guests already arrived when Mrs. Winchel . . ." He hesitated, seeing the expression on Gigi's face. "I suppose I ought to call her Miss Davenport to avoid confusion."

Gigi managed to hide her smile. "That's a good idea."

"Had any of the dinner guests already arrived," he continued, "when Miss Davenport went up to take her sauna?"

"No." Gigi grabbed the sponge from the sink and began wiping down the kitchen island, catching the crumbs in the palm of her hand. She couldn't stand being idle, and she couldn't stand mess.

"Who was in the house?"

Gigi wondered what all these questions were leading up to, but she knew better than to ask. She rinsed out the sponge and began wiping down the front of the refrigerator. "Let me think." Everything had gone blurry in her mind, and she had to concentrate to recall the events of the afternoon. "Mr. Winchel was here. Anja was here, but then she went out to get something." Gigi stopped with her sponge halfway down the front of the fridge. "Actually Anja went out before Felicity went into the sauna. But Derek was here. I'm honestly not sure about Alex Goulet, but Vanessa and Don Bartholomew were definitely here."

Mertz jotted some things in his notebook, his dark brows drawn together in concentration. He glanced up with an almost apologetic look on his face. "And when did you arrive?" He looked down again quickly as if to avoid Gigi's eyes.

"I got here yesterday. I'm staying here. I had a . . . a plumbing problem at home and couldn't use my kitchen. Felicity kindly suggested I come here."

Mertz nodded and continued with his note taking, his head bent over his notebook. Gigi thought she heard him sigh as if to say *Crisis averted*. She no longer blamed him for suspecting her in the death of her client, but she suspected he was still blaming himself.

Mertz glanced up, his brows still furrowed together, a solicitous look on his face. He put a hand on Gigi's arm. "Are you okay? This can't be easy for you."

His sudden concern brought tears to Gigi's eyes.

"Sure. I'm fine." She bent her head quickly and went back to her cleaning. She took a last swipe at the side of the refrigerator and worked up the nerve to ask the question that had been dancing around the fringes of her thoughts the whole time.

"But wasn't it an accident?"

Mertz's shoulders slumped in resignation. "We have reason to believe it was anything but."

Gigi was in the kitchen late the next morning when the back door opened. Anja backed into the room, attempting to subdue her umbrella, which the wind was toying with, trying to turn it inside out. Gigi shivered as a blast of cold, wet air blew across the room.

Anja finally managed to close her umbrella. She gave it a final shake out the door before propping it in the corner. "It is raining—how do you say it?—cats and dogs out there."

Anja's nose was bright red, and Gigi noticed that her eyes were as well. Was it the wind and the cold, or had she been crying?

Anja turned her back on Gigi, and Gigi thought she heard her give a loud sniff.

"Is everything okay?" Gigi asked tentatively. Anja was clearly a private person, and Gigi didn't want to intrude.

Anja turned around, and Gigi noticed she was dabbing at her eyes with a damp tissue. Anja's mouth worked for several seconds before she found her voice. "People in the town are . . . talking."

"Talking?"

Anja nodded her head vigorously. "They are all talking about Madam's death."

Gigi put a hand on Anja's arm. "It's natural they would be. I'm sure she was very well liked in Woodstone."

"No, no, you do not understand." Anja twisted the shred of tissue between her fingers and bit her lip. "They are all saying that she committed suicide."

"Suicide!" Gigi grabbed the kettle from the stove and began to fill it. She would make Anja some tea. The woman was shaking like a leaf. "That doesn't make any sense."

"I know." Anja collapsed in a chair at the kitchen table. "Madam would not do that. She had everything to live for."

"That's right." Gigi plunked the kettle on the stove. "What woman would go on a diet, buy a new dress and plan a party . . . all to commit suicide before she had the chance to enjoy any of it?" She adjusted the burner and leaned against the counter, her arms crossed over her chest. "The police did say it wasn't an accident," Gigi mused.

"Not an accident?" Anja looked startled. "But what else could it be? It's not suicide." Her jaw set in a firm line.

"I don't know," Gigi admitted. "Murder, perhaps?"

Later that morning Gigi decided she needed a break and headed into town and the Book Nook. Sienna was back, now that she was no longer working for Felicity, trying to catch up with all her responsibilities at the store.

Gigi was enveloped in the worn but comfortable sofa in the area of the store known as the coffee corner. Patrons often spent hours there thumbing through books. She nursed a mug of her favorite coffee. Rain continued to pelt the front windows of the shop, and the bright fall colors of the leaves outside were muted by ethereal strands of fog.

"Anja said everyone is talking about Felicity's death. Some have gone so far as to label it a suicide."

"Really?" Sienna looked up from her calculator where she was plugging in numbers. "I know everyone is gossiping about it, but I hadn't heard that. Hopefully that means they've stopped talking about the nonexistent affair between Felicity and Oliver."

"Mertz did say he was quite sure it wasn't an accident, but surely he can't be hinting at . . . murder." Gigi looked at Sienna. "One murder in Woodstone already seems . . . too much."

"I know what you mean." Sienna plugged in some more figures and hit total. She frowned. "Maybe she did commit suicide? On the other hand, the police could be wrong, and it was simply an accident."

"I hope so." Gigi took a sip of her coffee.

The bell over the front door jingled, and they both looked up, startled.

"It's miserable out there," Alice complained as she entered. She shook the drops of rain from her hair. "Where is that famous Connecticut autumn all the tourists come to see?"

"Have some tea." Sienna gestured toward the teakettle. "It will warm you up." Sienna herself was sipping a mug of her favorite herbal brew.

"I think I will, thanks." Alice picked up a mug, but before she could do anything more, her excitement obviously got the better of her. "You won't believe it!" she declared, looking from Gigi to Sienna and back again as if to judge their reactions.

"What?" they chorused.

"Joe, that's my Stacy's husband, stopped by the house, and . . ."

"And?"

"Well, you know Joe's on the force. He's got the inside scoop, so to speak. And he's always been really generous in sharing stuff with me. He's a good boy. A real good boy." She looked sad for a moment, as if she were reflecting on Stacy's marital discontent.

"And?" Sienna asked.

Alice's eyes glowed like diamonds. "You are not going to believe this!"

Gigi wanted to scream. Whatever Alice had to say, she wished she'd get on with it.

"Joe told me . . ." Alice lowered her voice and looked toward the front window of the Book Nook. The only thing visible through the streaks of rain was the hazy outline of Declan's Grille across the street.

Alice took a deep breath. "Apparently the police have reason to suspect that Felicity's death wasn't an accident," she finished triumphantly.

"That's what Mertz told me," Gigi said.

Alice looked deflated. She reached for a tea bag and added hot water to her mug, her face averted.

"Did he tell you why they suspect—"

Alice was already shaking her head. "I don't think he knew himself. He only knew this much by, you know, keeping his ear to the ground, so to speak." Alice smiled proudly. "He did say that there was something on the scene that had convinced Detective Mertz."

"I wonder what that was." Sienna glanced from Alice to Gigi. "I know Anja, Felicity's housekeeper, would be very relieved if it's proven Felicity's death wasn't a suicide. On the other hand, murder isn't much of an alternative."

Gigi was quiet. An idea was already percolating in her mind. Winchel had asked her to stay on for a bit and provide meals and ultimately a luncheon after Felicity's funeral. Anja also needed help in the kitchen since the police had asked Winchel's houseguests to stay in the area for a few days, and Winchel had insisted they stay with him. Besides, Hector's Plumbing and Heating still hadn't come up with the appropriate piece of kitchen pipe, so Gigi was glad of the offer.

Sienna regarded her with narrowed eyes. "Okay, give. What's up? You've got that look."

"What look?" Gigi asked innocently.

"The look. The one you get when you're about to suggest we do something insane like break into someone's porch for evidence."

"I had no choice," Gigi protested.

"Well, whatever it is, we can't let you do it alone."

* * *

Gigi spent the rest of the morning working on some recipes for Branston Foods. The good news was that she would serve the finished products to Winchel and the rest of Felicity's houseguests for lunch.

Anja was serving the meal, and everyone was in the dining room waiting to eat, when Gigi got out her cell and called Sienna and Alice. She reached Alice first and whispered into the phone, "The coast is clear," before hanging up.

She dialed Sienna and went through the same scenario. Then she hovered near the back door until they arrived.

"Oh, that rain refuses to let up," Alice declared.

"Sssh," Gigi and Sienna said in unison.

Alice's hand flew to her mouth. "Sorry."

"We can go straight upstairs." Gigi pointed to the back stairs, which went from the mudroom by the back door up to the second and third floors.

"This is so exciting," Alice said, and they shushed her again.

They got to the door of Felicity's bedroom, and Alice suddenly came to a halt. "I . . . I'm not sure I want to go in there." She swiped a hand across her eyes. "It was so . . . horrible, seeing that poor woman like that."

"Then you can stand watch," Sienna said decisively.

"Well, all right, I guess I'll go with you," Alice said, obviously not wanting to be left out.

They tiptoed across the acres of ultra-plush carpeting toward the master bath. Alice's head swiveled this way and that. "I didn't really get a chance to look around before. I was too upset. This is some setup, don't you think?" She plunged her hand into the cashmere throw that was casually draped across a rose-colored chaise longue.

"It's a little fancy for my taste." Sienna crossed the room quickly.

Gigi realized she couldn't even begin to imagine living in a room like this, so there was no point in thinking about it. The bedroom in her little cottage was perfect as far as she was concerned—small but homey and comfortable.

"Is this where it happened?" Sienna stood at the entrance to the bathroom.

Despite her earlier attack of nerves, Alice peered over Sienna's shoulder eagerly. Gigi was the only one holding back. Sienna opened the sauna door and peered in. The bench inside was large enough for several people. Gigi had never seen a sauna before, but this one looked as if everything was in order.

"Do you think it malfunctioned somehow?" Gigi examined the knobs and dials that she supposed set the temperature and the time.

"But that would make it an accident, and the police don't think it was for some reason."

"True."

Sienna pushed the door to the sauna closed and sighed in defeat. "I can't imagine what the police saw in here, can you?"

Alice shook her head, and Gigi was about to do the same when she stopped abruptly. She moved closer to the sauna door and examined it carefully, running her fingers across the smooth wooden finish.

"I think I know what they saw," she said, straightening up with a look of triumph on her face.

"What? Don't keep us in suspense," Sienna demanded.

"See that?" Gigi ran her hand across the wooden door again.

"What?" Alice adjusted her glasses on her nose. "I don't see anything."

"Feel it," Gigi suggested.

Alice delicately brushed her fingertips across the sauna door. "Feels like it's scratched."

"Exactly!" Gigi said.

Sienna shrugged. "So what?"

"So," Gigi explained, "I think someone might have put something in front of the door. To block it."

Alice's hand flew to her mouth. "Then it was murder," she said, her blue eyes round with shock.

"What do you think they used?" Sienna looked around the bathroom. "It had to have been something close at hand."

Gigi nodded. "My best guess would be a chair of some sort." She gestured toward the sauna door. "Wedged under the handle. Hardly foolproof, but if Felicity panicked . . ."

"But when I found Felicity"—Alice gulped hard, and her face blanched white—"she was already half out of the sauna."

"The killer must have hung around and removed the chair thinking the police would be none the wiser." Gigi wandered into the bedroom, and the other two followed. "It may have even been the killer who opened the sauna door to make it look as if Felicity tried to get out."

Gigi looked around the room. It didn't lack for chairs— plump chairs, straight chairs, reclining chairs. Any one of them could have been the one the murderer used. She wondered if there might be some sort of mark on the back, and began examining them one by one. Nothing.

She glanced at a chair in the corner that had an almost abandoned look, as if no one ever sat in it. Something caught her eye. Maybe . . . She moved around the room examining the other pieces of furniture.

"Well, Anja certainly isn't much of a housekeeper," Gigi declared suddenly. "But I think I've found our chair."

She was rewarded by the dumbfounded looks on the faces of Sienna and Alice.

"This is going to be good." Sienna sat down on the edge of the bed and put a hand to her back.

"How on earth?" Alice sputtered.

"If you look around"—Gigi waved a hand toward the furniture in the room—"you'll see that Anja, or whoever does the housekeeping, is in the habit of vacuuming around the bed, chairs and so forth."

"My mother always taught me to move everything to one side and do a decent job. *A job worth doing is a job worth doing well*," Alice quoted.

Gigi pointed at the carpet. "You can see that things haven't been moved. The carpet is so thick, the feet of all the furniture have left indentations in the pile. If," she added, feeling more like Miss Jane Marple by the minute, "the housekeeper moved them regularly, the marks would not be so distinct."

Gigi tilted the chaise longue slightly so they could see the deep well left in the thick rug.

"But this chair"—Gigi walked toward the chair orphaned in the corner—"is not in its exact former location. You can see the original craterous dents in the carpet, but the legs of the chair don't match up. They've begun creating a second set of marks in the pile."

"So the chair was moved!" Alice said, wide-eyed.

"It would seem so," Gigi said. "It also"—she gestured toward the chair back—"looks to be about the right height to have made that scratch on the sauna door."

Sienna slid off the bed and went over to examine the chair. "It's wood on back," she said, peering behind it. "And there are metal grommets along the top."

"Yup," Gigi replied. "Someone used that chair to bar the sauna door." She looked at Alice and Sienna and shivered.

"That's terrible," Alice said, plunking down into the

chaise and swinging her legs up. "Who would do such a thing?"

Gigi glanced at Alice and frowned. "Maybe we ought to get—" She cut off abruptly when a noise made the three of them swivel toward the door.

"Someone's coming!"

Chapter 6

Alice let out a tiny shriek and jumped up from the chaise. "Oh no, we're busted."

The sound of footsteps echoed on the wooden back stairs.

"Quick"—Gigi made a sweeping gesture with her arm—"let's hide in the bathroom. At least we won't be visible from the open bedroom door."

Together they beat a retreat toward the bathroom. Sienna promptly sat down on the wooden bench inside the sauna.

"I don't know how you can go in there." Alice shivered.

"I have no choice." Sienna stuck her legs out in front of her. "My feet are killing me."

She was wearing a tunic-length sweater and black leggings, and the front of her top was stretched as far as it could go.

"Another ten days." She sighed. "Although I've been having contractions on and off, so perhaps it will be early."

"Sssh." Gigi peeked around the edge of the door.

"Is someone coming?" Alice whispered, drawing back farther into the bathroom.

"It's Derek," Gigi said. She pulled her head back in suddenly and flattened herself against the wall behind the door.

"What's he doing?" Alice whispered.

Gigi shrugged.

They could hear him moving about in Felicity's room, opening and closing closet doors and drawers.

Very cautiously, Gigi peeked around the edge of the door. Derek had his back to her. Felicity's jewelry box was sprawled open on her dresser, and Derek was sifting through the contents one by one, his dark head bent over the task. Gigi watched as he held up two gold chains, palmed them, then stuffed them into the pocket of his jeans.

Gigi had to put her hand over her mouth to stifle her gasp of outrage. She knew that Derek sometimes raided Felicity's purse for a few dollars in cash, but this was much worse— stealing from the dead.

"What's going on?" Alice hissed when she saw the look on Gigi's face.

Gigi shook her head and peeked around the door again. Derek had replaced the other items in the jewelry box and was putting it back inside Felicity's lingerie drawer. Finally, he eased the drawer closed and sauntered out of the room, whistling softly under his breath.

Gigi felt steam gathering in her head and let out a huge breath. "Well!"

"Well, what?" Alice asked eagerly.

Sienna stopped rotating her ankles and looked at Gigi expectantly.

"That was Derek!" Gigi's fists clenched involuntarily. "He stole some pieces from Felicity's jewelry box."

Alice blew out a big breath, and her bangs flopped up and down. "Of all the nerve!"

"Felicity regularly complained about his taking money from her wallet." Sienna eased her way off the sauna bench with a hand to her back. "But I got the impression that she didn't really mind. She rather overindulged him in my opinion."

Alice nodded. "Trying to make up to him for not being his real mother."

"What happened to his mother?" Gigi had opened the mirrored medicine cabinet and was staring in awe at the contents. It looked like the cosmetics counter at Macy's.

"According to Felicity, she was an incredibly selfish, high-powered surgeon who ran off to join Doctors Without Borders and serve the underprivileged in darkest Africa." Sienna's mouth curved into a smile. "Instead of staying in New York and making millions of dollars performing plastic surgery on the rich and famous."

"In a way, it was a bit selfish of her not to think of her son," Alice put in.

"True." Sienna stretched her arms over her head and yawned. "But I gather Felicity has been trying to make it up to him ever since." She glanced toward the door. "Is the coast clear?"

Gigi peered into the now empty bedroom. "Looks good."

"That was close," Alice said as they dispersed into the hall.

"Yes, but it was certainly worth it," Gigi said. "We now know why the police think foul play was involved, and I'm inclined to agree with them."

Alice led the way down the dark, twisting back stairs, one hand on the railing, the other trailing against the wall.

"The killer must have turned up the temperature, too," Sienna said, feeling her way carefully down the narrow stairs. "There was this Russian fellow I remember reading about. He was in some sort of contest to see who could stay in this dreadfully hot sauna the longest. They turned the temperature up to two hundred thirty degrees. He lasted six minutes."

"What do you mean?" Alice said, stopping abruptly on the steps.

"He died. And his fellow contestant was seriously injured."

"Well then, I guess we need to find out who blocked the sauna *and* tampered with the settings," Alice said.

"Sure," Gigi agreed. "Easy peasy."

Gigi straightened up a final few things in the kitchen. She could hear voices coming from the dining room and the sounds of knives and forks on plates. Laughter mingled with the murmur of chatter. Gigi crossed her fingers. She hoped they liked the dishes she had prepared. With Felicity gone— the thought still gave her pause—she would have to line up some new clients soon. Fortunately there were several people on her waiting list. She would call them right away.

"Anything I can do to help?" Alice had one arm in her jacket sleeve.

"Not really." Gigi wrung out the dishrag and draped it over the faucet to dry. "Anja is taking care of cleaning up the lunch dishes."

"Speaking of lunch"—Alice stuck her other arm through the corresponding sleeve—"I'm starved. What do you say we get a bite to eat at that new place, Declan's?"

Gigi wrinkled her nose. "I've been dreading going in there since Al Forno closed."

"I know what you mean. But we can't avoid it forever."

Alice buttoned her jacket. "Come on. Let's go see what everyone's been talking about."

Gigi felt her heart thump as they approached the bright red awning announcing Declan's Grille. It wasn't going to be the same without Emilio and Carlo there to greet her. Alice went first, pushing open the heavy front door. The interior was dim, and they stopped for a moment to get their bearings. The bar area was paneled, and the bar itself was carved from a massive piece of highly polished wood. High, round tables surrounded the bar. A few scattered people still sat at the white-linen-covered dining tables, finishing up their meal. A blackboard over the bar announced the day's specials: shepherd's pie and ploughman's lunch. Gigi had to admit that the smells coming from the kitchen were tantalizingly delicious, and her mouth was watering already.

A man stood behind the bar. He appeared to be totaling up the day's receipts. He was tall and slim with broad shoulders and a narrow waist and had dark hair with a bit of a curl. Gigi found herself wondering two things: Was this Declan McQuaid, and was he as good-looking from the front as he was from the back?

He turned around, and she had one of her answers at least. The man had vivid blue eyes, thick, dark brows, even features and a delightful cleft in his chin. He smiled at Gigi and Alice, and Gigi found herself momentarily tongue-tied.

"Welcome to Declan's." He stuck out a hand.

"Declan, I presume?" Alice said as she accepted his handshake.

"The one and only." He smiled. "Would you ladies like a table, or would you care to sit at the bar and keep me company while I polish some glasses?" He glanced point-edly at Gigi.

Gigi cursed the infernal blush that always blossomed at exactly the wrong moments. Hopefully the dim lighting made it less obvious.

"I'd love to sit at the bar. How about you?" Alice nodded encouragingly at Gigi.

Why did everyone in Woodstone want to fix her up, Gigi thought, as she let herself be led, like a doomed sheep, toward an empty bar stool.

"I bet he's got more than a few notches in his belt," Alice whispered, tipping her head toward Declan. She perused the menu. "I love the sound of bubble and squeak, but I think I'm going to go with the grilled cheddar cheese sandwich on homemade bread with warm potato salad." She put the menu down. "How about you?"

Gigi's hunger had suddenly deserted her. She was hyper-aware of Declan's crooked grin as he watched them from behind the bar where he was polishing glasses that already sparkled with cleanliness. Gigi felt her telltale blush flame her face again, and she buried her head in the menu.

"I don't know," she mumbled from her protective cover. "I can't decide. It all sounds so good." She read through the options again and glanced up at the blackboard where the specials had been printed out in strong, block letters. "Maybe the ploughman's lunch."

"What is that?"

Declan must have heard Alice because he approached them, his cloth slung over his right shoulder. "That's an old English favorite." He smiled, his eyes on Gigi's. "My ances-tors may be Irish, but I grew up in England. A ploughman's lunch centers around a chunk of homemade bread, a wedge of fine cheddar or Stilton, a piece of good ham and, last but not least, Branston pickle. Our very own recipe, of course."

Gigi fought the urge to fan herself with the menu. "What's Branston pickle?" she asked in an attempt to divert Declan's attention from her.

"It's more *pickled* than *pickle*," he said, smiling in such a way that the cleft in his chin deepened. "It's a combination of vegetables and fruits—apples, cauliflower, carrots, onions, garlic, swedes—I think you call those rutabagas—courgettes—" He ducked his head. "I must learn that when in Rome . . . courgettes are what you call zucchini, I believe." He looked at Alice.

She shrugged. "Ask Gigi, she's the expert."

Declan raised his eyebrows, causing Gigi's blush to intensify. She cursed Alice under her breath.

"I do like to cook."

"Ha!" Alice guffawed. "That's an understatement." She poked an elbow in Gigi's direction. "She's really good. Her stuff is delicious."

"I hope I get to try it sometime." Declan lowered his voice so that he and Gigi were wrapped in their own bubble.

"I'll have the ploughman's lunch, then." Gigi snapped her menu shut.

Declan's face returned to a neutral expression, and he moved back away from the bar. "I'll put your order in. It shouldn't be long."

"Now why on earth did you go and—"

Gigi cut Alice off. "He was making me uncomfortable."

"You're never going to find a man if—"

"I don't want to find a man," Gigi all but screamed even though she realized she didn't mean it even as the words came out of her mouth. What she didn't want was another Ted. Another heartbreak. Another divorce. And Declan

McQuaid had all the hallmarks of the "*love 'em and leave 'em*" type. This time she wanted something permanent . . . or nothing at all.

Gigi's cell phone rang as she was about to pull away from the curb after dropping Alice off at the police station. She didn't normally work Saturdays but was covering for someone who had a funeral to attend. Gigi answered the call quickly—it seemed that Hector's Heating and Plumbing had finally secured the correct piece of pipe for the one-hundred-year-old plumbing system under her cottage's kitchen sink.

Gigi was glad she would soon be able to escape Felicity's posthumous hospitality. Tension crackled in the air between the guests, and it was hardly a comfortable place to be.

After several days of rain, sunshine finally filtered through the vibrant leaves on the trees and formed dappled patterns on the sidewalk. There was a brisk breeze—it was light coat weather, but still comfortable.

Gigi had half an hour before Jackson was expected at the cottage with the piece of pipe that was going to put everything back in working order. *At least until something else springs a leak*, a small devilish voice whispered in the back of Gigi's mind. She felt her stomach clench. She had to sign some new clients soon. The deal with Branston Foods looked as if it was going to go through, but she'd learned long ago not to count her chickens before they hatched.

Gigi pulled up in front of Bon Appétit, Woodstone's cookery store and gourmet shop. Fortunately, there were two spaces in front of the store, so she didn't have to attempt to parallel park. Gigi's face reddened annoyingly as she remembered another occasion when she was trying to park and making a complete mess of it. As luck would have it,

Mertz had come along in time to witness her humiliation. She'd vowed never to try parallel parking again, even if it meant parking a mile away and walking back.

Evelyn Fishko was behind the counter at Bon Appétit as always, her dark hair in its short bob held back off her face with a bright red headband. If something happened in Woodstone, there was no keeping it from Evelyn.

"Howdy, stranger," she said as Gigi approached the counter. Gigi did her big shopping trips at the Shop and Save outside of town, but there were certain items like truffle oil and fresh pâté that couldn't be had anywhere except at Bon Appétit.

Evelyn looked eager to see Gigi, and Gigi thought she knew why. There had been a brief mention of Felicity's death in the local paper. Evelyn, no doubt, planned to pump her for the in-depth details.

"Hello, yourself." Gigi smiled as she approached the counter.

"What can I get for you today?" Evelyn leaned her elbows on the counter.

Gigi pulled a short list from her purse and consulted it. "Not much, really. I'm out of pine nuts, and I'm running low on that lovely balsamic vinegar you carry."

Evelyn glowed at the compliment. She prided herself on the top-notch quality of her selection and did all the buying herself. She fetched the two items and put them down on the counter.

"And?"

"That's it for now."

Evelyn thumbed two pieces of tissue from the stack on the counter and carefully wrapped Gigi's items. She pulled a black and white striped bag with *Bon Appétit* written on it in script from under the counter and placed Gigi's order inside. But instead of handing over the package, she leaned her elbows on the counter again and got comfortable.

Gigi sighed. She knew what was coming.

"I read about your client, that soap opera star, in the paper. Shame. Awfully young, wasn't she?"

Gigi smiled and nodded her head.

"And didn't she take up with that friend of yours' husband? The one who runs the Book Nook down the street?"

"Sienna?"

"That's the one. Someone left a copy of the *New York Post* on the bench outside the shop." Evelyn shook her head. "I don't understand some people . . . there's a trash can not five feet away. Anywho, I glanced through it before throwing it away. Do you think it was true? I know a lot of these actress types take up with a boy toy."

Somehow Gigi had never pictured Oliver as a "boy toy," and she had to suppress a giggle. "No, it wasn't true at all. Just a publicity stunt. Sienna says it happens all the time."

"That's what I thought. Hey, weren't you catering that big shindig Miss Davenport had?"

Gigi reluctantly acknowledged that she had.

"I suppose you know all about what happened that night," Evelyn hinted.

"Not really," Gigi murmured.

"Real shame for the Woodstone Players. They were counting on her to bring in the crowds. And the—" She rubbed two fingers together. "Of course, I heard that her manager covered his own you-know-what by taking out some kind of policy on her."

"Really?" Now Gigi was listening in earnest, her own elbows resting comfortably on the counter, her groceries forgotten.

Evelyn nodded vigorously, causing her bob to swing to

and fro. "Yes. I guess it's *S-O-P*—standard operating procedure—in that business. If for some reason Miss Davenport doesn't show up, takes ill, walks off, whatever—you know how temperamental those actor types can be—then he gets the money from the insurance policy."

What she wanted to say was *How on earth did you hear about that?* but she settled for, "How interesting. I suppose you're sure . . ."

Evelyn nodded her head vigorously. "Hunter Pierce was just in buying some herbes de Provence. I overheard him talking to his companion—some young man I didn't recognize—I suppose he came out from the city."

Evelyn said *city* as if it were a four-letter word.

"He was complaining about it," she continued, leaning closer toward Gigi. "About how Felicity's manager was going to get all this money, and once again the Woodstone Players were going to be left in the hole."

Well, she was certainly leaving with more than just her groceries, Gigi thought, as she exited Bon Appétit and headed toward her car. She sat in the MINI for a minute contemplating what Evelyn had told her. If, and it was a big *if*, what Evelyn told her was true, then Don Bartholomew, Felicity's manager, had a very good reason for wanting his client out of the way. Felicity had been Don's golden goose for many, many years, but she was getting too old now to lay any more golden eggs. Parts for middle-aged women were notoriously few and far between. Don's prize client had become more of a liability than an asset.

Gigi glanced at her watch and realized she needed to hurry, or she might miss Jackson and his arrival with the life-saving pipe. She put the car in gear and pulled away from the curb.

She was passing the Woodstone Police Station when

something caught her eye. She slowed and looked again and realized it was Alice, standing on the sidewalk, her rather unruly hair blowing every which way. She waved crazily at Gigi.

Gigi slowed and pulled over to the curb, double-parking next to a red Honda. She buzzed down her window.

Alice was nearly gasping by the time she reached Gigi's car. "I'm so glad I caught you!" She gripped the edge of the window, attempting to catch her breath.

"What's wrong?" Gigi felt herself catching some of Alice's anxiety even though she had no idea what was going on.

"It's Sienna."

Gigi's hand flew to her mouth. "Oh no. Has something happened to the baby?" Her hand inched toward the ignition. If something was wrong with Sienna, she had to get to her right away.

Alice shook her head, her blues eyes nearly bulging in excitement. "No, no, the baby's fine. It's Detective Mertz." She paused to catch her breath.

Now Gigi was more confused than ever. Detective Mertz?

"He's . . . he's . . ." Alice said, trying to get the words out. "He's on his way to arrest Sienna for Felicity's murder."

Chapter 7

By the time she pulled into Sienna's driveway, Gigi's heart was clamoring in her chest, and she knew her face was as red as her scarlet MINI Cooper. Her Irish was rising, and her Italian was right on board. She wouldn't have been surprised to see steam spewing out of her nostrils.

Mertz's Crown Vic was already in the drive, pulled up to the front door of Sienna and Oliver's renovated carriage house. Everything was quiet except for the rustling of the wind in the leaves and the *rat-a-tat-tat* of a woodpecker hammering at a tree.

Gigi stormed up the front steps of the fieldstone and half-timber house and slammed the pineapple-shaped knocker against the bright red door.

When Sienna yanked it open, Gigi was shocked to see how white-faced she was. Her first thought was for the baby and what this might be doing to it. She felt her anger rise another notch.

"What's going on?" Gigi asked in alarm. "Alice told me—"

"Detective Mertz is just here to ask a few questions." Sienna put her hand on Gigi's arm reassuringly. "I'm sure it will all be straightened out in no time."

"Is Oliver here?"

Sienna nodded. "He's in the kitchen with Mertz."

They heard male voices approaching the door and turned toward the hallway that led to the kitchen. Mertz came around the corner and froze when he saw Gigi. His posture was as ramrod straight as ever, but his light blue eyes had an apologetic look in them.

Part of Gigi's brain recognized how attractive Mertz was, but the other part ordered her to stiffen her back and greet him with an icy glare.

Gigi and Sienna stood aside and watched silently as Oliver followed Mertz to the door and ushered him outside, then closed the door and leaned against it, his hands hanging limply at his sides, his eyes closed.

"Let's go make some tea." Sienna took Gigi by the arm.

The kitchen was bright and airy, dominated by a limestone-topped island over which hung a pot rack filled with shiny copper pots. Gigi pulled out one of the stools and sank down onto it. She'd been in such a state since Alice pulled her over on High Street that she was now exhausted.

Some color had returned to Sienna's cheeks. Gigi watched as she held a brass teakettle under the tall, curving faucet and set it to boil on the stove. Sienna kept her back to Gigi as she fussed with cups and saucers, tea bags and cream and sugar, and Gigi had the impression that she was using the time to compose herself. When Sienna turned around with the tray set with tea things, she looked almost normal. Gigi bit her tongue and waited as Sienna poured tea, offered cream and sugar and had her first sip. Finally, Sienna set her teacup down. It rattled slightly in the saucer. She pushed a hand through her mass of golden hair and sighed heavily.

"Your Detective Mertz seems to think I had something to do with Felicity Davenport's death."

"He's not *my* Detective Mertz," Gigi sputtered. "Why on earth would Mertz think you had anything to do with what happened to Felicity?"

Sienna looked away and kept her head averted as she spoke. "Well, that article in the *New York Post* for starters."

"True."

Sienna turned around, and her face definitely had color now. "I can't imagine what Felicity thought she was doing with that outrageous scheme of hers. Unfortunately"—she smiled sadly at Gigi—"Mertz seems to think it gives me a motive for murder."

"He can't be serious!" Gigi exploded. "No one in their right mind—"

"Unfortunately, there's more." She stared into her cup of tea as if trying to read her future in it. "There was evidence that someone came up the back stairs that afternoon—some wet leaves stuck to the steps and some small puddles of water."

"But anyone could have left those!" Gigi protested.

Sienna shrugged. "It seems that everyone else has some sort of alibi, while I . . ."

"You don't?"

Sienna shook her head. "It's not that." She looked up at Gigi, and Gigi was shocked to see the tears in her eyes. "I can't tell anyone where I was that afternoon. I just can't."

Gigi left Sienna's house more perplexed than when she had arrived. What on earth had Sienna been up to that she couldn't tell Gigi, one of her oldest friends? Gigi shivered, and it wasn't from the sudden icy edge to the breeze nor from the line of clouds that suddenly masked the sun.

Gigi was putting her key in the car door when she remembered Hector's Plumbing and Heating and her date with the laconical Jackson. She glanced at her watch. She was twenty minutes late. Hopefully Jackson had waited.

Gigi was relieved to see Jackson's truck in her driveway when she pulled in. Jackson himself was asleep in the driver's seat—head tipped back, mouth open slightly.

Gigi knocked on the window of the truck and watched as Jackson slowly came awake. He rubbed the back of his neck and reached for his tool box.

"Sorry," Gigi said as soon as his door was open. "I was held up."

"S'all right." Jackson reached into the back of the truck and pulled out a section of shiny, new pipe.

While Jackson fiddled under the sink, and Reg stood guard nearby, Gigi flipped through her notebook for the names of the people who had asked to be added to her waiting list. She could handle only a certain number of clients at once, but if the deal with Branston went through, hordes of people would be able to access her low-calorie gourmet food. Gigi hoped that some of them would still want the personalized service and fresh ingredients of the real thing.

A half hour later, Gigi hung up the phone and sighed with satisfaction. She'd signed six new clients. It looked like she'd be able to keep the lights burning for another month.

Gigi had almost forgotten about Jackson when he grunted and backed out from under the sink. He rose slowly to his full six feet, one hand on his lower back.

"Sink's fixed. I'll just go turn your water back on for you.

Valve in the basement?" He pushed his dark blue *Yankees* baseball cap farther back on his forehead.

"I'll get it." Gigi opened the door to the basement. By the time Jackson got downstairs, found the valve and came back up, the sun would have set.

There were fewer cobwebs to contend with this time, and Gigi quickly turned the water back on and raced back up the stairs.

Jackson turned the tap, which hissed and spit before finally spewing forth a stream of water.

Gigi had to restrain herself from clapping her hands. Never before had she appreciated water quite so much. Gigi gladly wrote Jackson a check—she had to pay extra because it was a Saturday, but it was worth it. She'd still be spending a fair amount of time in Felicity's kitchen—it made sense to prepare for the funeral lunch on the spot—but she'd be able to sleep in her own bed again, with the windows open to the scent of lavender from her garden.

Sunday was a quiet day. Gigi slept late and headed to Winchel's in the late afternoon to prepare a light supper of soup and sandwiches. She was surprised at how tired she was and was glad to be able to have an early night. She would be meeting one of her potential new clients on Monday morning. Gigi felt the same stirrings of excitement as she had the time she had scored her very first client and had realized Gourmet De-Lite was off and running. As much as she'd loved working in New York City for *Wedding Spectacular* magazine, she was relishing the opportunity to grow her own business.

Her newest client was a paralegal at the offices of Simpson and West. Gigi knew the office well—the attorneys there had handled Martha Bernhardt's estate. Martha had been a client of Gigi's and the original owner of Gigi's cottage. Gigi had been awed by her first visit to their office—the walls were paneled in fine wood, the furniture was all antique and the rugs were silk Orientals. An expensive hush hung over the entire place as if everyone had been forbidden to speak above a whisper.

Gigi pulled into the miniature five-car parking lot in back of the building and was relieved to get the last space. She pulled her collar up against the now chilly wind and walked around to the front of the building. Simpson and West occupied the second and third floors above the Knick Knack Shop.

The offices were as she remembered them—quiet, tastefully expensive and subtly forbidding. Gigi gave her name to the receptionist, who sat behind a huge mahogany desk devoid of anything but a telephone and a blotter. Gigi's client, Madeline Stone, was on the third floor. Gigi was directed up the interior spiral staircase that linked the two floors.

The third floor was as hushed as the second, but here the offices were smaller, and there were a number of cubicles piled high with law books and manila folders. Madeline had a tiny office, hardly larger than a broom closet, with no window and barely enough room for an extra chair.

Madeline was in her early thirties with long, dark hair. She was pretty, but Gigi noticed that the fabric of her skirt was stretched tightly across her hips. She jumped up from her chair when she saw Gigi coming.

"Hi, I'm Madeline." She stuck out a hand and pumped Gigi's own energetically. "Have a seat. Sorry there's so little room."

"That's okay." Gigi took a green folder off the chair, put it on the corner of Madeline's desk and sat down.

"I've heard wonderful things about you," Madeline gushed.

Gigi ducked her head. She found compliments embarrassing. "I do my best to make the food taste good. My clients are the ones who do all the work."

"I do hope your diet will work for me." Madeline twirled a long strand of hair around her finger and leaned toward Gigi. "Everyone around here is so perfect." She inclined her head toward her open door. "All the women are thin, and dress perfectly and have their hair and nails just so."

Gigi nodded encouragingly.

"I'm kind of afraid"—Madeline lowered her voice even further, so that Gigi had to lean forward to hear—"that someone"—Madeline raised her brows up and down as if transmitting secret code—"is going to decide that I don't quite fit the Simpson and West image, if you know what I mean." She glanced around again like a secret agent in an old Cold War movie. "It's happened before."

Gigi nodded understandingly.

"Anyway," Madeline continued, "a friend of mine, Beth Taylor, used your services and dropped a ton of pounds, and she said it was easy. And I've heard that you were hired by that actress, Felicity Davenport, who lives here in Woodstone, and I thought if you're good enough for her, wow, you're sure good enough for me."

Something had unleashed the floodgates of Madeline's conversation, and Gigi drew back in alarm as her voice got louder. She half expected some Simpson and West gatekeeper to come along and tell her to shush.

"What a shame about that poor woman dying the way she did." Madeline's face was getting flushed in her excitement. "Back before I started working I always watched *For Better or For Worse*, and sometimes now I even record it." Her voice dropped back to a conspiratorial level.

"Really?"

Madeline nodded her head. "People tell me they see Felicity around town all the time, seeing as her country house is here and all, but I only saw her the once. Only she actually came *here*." Madeline was almost breathless. "Waltzed in wearing this heavenly fur coat that must have cost a fortune! Of course, she *has* a fortune. I guess that stepson of hers, Derek, is getting half of it. The rest will go to her husband, of course."

Gigi, who had been thinking of something else altogether, felt her ears perk up. "Derek? Really?"

Madeline nodded. "Mr. Simpson himself handled the will. And he asked specifically for me as his assistant."

Gigi could barely focus after that. If Derek stood to inherit most of Felicity's money, didn't that give him a darn good reason for killing his stepmother? Gigi remembered watching as Derek lifted the gold jewelry from Felicity's room. She couldn't imagine what he needed the money for. Felicity said he received a generous allowance, and they paid all his charges around town. Did he need money desperately enough to kill?

Don Bartholomew had also gained from Felicity's death—a nice hefty check from the insurance policy he'd had the brilliant forethought to purchase. Gigi felt a tingle of excitement. She now had not one but two likely suspects to present to Detective Mertz.

Surely this would make him realize that Sienna couldn't possibly have had anything to do with the murder.

Chapter 8

Gigi drove down High Street, past the Book Nook, past Abigail's, past the Silver Lining, rehearsing what she would say to Detective Mertz when she got to the police station. He'd discounted everything she'd discovered last time—when Martha Bernhardt had been the victim. Would this time be any different? She found herself dragging her feet.

Maybe she ought to talk to Sienna first? She felt like a coward as she pulled into the tiny parking lot next to Declan's Grille and turned the car around. She couldn't help glancing at the window shaded by the bright red awning. She didn't want to admit it, but she wouldn't have minded catching a glimpse of Declan again.

She was about to pull back out onto High Street to head in the other direction when she realized that perhaps she ought to call Sienna first. She backed up, pulled into the closest vacant spot and, after much scrambling, dredged her phone from the bottom of her purse.

The phone rang half a dozen times before Sienna picked up.

"Gigi. I'm glad you caught me. We were just about to go out."

"I won't keep you, then. I just wanted to give you some good news. I think I've uncovered another potential suspect in Felicity's death."

"Really? Hang on a sec."

Gigi heard the muffled sounds that indicated Sienna had put her hand over the receiver.

"Oliver just got home. We're headed to Declan's for dinner. Why don't you join us?"

"Declan's?" Gigi heard the squeak in her voice.

"Yes. We haven't been yet, and Oliver is anxious to try it. We've heard some really good things about the place." Sienna lowered her voice. "And about the owner, too. I gather he's gorgeous."

"He is. I've met him."

"Then this will give you a chance to see him again," Sienna said decisively.

"I don't think he's the type I want to get involved with."

"Why not? He's good-looking and employed. A winning combination."

"He just seems like he might be a player."

"Why? Just because he's gorgeous? Don't be silly. You can't judge a book by its cover."

"All right." Gigi reluctantly agreed to meet them in five minutes.

Gigi felt rather ridiculous sitting in her car waiting, but there was no way she was going into Declan's alone. The very thought made her shiver.

People gave her funny looks as they drove into the parking lot, and some even hesitated, wondering if she were leaving and they could have her space. Gigi was about to slink down in her seat so no one would see her when Sienna and Oliver pulled into the lot in the new BMW Oliver had leased. Gigi was surprised to see that Oliver still had the car. With Oliver's law practice slow to take off, Sienna had mentioned cutting back on any number of things.

Gigi had a thought that sent her stomach into a tailspin. Was there any financial gain for Sienna in Felicity's death? She couldn't think of anything, but who knew what the police might drum up. Suddenly, she wasn't half as hungry as she'd been a few minutes earlier.

Gigi felt slightly better walking into the restaurant under the cover of dinner with Oliver and Sienna. Perhaps Declan wouldn't notice her. Maybe he'd be busy in the kitchen or behind the bar.

Steak and Guinness pie was the special of the day, and the place was crowded with diners anxious to try this new dish.

"Anything with beer in it is fine by me," Oliver remarked as he gave his name and the number in their party to the hostess—a beautiful young woman with auburn hair slightly lighter than Gigi's.

Gigi cringed when Declan spied them and quickly made his way through the crowd around the bar.

"Welcome to Declan's." He smiled at Gigi. "I'm glad to see you came back."

Sienna raised her eyebrows at Gigi, and Gigi mouthed *later.*

"We can't have you standing, can we?" Declan nodded at Sienna's swollen belly.

"See what you can do," he said to the hostess, who stood patiently waiting.

She disappeared toward the back of the dining room, and Gigi noticed her snapping her fingers at some busboys who hastened to clear a recently vacated table.

"Please." Declan put his hand lightly on Sienna's shoulder and led them toward the waiting table.

Several patrons gave them dirty looks, and Gigi ducked her head as they wended their way through the packed dining room.

"So what's the big news?" Oliver asked after the waitress had brought their drinks and left menus on their table.

Gigi pushed her menu to one side and leaned her elbows on the table. "I have not one but two"—she counted on her fingers—"possible suspects for Mertz to chase instead of Sienna." She nodded toward her friend, who was sipping a glass of sparkling water. She was wearing a long, brightly colored silk blouse over a pair of leggings. Sienna managed to make even pregnancy look exotic, Gigi thought.

Oliver's eyebrows shot up over the rims of his round, tortoise-framed glasses, and he brushed a hand through the hank of dark hair that fell over his forehead. "Really?" He glanced at Sienna with an encouraging smile.

Sienna didn't look up but continued to twirl the ice cubes around and around in her glass with her index finger.

"Who are your suspects?" Oliver asked encouragingly.

Gigi suspected that he was humoring her, but she didn't care. She was confident that she was on to something. "First off, there's Felicity's manager, Don Bartholomew."

"But she's his star client. Why would he want to get rid of her," Oliver said, licking the foam off the top of his beer.

Gigi explained to both of them about the insurance policy and the hefty payout.

"Sounds like a serious suspect to me," Oliver agreed. "Does he have an alibi?"

Gigi shrugged. "I have no idea. I am going to try to find out, though." Even as she said it, Gigi realized she had no idea exactly how she was going to do that. If only Mertz would get his mind off Sienna and start looking into some real suspects!

"Okay, I agree this Bartholomew character makes an excellent suspect," Oliver said as if he were summing up in court, "now tell us who the second one is."

Gigi spread her hands out on the table. "I was at the attorney's office—"

Oliver raised his eyebrows.

"Simpson and West," Gigi supplied.

Oliver made a face, and Gigi shrugged apologetically. "I have a new client there."

Oliver looked slightly mollified.

"Go on." Sienna was paying attention now and leaned forward eagerly.

"I was meeting with my new client, Madeline Stone. She's a paralegal there. We got to talking, and she let slip that Felicity's stepson, Derek, will inherit half of her estate."

Oliver let out a long, low whistle, and several diners at nearby tables turned to look at him. He swiveled toward Sienna. "Looks like Gigi's done some amazing detective work." He put his hand over his wife's, and she smiled wanly at him. "When do you plan on bringing this new information to Detective Mertz?"

Gigi looked down at the table. "Soon. Very soon." *As soon as I get up the nerve*, she thought to herself. Mertz hadn't believed her before, why would he now?

"I'd recommend the special tonight." Declan glided up to their table. His smooth voice and lilting accent cut into Gigi's thoughts. She willed her face not to get flushed, but it was one of the downsides of having red hair that she had never been able to conquer.

Sienna looked at the menu doubtfully. "I don't think I should have the steak and Guinness pie."

"Don't worry. The alcohol burns off. On the other hand, if that concerns you, I'd suggest the hanger steak with sweet potato fries."

Gigi tried to focus on the menu, but the words morphed into a fuzzy haze the harder she tried. She was hyperaware of Declan standing beside her and was sure she could feel the heat coming from him. Then again, maybe it was her annoying telltale blush that was making her so warm.

"I'll have the special," she said decisively when Declan came around to her. She was so flustered, she'd completely forgotten what the special was. Well, surprises were always good, weren't they?

"Same for me," Oliver said, putting down his menu.

"Excellent choice," Declan assured them as he collected their menus and handed the order to the waitress who had been hovering nearby.

"Looks like we're getting some pretty special treatment. Or does the owner go around to every table?" Oliver shook out his napkin and spread it on his lap.

Sienna's face brightened for the first time that evening. "I do think Declan fancies you," she said to Gigi after Declan had turned the corner. "That is the British term for it, isn't it?"

Gigi protested, but she was actually rather pleased. She thought of Mertz and his ruggedly good-looking features and then she thought of how mad he'd made her, and she decided right then and there that if by some wild miracle, Declan McQuaid asked her out . . . she would say yes.

The next morning, Gigi awoke early. She stretched luxuriously and breathed deeply. Fragrant lavender-scented air drifted in through the partially cracked window. The breeze had a delicious chill to it, and she snuggled contentedly under her huge down comforter. It felt so good to sleep in her own bed, under her own roof. Not that Felicity's guest room had been anything but supremely comfortable—there was just something about your own place that was special.

Once again, Gigi thanked her lucky stars for bringing her to Woodstone and making it possible for her to buy her cottage. It was tiny but full of charm, and the kitchen had been completely updated before she moved in.

Gigi stretched again, and her leg bumped up against something solid. Reggie grunted and rolled onto his back. "Hey you, sleepyhead." She reached down and scratched his belly.

She slid out of bed and was surprised to find that the floor was chilly beneath her bare feet. Autumn had obviously arrived in earnest. Gigi dug her slippers out from under the bed where she'd accidentally kicked them, and pulled on her robe.

Coffee first. She filled the pot with her favorite Sumatran blend, added water and pushed the start button. Within minutes, the machine was gurgling happily and the scent of freshly brewed coffee filled the kitchen.

Madeline Stone had been anxious to begin her diet immediately, so Gigi had agreed to start her off with this morning's breakfast. She decided that it made the most sense to double the recipe and enjoy the same meal herself. She cracked two eggs into a bowl and added four separated egg whites along with a splash of skim milk and a good grinding of black pepper. She cut up some green pepper, diced part of a tomato and a smidge of a jalapeno and grated a handful of low-fat cheddar cheese. She added it all to the eggs and then poured the mixture into a hot pan coated with cooking spray. It sizzled briefly before settling down and beginning to form into soft curdles. Gigi planned to spoon the mixture into warmed, low-fat tortillas. She would serve them with some berries topped with a spoonful of Greek yogurt. The meal should keep Madeline full and energized until it was time for her mid-morning snack—a handful of almonds, a banana or a piece of string cheese.

Gigi ate her tortilla while she perused the morning paper. The other tortilla and the fruit salad were packed in Gigi's signature white box with *Gigi's Gourmet De-Lite* written in silver script across the top. Madeline wanted her breakfast delivered to the office, so Gigi had planned something that she could easily reheat in the law firm's microwave.

Gigi took a quick shower and jumped into a pair of jeans and a cotton sweater. Most of her clothes these days could be washed and worn—even with an apron on, she was prone to making a mess of her things. She felt a brief moment of yearning for her days in New York City and her wardrobe of cute outfits, but the feeling passed quickly when she looked around her new home.

She pulled a brush through her hair, attempting to subdue its natural wave and curl, then gathered it into a low ponytail to keep it off her face and out of the way. She would be working in Felicity's kitchen that morning. It made more sense than carting things back and forth. The funeral was that afternoon at the Woodstone Episcopal Church and a reception would follow at Felicity's house.

Reggie hovered near the door nervously until Gigi reassured him that he would be going along to play with his newfound friend, Tabitha. He bounded down the path behind her and into his accustomed seat in the MINI, his nose pressed against the window.

Gigi had to pass Declan's on her way to Simpson and West, and she tried hard not to look, but her eyes seemed to swivel of their own accord toward the bright red awning. She felt a strange sensation in the pit of her stomach— excitement? Maybe it was time she put her heartache over Ted aside and began to live again.

Madeline rushed downstairs as soon as she saw Gigi's red MINI pull into the parking lot, and Gigi was quickly on her way again toward Felicity's house. She turned into the long, winding driveway and almost backed out again when she noticed Mertz's Crown Vic pulled up next to Winchel's Escalade. She would have turned tail and run, but she had far too many things to get done before Felicity's service. Hopefully, she could skulk into the kitchen through the back door and avoid Mertz altogether. She needed to get up her nerve to present her discoveries to him.

Mertz was standing at the front door as Gigi got out of her car. She avoided looking in his direction. She rounded the corner of the house with a sigh of relief and slipped in through the back entrance.

The kitchen was in shadow, so Gigi flipped all the switches, instantly flooding the room with light. She felt uneasy for some reason. Perhaps that was to be expected considering Felicity's death.

She hastened to get to work. Chopping and peeling and sautéing always helped to take her mind off unpleasant things. No wonder she had become particularly passionate about cooking after Ted's departure. Gigi had minced, diced and chopped her fingers to the bone. Fortunately, she'd been too depressed to eat much or she'd now be a lot more than five pounds over her normal weight. Hardly a good adver- tisement for someone selling diet gourmet food.

A knock on the back door startled her. Gigi pushed aside the curtain to see Alice's round face topped with its frizz of curly gray hair.

"Sorry I'm late." Alice had taken off her jacket and donned an apron before Gigi could even say a word.

Gigi opened her mouth but then shut it again. Something was wrong with Alice. She could tell just by looking at her expression.

"What are we making?" Alice peered into the pot Gigi had bubbling on the stove.

Gigi had the impression she was trying to hide her face. "There's butternut squash soup to start." She indicated the pan Alice was sniffing.

"Perfect weather for it. The wind has quite an edge today, and I noticed a lot of leaves fluttering off the trees."

"Really?" Gigi glanced over her shoulder at Alice. "How is Stacy, by the way?"

Alice gave a small sob—almost like a hiccup. "Joe has had a terrible accident. He was cleaning out the gutters on their new house, and he fell off the ladder."

"Oh no." Gigi's hand flew to her mouth. "Is he okay?"

"His leg's broken in two places." Alice kneaded her apron between her hands "He's going to be laid up for months."

"I'm sure he must have some sort of disability insurance . . ." Gigi trailed off. She didn't know much about those things herself.

"He'll be getting something." Alice began smoothing out the wrinkles she'd created in her apron. "But I don't know if it'll be enough to keep up that big house they bought. Joe did a lot of jobs on the side—bringing in some extra, you know."

"Maybe Stacy can get work?"

Alice shrugged. "I think she's going to have to. She quit her job at the diner to get them moved into their new house, and now I was kind of hoping that there'd be a baby soon, but with this happening . . ."

"Stacy is young. She has plenty of time."

Alice nodded. "True enough." She clapped her hands briskly. "Enough of that. What can I do?"

"If you wouldn't mind peeling the potatoes." Gigi gestured toward a bag of red-skins on the counter.

"Wasn't that Detective Mertz's car in the driveway?" Alice inclined her head toward the front of the house. "Thank goodness he didn't arrest Sienna. I can't imagine what that would do to her in her state."

"Just questioning her was bad enough."

"What's he doing here? I wonder."

"He must be talking to Mr. Winchel about something." Gigi shook her head. "I wish he weren't so stubborn. I have some leads for him, but there's no point in even bringing it up." She thought for a moment. "Maybe if I had something concrete . . ."

Alice nodded. "Policemen have very analytical minds. They like the facts and nothing but the facts."

"It might help to know what he's talking to Winchel about."

Alice's face brightened for the first time. "I agree. Is it possible to eavesdrop?"

"I think so." The thought of getting caught with her ear to the proverbial door made Gigi's stomach suddenly turn over. "They're in the dining room. Mr. Winchel was finishing up a late breakfast when Mertz showed up. I heard Anja showing him in. If we're very quiet we can stand in the butler's pantry and ease the door open slightly."

Alice all but rubbed her hands together in excitement. She followed close on Gigi's heels as Gigi pushed open the door between the kitchen and the butler's pantry. It was a smallish room lined with glass-fronted cabinets filled with serving pieces and glassware. Under the counter on one side were rows of specially lined drawers for silverware, and on the other side was a dishwasher, and next to it, a full-size refrigerator. Felicity had liked to entertain and had made sure her house was well equipped for it.

The swinging door to the dining room was partially glass, but the glass, which was original to the house, was etched in a lacy pattern that obscured a clear view and turned everything beyond into shadows. Gigi hoped it would be enough to prevent Mertz and Winchel from seeing her and Alice. She eased the door open an inch and leaned as close as she could to the crack. Alice was right behind her—she could feel her breath on the back of her neck.

Winchel and Mertz were seated at the dining table, Winchel relaxed in his chair at the head, his breakfast things pushed to one side. Mertz was stiff and formal. Gigi got the impression that he would have been much more comfortable standing. Their voices were low and barely discernible. Gigi closed her eyes in concentration.

"What are they saying?" Alice whispered into her ear.

"Shhh." Gigi strained even harder. This time she caught a few disjointed words . . . *autopsy* . . . *findings* . . . *report*. "Something about an autopsy," Gigi whispered as quietly as she could.

She closed her eyes again and tried to focus. Mertz's voice rose slightly, and his words drifted toward Gigi loud and clear. Alice must have heard, too, because she gasped and accidentally leaned against Gigi.

Gigi lost her balance and fell forward, swinging open the door and catapulting herself into the dining room with Alice close behind.

Chapter 9

Gigi had experienced many awkward moments in her life. Not to mention many embarrassing ones. But on a scale of one to ten, this latest rated at least a seismic twenty. It was the tsunami of embarrassments. She was quite certain she would be having nightmares about it for years to come.

Fortunately, her Irish and Italian ancestors had equipped her with a quick wit and even quicker tongue. As soon as she ceased her jet propulsion forward toward the dining table and had regained her balance, she asked in a perfectly calm voice, "Is there anything else I can get you?"

"Perhaps some more coffee?" Alice gestured toward the pantry from which they had come.

The startled look on Winchel's face turned to one of dismissal, and he shook his head. "No, thank you. That will be all for now."

Gigi and Alice backed hastily into the butler's pantry and breathed a collective sigh of relief when the door swung to in back of them. Then they burst into giggles and laughed until tears ran down their faces.

When Gigi finally collected herself, she grabbed a tissue from the box on the counter and blew her nose. Alice dabbed at her eyes with the edge of her apron.

"Oh my goodness, I can't believe we did that."

"Neither can I," Gigi said before turning serious. "But did you hear what Mertz told Felicity's husband?"

"No, I'm afraid I didn't."

Gigi motioned for Alice to come closer. "The results of the autopsy came back. And Felicity was drugged before she was put in the sauna. Some kind of tranquilizer. Apparently it was her own prescription, but they found more than ten times the normal amount in her system."

"Enough to make her too drowsy to rescue herself from the sauna?"

"It would seem so."

Gigi thought about this latest nugget of news as she chopped and diced and roasted and stirred. The butternut squash soup was ready to be put on the sideboard so guests could help themselves. She would offer it with a dollop of Greek yogurt on top—far fewer calories than heavy cream or sour cream—and a sprinkle of candied pecans. She had a platter of chicken ready—breasts pounded thin and rolled around a stuffing of diced tomatoes, spinach sautéed with garlic, and feta cheese—along with an orzo salad tossed with lemon zest, olive oil and sliced black olives.

Gigi tried to focus on what she was doing, but her mind kept circulating pictures of poor hapless Felicity asleep in the increasing heat of the sauna, unable to save herself. Then her thoughts turned to Sienna, and her stomach gave an uncomfortable lurch. She knew Sienna hadn't had anything to do with it. But how to convince Mertz of that?

Alice was going to help Anja serve, but meanwhile she was taking a short break, her apron put aside, her feet up and her nose buried in the *Woodstone Times*. Gigi could hear the clink of silver and the occasional ping of china from the butler's pantry where Anja was organizing the serving pieces for the lunch.

Gigi was putting the chicken in the oven when a car turned into the drive, quickly followed by another and another. The service was over and the guests were arriving.

Moments later, they heard the front door open, and Anja scuttled out of the pantry toward the foyer to help with coats. Drinks were being served in the formal living room, and Alice was going to help Anja with that, too.

Gigi bent over the stove, making the final preparations. Putting together a multicourse meal was like conducting an orchestra—each dish coming together at the right moment and in tune with the others. The oven timer pinged, and Gigi removed the chicken and tented it with foil. In turn, she slid a pan of apple cake batter into the oven. It was a simple dessert that she would dress up with a side of crème anglaise.

Gigi fanned her face with an oven mitt. With the burners going and both ovens lit, the kitchen was getting warm. She stepped into the hall briefly, which was still slightly chilly from the front door's opening and closing. Winchel came down the corridor, a glass of amber-colored liquid in his hand.

"Miss Fitzgerald. Why don't you join us?"

Gigi had no desire to face the crowd in the living room, but it would be a good opportunity to snoop. She ditched her apron and ducked into the powder room. She'd brought along a change of clothes in case Anja or Alice needed help serving—plain black slacks and a simple beige sweater. She donned them quickly, checked the security of her ponytail and tried to slip into the gathering as inconspicuously as possible.

Winchel was in the corner, surrounded by tall men in suits. Their expressions were uniformly grim, and Gigi wondered what they were discussing. An onlooker would have thought that Vanessa must have been an extremely close relative. She was the only person in the room dressed in unrelieved black, although how appropriate the dress was, Gigi wasn't sure. It was long sleeved but low cut, and hugged her curves tightly. Vanessa was in an intense tête-à-tête with Don. Gigi caught a flash of brilliance as Vanessa waved her hand in the air. A huge diamond flashed from the ring finger of her right hand. Had Don already cashed in the insurance policy on Felicity?

Gigi took her glass of wine and sidled as close as she could get to the two of them.

"You've got a lot of nerve," Gigi heard Don say, but not without a note of admiration in his voice.

Vanessa faked a very attractive pout and waved her hand around in front of Don's face. "It was worth it, don't you think?"

Anja slid between Gigi and the couple with a tray of bite-size croquettes. Gigi felt like swearing. What had Don and Vanessa been talking about? Had Vanessa had something to do with Felicity's death? Gigi knew she wanted to be the star of *For Better or For Worse*, but to Gigi it seemed as if all she had to do was bide her time until Felicity was eased off the show. Surely she hadn't resorted to murder.

"We have too many suspects," Gigi murmured to Alice when they were back in the kitchen dishing up bowls of butternut squash soup.

"Don and Derek . . ." Alice counted on her fingers. "Is there someone else?"

Gigi nodded. "I heard Don and Vanessa talking in there. It sounds as if Vanessa may have had a hand in things."

Alice sighed. "Does no one mourn that poor creature? It's so sad."

For the next hour, they were all run off their feet and had no time for anything else. Finally, the last plate of apple cake was taken out to the dining room, and Gigi sank into a chair. She kicked her shoes off and rubbed the balls of her feet. Cooking was sometimes more of an endurance sport than anything else, she reflected. Maybe she needed to start exercising to build up her strength?

Anja came into the kitchen. Her face was drawn, and there were dark circles under her eyes.

"Why don't you get some rest?" Gigi suggested. "The dishes are done, and you can put them away later."

"I promised to take Derek a cup of tea with honey. He is not feeling well."

"I'll do that," Gigi offered. "You go lie down for a bit."

Gigi wondered what was really wrong with Derek as she boiled water and steeped an Earl Grey tea bag in the pot. Was he feeling remorseful over stealing from Felicity after all she'd done for him?

Gigi found a tray in the butler's pantry and arranged the teapot, cup and saucer along with cream, sugar and honey. She had no idea how Derek took his tea, but he was welcome to make his own.

Winchel was still closeted in the library with the serious-faced men who had been at the funeral, so Gigi decided to go up the back stairs. She thought about the leaf Mertz's team had found on the steps and wondered again how he could possibly tie that to Sienna. Certainly Sienna did go up and down those stairs to get to her office, but so did any number of other people.

Derek's door was partially open. Gigi knocked softly and waited. Nothing. She knocked again. Had he fallen asleep? If so, then he certainly didn't need his tea. She pushed the door an inch or two and peered into the room. Heavy tasseled drapes had been pulled haphazardly across the large windows. The bed was unmade, its dark red velvet spread bunched up at the foot. The room was clearly empty. Clothes were scattered in a path from the dresser to the en suite bathroom. That door was open as well, and although Gigi listened, it didn't sound as if anyone was in there.

She would leave the tea on the bedside table. She pushed aside a graphic novel that was bent open to a page in the middle of the book, a television remote control and an empty eyeglass case. Her hand brushed something and knocked it to the floor.

Gigi grumbled under her breath and got down on her hands and knees to search for whatever it was she'd knocked off the table. Although how likely Derek was to notice anything missing, she couldn't begin to guess. She lifted up the drooping top sheet and peered underneath the bed. Something was there, but it was too dark to see. She swept her hand along the rug until she was able to grasp the object by feel.

She edged her hand out from under the bed and leaned back on her heels to examine the object she had retrieved. It was a prescription bottle—for a generic brand of a well-known tranquilizer. But instead of "Derek Winchel" on the label it read "Felicity Davenport."

And the bottle was empty.

Chapter 10

Gigi stared at the bottle for a long minute before dropping it on the carpet as if it had suddenly turned radioactive. She had added her fingerprints to the potential murder weapon! And she had possibly destroyed some real concrete evidence. She groaned. Why hadn't she left the bottle under the bed and called Mertz?

Gigi decided she had to tell Mertz about the bottle even though it meant risking his wrath. She crept back down the stairs to the kitchen. Voices still emanated from the library, and Anja was nowhere to be seen. The bicycle she often used to ride into town wasn't leaning against the back railing where she tended to keep it.

Gigi slipped into her jacket, pocketed her phone. She decided it would be safest to phone Mertz from her car. A strong breeze whipped her hair back from her face when she opened the back door, and she paused for a moment to catch her breath. Swift clouds scudded across the gun metal gray sky, and a few plump drops of rain spattered onto Gigi's windshield as she slid into the front seat. She pulled her cell from her pocket and dialed the police station. She punched in the last number and hesitated. She really, really didn't want to hear what he was going to say, but she stabbed the talk button decisively.

It took three tries to route her to Mertz's phone. His economical "Hello" gave nothing away. Gigi crossed her fingers and prayed he would be in a good mood.

"I think I found some evidence that relates to Felicity Davenport's death," Gigi said after introducing herself.

Mertz groaned so loud that Gigi pulled the phone away from her ear.

"We always appreciate it when the public comes forward with information," Mertz said, sounding as if he were reading from a handbook of some sort. He sighed and his tone softened. "Look, I haven't had anything to eat all day. I'm headed out for a bite. Can you meet me at Declan's?"

This time Gigi groaned. Why did everyone want to eat at Declan's? What was wrong with the Woodstone Diner for a change?

"Well?"

"Sure," Gigi said reluctantly. "I'll meet you there."

Gigi clicked off the call and tossed the phone onto the passenger's seat. She let her head drop forward until her forehead rested against the steering wheel. It was really difficult, but she managed to resist the incredibly strong urge to smack her head repeatedly against the wheel.

Gigi had a Gourmet De-Lite package ready to deliver to Madeline Stone for her dinner. She'd made some extra butternut squash bisque and had included a portion of the chicken and spinach rollatini with lemon orzo. It was easy enough to drop it off on her way to Declan's.

Gigi drove slowly down High Street, dreading the moment when Declan's would come into view. Her feelings were in a complete state of tumult. Her heart beat just a bit faster when Mertz was around, and she found him incredibly attractive, but so far he had shown no interest in taking their relationship beyond casual acquaintance.

She certainly found Declan McQuaid attractive as well, but Gigi guessed him to be the "here today, and gone tomorrow" type no matter what Sienna said. And she'd already had more than enough of that with Ted.

Gigi reluctantly pulled into the tiny parking lot between Declan's and Gibson's Hardware next door. Mertz's Crown Vic was nowhere in sight.

Gigi pushed open the front door and a rush of air, scented with the aroma of roasting meat and browning garlic and onions, wafted over her. Declan was in his accustomed spot behind the bar, and Gigi avoided his eye as she scanned the room for Mertz.

Suddenly Declan appeared at her elbow. "Lovely to see you again." He gave her a smile that made her feel woozy.

He put a hand toward Gigi, and she instinctively flinched.

"I didn't mean to scare you, but there's a leaf caught in your beautiful hair." He leaned closer and plucked a brown-tinged maple leaf from Gigi's locks.

"See?" He handed it to Gigi. "I've only dated one or two redheads in my life." He leaned against the hostess stand, and the look he gave Gigi made her feel as if they were the only two in the room. "But they were always a lot of fun. Up for the moment, you know what I mean? Maybe one of these days we could . . ."

Gigi heard someone clear his throat, and they both turned

to see Mertz standing a foot away. He moved closer until his elbow was nearly touching Gigi's.

"Could we have a table please?"

Declan gave Gigi a rueful smile. "Certainly." He grabbed two menus from the hostess stand. "If you'll follow me."

"There's something about that fellow," Mertz grumbled as he looked over his menu at Declan's departing back.

Gigi unfurled her napkin and put it in her lap. Was Mertz *jealous*? she wondered. He still hadn't asked her out, although he'd hinted often enough that he found her attractive. Maybe this would be the push he needed?

Mertz slapped his menu closed. "I'm going to have the roast beef. At least there are things on this menu I recognize. Not like when it was that Eye-talian place."

A retort nearly burst from Gigi's lips, but she quelled it in time.

"What are you going to have?"

"I don't know. I had a big lunch, and it's not nearly dinnertime yet."

"I didn't have any lunch, and who knows if I'll get dinner. The sorry lot of the policeman."

Gigi looked at him sharply.

"You're supposed to feel sorry for me." Mertz made a comically sad face.

"Don't worry, I do, I do." Gigi laughed.

Mertz gave his order to the waitress, with Gigi settling on just a glass of sauvignon blanc. When the waitress turned away, they were left staring at each other.

"Well," Mertz said.

Gigi's nerves had ratcheted up like a tightened piano wire. She knew what she had to say, but she was loathe to say it. The silence lengthened until it became as uncomfortable as the chafing of a scratchy garment.

"I found a prescription bottle in Derek's room," Gigi blurted out to break the awkward pause.

Mertz closed his eyes briefly, and Gigi saw his hands clench on the table. "A prescription bottle?"

Gigi kneaded the napkin in her lap as if it were bread dough. "Yes. For tranquilizers—probably the same ones that were found in Felicity Davenport's system."

Mertz steepled his fingers on top of the table. "And how do you know about that?" There was the hint of a smile tugging at the corners of his mouth.

Gigi looked down, trying to avoid his piercing blue eyes. "The maid, Anja, heard you talking to Mr. Winchel, and she told me about it."

Mertz shook his head back and forth slowly. "And you . . . swallowed . . . this information?"

Gigi jerked upright. Was Mertz making fun of her? He didn't believe she'd uncovered anything useful. She felt her Irish rising to epic proportions. "The prescription happened to be for Felicity, not Derek. And the bottle was empty."

So there, Gigi thought. Let him chew on that one for his meal.

Mertz sat up straighter in his seat if that was even possible. "Did you touch it?"

Gigi felt her telltale blush flood her face with color. "Yes," she admitted.

Mertz groaned as if he had been shot. "Figures."

"What do you mean by *that*!"

But before he could answer, his phone buzzed. He smiled apologetically and pulled it from his pocket.

Gigi fiddled with her fork, turning it over and over and over again.

Mertz spoke quietly for a few moments and then ended the call. He tossed his napkin on the table and got up.

"I'm sorry. Something critical has come up at the station, and I need to get back. Tell the owner"—he jerked his head in the direction of the bar where Declan was pulling beer—"to send the bill to me at the station." He gave Gigi a crooked smile. "Let's try this again sometime, okay?"

Before Gigi could say another word, he was gone.

She wondered if it was too late to cancel their order and leave, but before she could summon the waitress, Declan slid into the seat vacated by Mertz. He jerked a shoulder toward the door.

"What happened? You guys have a fight?" His deep blue eyes were concerned.

She shook her head. "He had an emergency."

"Mind if I join you, then? I haven't eaten yet."

Gigi groaned inwardly. The last thing she wanted to do was to become any more ensnared by the charm of Declan McQuaid. He'd made it obvious that he was after a good time. With Gigi's biological clock ticking so loudly, she couldn't afford that sort of relationship. She wanted to enjoy her glass of wine in peace and then go home to her sweet, little cottage.

But instead she said, "Sure."

The waitress put a glass of white wine in front of Gigi and slid a plate in front of Declan. Gigi glanced at Declan's dish. A huge T-bone steak covered half of it, and the other half was hidden beneath a pile of thin, crispy fries.

Declan turned out to be a very amusing companion, and more than once, Gigi found herself laughing out loud. They talked about everything from their Irish ancestors to his youth in England and hers in Massachusetts. Gigi was surprisingly disappointed when Declan finished his last bite of steak and it was obviously time to go.

She glanced at her watch. She was glad she'd dropped

Reg at home earlier in the day and had arranged for the young girl down the street to give him a walk and feed him his dinner. He expected to be fed promptly at six P.M., and Gigi swore he could tell time better than most humans. He did not brook any tardiness in having his bowl filled.

Gigi said good night to Declan—an awkward moment where she wondered if she ought to stick out her hand to be shaken. She almost fainted when Declan pulled her close and gave her a kiss, European style, on both cheeks. Gigi knew those cheeks were burning red as she backed awkwardly out the front door.

She got into her MINI and slammed the door shut. Would she never learn to play it cool and sophisticated? She was pulling out of the driveway when her cell phone rang. She eased over to a vacant spot at the curb and pulled the phone from her handbag.

It was Mertz.

"I want to apologize about dinner."

There was a long pause, and for a moment, Gigi thought they had been cut off, but then she heard Mertz clear his throat several times.

"I hope we can do it again sometime. When I'm not on duty, and we won't be interrupted."

Gigi gulped. Was Mertz . . . asking her out?

She mumbled something incomprehensible and ended the call, pulling away from the curb with the car jerking as if she were driving a manual shift and not an automatic.

How had she gone from zero men interested in her to two in less than half a day?

Gigi's sleep was disjointed and fitful to the point where Reg jumped off the bed and made himself comfortable in his dog bed, sighing loudly. The faces of Declan and Mertz rotated through Gigi's mind and dreams until she pulled the pillow over her head and groaned loudly. Men were such a distraction! Did she really need that in her life?

She finally rolled out of bed and convinced a sleepy and reluctant Reg to go for a walk. Her cottage was within walking distance of Woodstone's main street, and they headed in that direction. The sidewalks and street were deserted except for a delivery truck pulled up in front of the newsstand opposite Abigail's. A man in a cap was wheeling a hand truck loaded with a stack of the day's newspapers toward the store.

Wisps of early morning fog hovered slightly above the ground and clung to the branches of the trees. Gigi pulled up the hood of her sweatshirt and stuck her hands in her pockets. Reg sniffed every parking meter, planter and garbage can he could find while Gigi enjoyed looking in the windows. A beautiful silver cuff bracelet in the window of the Silver Lining caught her eye as well as an exquisite fawn leather jacket displayed on a mannequin in Abigail's.

Someday, she thought to herself. Someday, she'd be able to afford things like that.

By the time she and Reg got back to the cottage they were both starved. Once again, Gigi created a breakfast that both she and Madeline would be able to enjoy—poached eggs— she did them in a mold in the microwave—on an English muffin with a slice of low-fat sharp cheddar cheese. A small fruit salad rounded out the meal. She packed Madeline's portion in one of her signature Gourmet De-Lite containers and went to take a shower.

The phone was ringing as Gigi wrapped her wet hair in a towel. She hurried down the hall and grabbed it on the fifth ring. She listened intently, made a few comments and hung up. The call sent her scurrying to her desk where she turned on her computer. While it was booting up, she poured a cup of Sumatran brew from her automatic coffeepot that she filled and set every night.

Finally, her computer sprang to life, and she perched on the edge of her desk chair and clicked open her spreadsheet of expenses and deposits. She stared at the number on the screen. According to her accounting, she ought to have plenty of cash left in her account. But according to the bank manager with whom Gigi had cultivated a relationship since she borrowed a small sum to start her business, she was woefully overdrawn. Something was wrong.

Fortunately Deborah had agreed to meet her in her office in an hour. Gigi delivered Madeline's breakfast and drove the rest of the way down High Street toward the bank. She couldn't imagine what had happened to her account. She was very careful about entering everything into her checkbook, balancing it promptly and checking her balance daily before going shopping. There must have been some glitch in the system.

The parking lot was almost empty save for a few cars in the employee slots. Gigi hurried inside, relieved to see that Deborah was alone in her office.

She looked up and smiled when she saw Gigi. She was wearing the requisite dark suit but with a sapphire blue blouse that set off her carefully coiffed blond hair and her blue eyes. She rose and extended her hand as Gigi walked into the room.

"So good to see you again." She gestured toward the armless chair in front of her desk. "Please have a seat."

"Thanks." Gigi was nervous. What if she'd made some sort of hideous mistake on her account? Since the day years ago when she transferred her savings from a piggy bank to a real bank, she'd never overdrawn even once.

"Let me bring up your account." Deborah reached for the glasses that dangled from a gold chain around her neck.

Gigi kneaded her hands in her lap as she waited.

"I see what the problem is." Deborah whisked off her glasses and let them drop against her chest. She turned the computer screen so that Gigi could see, too.

"Right here." Deborah tapped the screen with a long, red fingernail. "One of the checks you deposited bounced. That's what's caused all the trouble."

Gigi squinted at the screen and could just make out the letters.

Deborah tapped the screen again. "The check from the Woodstone Group. That's your culprit right there."

Gigi had to think for a minute. "The Woodstone Group?"

Deborah nodded her head.

"Oh," Gigi said as realization dawned. That was the check Jack Winchel had given her for catering Felicity's funeral luncheon and for all the other work she'd done.

"It bounced?" she said in disbelief.

Deborah shook her head. "There's been some scuttlebutt in the papers lately about the Woodstone Group. Seems they're skating on thin ice."

How could that be? Gigi thought. There was that big house, the fancy cars . . . maybe Felicity was the one paying for all that?

"I'm sure if you'll explain to them what's happened, they'll make good on the check." Deborah smiled sympathetically across the width of the desk. "Meanwhile, I can set you up with some overdraft protection that should cover the shortfall for the near term."

Gigi nodded dully. She really had to get this deal with Branston Foods. She hated living so hand to mouth. It made her nervous. Fortunately, she had five new clients starting her regimen next week. That would certainly help.

"I guess that's what I'll do," she said as she rose from the chair.

Deborah held out her hand, and Gigi shook it.

She was halfway through the revolving door when the implications of what she'd learned struck her. If Winchel's company was skating on thin ice, to use Deborah's term, didn't that give him a darn good reason for murdering Felicity? A good portion of her estate was going to Derek, but Winchel was still in for a substantial sum of money.

Chapter 11

Gigi's head swirled as she pulled out of the bank parking lot onto High Street. Traffic had picked up, and several people were already out and about poking into the shops.

She had to find a way to eliminate some of the suspects. There were entirely too many! First Don Bartholomew, then Derek, and now Winchel.

Gigi continued down High Street until she was in front of Simpson and West. It took barely five minutes to park and drop off Madeline's breakfast. She was walking back toward her car when she noticed Mertz coming in the other direction. A few long strides and he had caught up with her.

"Good morning."

"Good morning," Gigi said, falling into step beside him. She tried to remember whether she had bothered with lipstick or not. At least she remembered pulling a comb through her hair.

Just ahead of them several people stood around a tree, looking up and pointing.

"I wonder what's going on," Mertz said, quickening his pace.

They approached the three women and one man who were staring into the branches. All but a handful of leaves had fallen, and those that remained were brown and dusty looking.

Gigi maneuvered her way into the small group and followed their gaze but didn't see anything.

"What is it?" Mertz asked the nearest woman.

She turned worried blue eyes on him. "A kitten. There's a kitten stuck in the tree. How it got up there, I can't begin to imagine. I think it's afraid to come down."

Mertz narrowed his eyes and stared up through the remaining leaves. "That it there?"

"Yes. Poor thing. It must be frightened half to death."

"And cold and very hungry," said one of the other women. She made a tsking sound under her breath and shook her head.

Mertz slipped out of his black parka and handed it to Gigi. "Here. Hold this for me, would you?"

"What are you going to do?"

"Can't let the poor little thing starve, can I?" He grasped the lowest tree branch and quickly hoisted himself up.

"Be careful." Gigi bit her lip.

Mertz smiled back at her. "Don't worry. Of all my brothers, I was the best tree climber." He reached for the next branch and disappeared somewhere over Gigi's head.

Everyone heard the loud meow the kitten gave, and necks craned as they tried to see what was going on. Within moments, Mertz was making his way back down the tree, the kitten tucked safely into the breast pocket of his shirt.

He landed at Gigi's feet with a soft *thud*. The small crowd broke into applause, and Mertz's face reddened. He took the kitten from his pocket and cuddled it in his hands. It was very tiny with soft gray fur and eyes that were almost violet.

"It's so pretty." Gigi reached out a finger and stroked it. "I wonder where its mother is."

"Probably scampered by now." Mertz held the kitten close to his chest to warm it. "Do you think . . ."

"What?" Gigi asked when he didn't continue.

"Do you think I could keep it? Cats aren't like dogs so it shouldn't mind that I'm not home all the time."

"Of course. And they use a litter box so no need to worry about walking it."

"Maybe that wouldn't be fair to it. Maybe it should go to a home where someone would be there to keep it company all the time?"

"I don't think that's necessary. I think you should keep it. What will you name it?" Gigi smiled at Mertz.

"I don't know. Whiskers?" He gave a self-conscious laugh. "Probably half the cats in the world are named that. I'm not very creative, I'm afraid."

"I think Whiskers is just fine. Besides, he does have awfully long ones—look." Gigi brushed the kitten's long white whiskers with a gentle finger.

"Hey, Whiskers, want to come home with me? If I take him back to the station, perhaps Alice will watch him until my shift is over."

"I'm sure she wouldn't mind at all." Gigi smiled as she watched Mertz rub noses with the tiny kitten. It was a side of him she'd never expected to see.

"I'd better be going." Mertz held the kitten toward Gigi. "Want to say good-bye to Whiskers?"

She gave the kitten a final pat on the head and then watched as Mertz loped off down the street.

* * *

Gigi had some time to kill, so she thought she would visit Sienna and check up on her. She drove into the parking lot next to Declan's to turn around. Declan's didn't open till lunch, but the front door was propped wide, and she could see the lights were on. They were obviously already cooking and setting up for the lunchtime work crowd and the ladies-who-lunch bunch. The place had become quite popular with them, Gigi had heard, since Declan had such a way with women.

Gigi turned around in an empty space and headed back out, in the other direction, on High Street.

The trees overhanging Sienna and Oliver's cottage were bursting with color—red maples, yellow birches and purple pear trees. A large pumpkin and a big pot of mums sat on the front step in front of the cherry red front door.

Gigi knocked and stepped back to wait. Moments later Sienna opened the door. She was in an old, worn bathrobe that barely closed around her expanding middle. She was pale and looked as if she'd been crying.

"What's the matter?" Gigi blurted out as she followed Sienna inside. "Have the police been bothering you again?" She felt her fists clench at the notion.

"No, no." Sienna shook her head, hastening to reassure Gigi. "It's not that. Not that at all."

"Not . . . Oliver again?" Gigi had held Sienna's hand through last year's crisis when she thought Oliver was seeing someone else.

"No, not that either."

That left only . . . the baby, Gigi thought. "Not the baby?"

"Not exactly, no." Sienna gestured toward the kitchen. "Let's get a cup of tea."

Gigi followed Sienna into the kitchen. Sunlight glanced

off the hanging copper pots and puddled on the warm, wood floors. Gigi slid onto a stool at the kitchen island. Sienna took the teakettle that was whistling on the stove and added two tea bags.

Sienna must have noticed the worried look on Gigi's face. "It's not that bad, really." She gave a brief, half smile. "It's quite common actually. Especially in women my age."

"Your age? But you're young!" Gigi felt her hackles rise. She and Sienna were the same age, and she refused to think of herself being . . . not young.

"When it comes to maternity, I'm a dinosaur." Sienna poured the brewed tea into mugs with *Book Nook* written on them and carried them to the island.

"Well, what is it?" Gigi needed to stop the whirlwind of tragic pictures running through her mind.

"It's called gestational diabetes."

"Oh." Gigi wracked her mind for any information she might have stored away on that topic, but nothing came to the forefront.

"It's a form of diabetes that pregnant women can get in the last trimester." Sienna patted her stomach.

"Can you take something for it? A pill?"

Sienna nodded. "The doctor is putting me on insulin."

Gigi gulped. "You'll have to take shots?"

"They're not so bad." Sienna smiled reassuringly. "The needles are very short and very slim. I hardly feel them." She sipped her tea. "It's a small price to pay for a healthy baby."

"Will it go away after the baby is born?"

"It should. I'll have to watch my diet, too, but with any luck everything will be back to normal as soon as I give birth."

Gigi noticed that a tear was making its way down her friend's cheek. Sienna brushed at it impatiently.

"This is bothering you, isn't it?" Gigi put her hand on Sienna's arm.

"It's just that I wanted everything to be perfect. We've waited so long . . ." Sienna gave a small sob. "I know every-thing's going to be fine, but it was a shock when the doctor told me." She pulled a tissue from the pocket of her robe and blew her nose. "I mean, I felt great. I had no idea anything was . . . wrong." She stuffed the tissue up the sleeve of her robe. "And this whole business of Felicity's death has unnerved me, I think. Besides the fact that I'm not going to get paid now, and we were counting on that money. Plus it seems I'm still Detective Mertz's prime suspect."

"That's ridiculous," Gigi exploded. "I can't believe all this stress is doing you any good. I'm going to have to talk to him." Gigi's knees weakened at the prospect. She hadn't gotten very far that evening at Declan's. Well, she'd have to try harder.

Gigi took a cautious sip of her steaming tea. "I still think Derek is the most likely suspect." She filled Sienna in on having found the prescription bottle in his room. "And then this morning, I learned that Winchel's check to me had bounced. The bank manager told me that rumor has it his company is in trouble."

"That's the Woodstone Group, isn't it?" Sienna paused with her mug of tea halfway to her lips. "Maybe Oliver knows something about it."

"About what?" Oliver rounded the corner then and stopped to plant a kiss on his wife's cheek.

"About the Woodstone Group. Gigi's heard that they aren't doing well."

"That's Winchel's company, right?" Oliver scratched his chin. "I read something the other day in the *Connecticut Business Journal*. I think Gigi's source is right."

"So, he probably needs money."

Sienna and Oliver both nodded agreement.

"This is getting very interesting." Gigi absentmindedly twirled a piece of hair around her finger. "We now know that three people benefited from Felicity's death." She shrugged her shoulders. "The question is, which one of them actually did it?"

Gigi pulled into the driveway of her cottage with a feeling of relief. She could hear Reg barking. He was probably lunging at the front door. He'd already scratched most of the paint off the bottom section.

Gigi greeted him and scurried into the kitchen to package up Madeline's lunch. She had left a hearty but low-fat split pea soup simmering in the slow cooker since early that morning. Gigi would give Madeline some homemade croutons to top it off. She bought up stale loaves of good bread at Bon Appétit and turned them into croutons to garnish soups, salads and stews. The soup would be filling, but there were enough calories left over for dessert. Gigi sliced half an apple paper thin, fanned the slices out on a small plate and drizzled them with the barest touch of caramel sauce. It would help satisfy Madeline's sweet tooth while not adding too many calories.

As she worked, Gigi thought of the myriad of suspects she'd uncovered so far. She wondered about that policy Don had taken out. Maybe Madeline would know something about it? Her boss handled Felicity's other affairs, so perhaps he was involved in that sort of thing as well.

The more she thought about it, the more excited Gigi became. She would deliver Madeline's lunch, but this time she would stick around for a chat.

* * *

Madeline wasn't waiting in the parking lot as usual, so Gigi climbed the stairs to her third-floor office. Madeline was nearly hidden behind a stack of folders. She looked up when she sensed Gigi standing in front of her.

"Oh my goodness, is it lunchtime already?" She glanced at her watch. "I can't believe it. Usually I'm starved by now, but your breakfasts really fill me up."

Gigi handed her the Gourmet De-Lite container. "The soup was hot when I left, but you might want to give it a minute in the microwave."

"I'm sure it's fine." Madeline sighed and blew a lock of hair off her face. "We have a big case coming up next week, and I'm literally buried." She waved at the stacks of files on her desk. "I haven't even had a chance to get my nails done." Madeline brandished her fingers, and Gigi noticed that the dark red polish was chipped in spots.

"I'm just waiting for someone to say something." Madeline scowled.

Gigi's glance happened to fall on one of the folders on Madeline's desk. She could plainly see the name "Felicity Davenport" printed neatly on the tab. She gestured toward it. "Follow-up work on Felicity's estate?"

Madeline nodded. "It's one of the cases we're working on at the moment."

"I heard that she was going to be in a play at the Woodstone Theater. And that her manager had taken out some sort of insurance policy on her."

"Oh, him." Madeline scowled. "Just between you and me"—she leaned toward Gigi—"Felicity wasn't very happy with him. I heard her talking to Mr. Simpson about it." Madeline's eyes widened. "Her last contract wasn't nearly as good as the others, and then when she found out about that other actress, Vanessa Huff? She blew her stack. Mr. Bartholomew had signed her as well, and according to Felicity, he got her a much better deal."

Gigi tried not to look as interested as she felt. "What did Mr. Simpson say about that?"

"He told her it was high time she changed managers no matter how much history she and Mr. Bartholomew had."

As Gigi pulled out of the parking lot, she thought about the word *history* and wondered what Madeline meant by that. Romantic history? Business history? Family history? She suspected a combination of the two former. She needed to learn more about Don Bartholomew. Alex Goulet, Felicity's leading man, came to mind. He'd been on the soap almost as long as Felicity had. But what pretext could she use to see him, let alone engage him in conversation?

She thought about it as she drove along aimlessly, turning this way and that, enjoying the bright colors of the leaves and the crisp autumn smells coming in her open window. But, as the old adage had it, "Desperate times call for desperate measures."

As Gigi drove, her mind turned toward the new recipe she was working on for Branston Foods. That's when the idea struck her, and she nearly hit the old elm tree on the corner of High Street and Beacon Road. She would ask Alex for dinner under the pretext of having him sample her new recipe and giving an unbiased opinion. Sort of like a one-person focus group.

Gigi pulled into the nearest driveway and dug out her cell phone. She saw the lace curtain in the front window of the house twitch and braced herself for some homeowner to come out and ask her what she was doing. She punched in the number of Felicity's house and was relieved when Anja answered on the second ring. It took a couple of precious seconds to explain to Anja that she wanted to speak to Alex, who was, by last account, still staying at Felicity's house.

Alex finally came on the line, and Gigi outlined her proposal. She could tell by the slightly oily tone of his voice that he thought she was coming on to him. *What have I gotten myself into?* Gigi thought as she reversed out of the drive just as the front door opened and an older woman emerged. She gestured at Gigi, but by then Gigi had the car in drive and was pulling away.

Chapter 12

Gigi stood in her kitchen amidst a stack of notebooks, cook-books, magazines, notes and all sorts of other things. Nor-mally her kitchen was her retreat, the place she went when she needed to be soothed or wanted to relax. But this time it wasn't working. She failed to take comfort in the sunlight spilling through the window and casting a rainbow of colors on her glass cabinet doors, or the faint scent of herbs and spices that perfumed the air.

She slumped at the kitchen table, a mug of lukewarm tea in her hand, and wondered for the second time what on earth she had gotten herself into. Inviting Alex Goulet to *dinner*? What was she thinking? Women threw themselves at him wherever he went. He probably thought she was doing the same.

Gigi straightened her shoulders, put on her most stoic face and went back to her recipes. She was slightly behind in recipe development for Branston Foods, and this was a wonderful opportunity to preview one of her dishes and get some feedback. She tried to concentrate on that thought as she scrolled through the dishes she had already created.

Men usually liked a meal that felt substantial even if it was low in calories. That usually meant meat, preferably beef. With the colder touch to the air, a stew would be a welcome entrée. She would use a very lean cut of meat, plenty of vegetables to bulk up the stew, and plenty of fresh herbs, particularly thyme, for a real blast of flavor. She would give Alex some crusty bread to sop up the gravy since he wasn't actually on a diet, and she'd make a fruit compote for dessert. Alex could have his over a slice of angel food cake.

Gigi got busy and within minutes had forgotten all about her attack of nerves. She measured, stirred and sautéed her heart out. Finally the stew was bubbling softly on the stove, and she leaned forward and took a long, deep sniff. She could smell the earthiness of the mushrooms, the freshness of the thyme she'd picked herself from a pot on the windowsill, the richness of the garlic and onions. She closed her eyes in rapture. If this didn't win Alex over, nothing would.

The clock struck five, and Gigi realized she had barely enough time to dash into the shower, slap on some makeup and get dressed. She would take Madeline a container of the stew and compote for her dinner and then race back to be ready to greet Alex.

As Gigi lathered up in the shower, she auditioned ways she could broach the topic of Don with Alex. They all seemed contrived. She would have to hope for on-the-spot inspiration. Like those lightbulb moments in the comics.

Gigi made it back to her cottage as the clock ticked over to six. There was no sign of Alex's sports car, and she breathed a sigh of relief. She fiddled with the table settings and momentarily wished she'd asked someone else to join them. Sienna and Oliver, for example. But would that have been worse? Would it have looked more like a dinner party and less like a strange sort of gourmet focus group? At any rate, it was too late now.

Gigi had fallen asleep and was slumped comfortably in her old armchair when the bell rang. She glanced quickly at the clock. It was already after seven P.M. Alex was very, very fashionably late.

Gigi pulled open the front door and took a step backward. Alex was clutching a bunch of tissue-wrapped flowers. He wore a black velvet smoking jacket with a paisley print silk ascot. His costume put Gigi in mind of that line from count-less old movies, uttered by the leading femme fatale: *Let me slip into something more comfortable.* There certainly wouldn't be any of that tonight, no matter what Alex Goulet had in mind!

Things started out well enough. They enjoyed a drink in the living room, Gigi on the sofa and Alex in her armchair, his long legs stretched out in front of him, drink balanced on his flat stomach. He was actually quite interesting and knew a lot about theater history and a fair amount about cooking. Gigi suddenly became nervous about the meal she'd prepared and had to remind herself that she hadn't *really* invited Alex for his opinion.

Every time she thought there was an opportunity to intro-duce Don, Alex would veer away onto a different topic. Gigi refilled his glass twice before it was time to serve her stew.

Alex tucked the linen napkin into the open collar of his shirt and prepared to dig in. Gigi ladled out steaming bowls of heavenly smelling stew and cut them each a chunk of crusty French bread.

"Butter?" She pushed the dish across the table toward Alex.

"Oh, this is delicious." He closed his eyes in delight. "Absolutely delicious. You did say this was low calorie?"

Gigi nodded. She could feel the grin spreading across her face. No matter how much cooking she did, she still relished compliments.

"I can't believe you can cook like this and"—Alex looked around Gigi's tidy cottage—"you don't have a man hidden somewhere."

Gigi cursed the blush that rose automatically to her face.

"The way to a man's heart is through his stomach, you know."

Gigi hastened to change the subject. "What's going to happen on the show in light of Felicity's . . . death."

Alex tore off a piece of bread and swiped it across his now empty bowl. "Felicity will be written out. And Vanessa will be written in. They've been waiting forever to do that as it is. Felicity's fans are the only thing that have kept her alive." He paused for a moment. "No pun intended."

Gigi cleared her throat. This was it. Her big opening. Time to go for broke. "Isn't it up to her agent to see that she keeps her job?"

Alex stretched. "How about we take the rest of that excellent Bordeaux you've been plying me with and get comfortable in the living room?"

Gigi's first thought was to scream *No*, but she reined in that impulse and grabbed the bottle of wine instead. Alex took her glass and his, and she followed him meekly into the other room. He sat down on the sofa, extremely close to the dividing line between the two sides and waggled his eyebrows at Gigi.

She thought of the expression "Think of England" and

plopped down next to him but still as far away as she could manage.

Alex held his glass out for a refill. Gigi obliged and he held it by the stem, twirling it around and around between his fingers. "Don and Felicity go way back," he began. "Before she met Mr. Wall Street, Jack Winchel." He made a face. "They were starting out together, and you could almost say they made each other's careers. But Felicity got bigger and bigger, and Don effectively went nowhere. He was content to tie his string to her kite and ride the air with her instead of looking for more clients to develop to beef up his stable." Alex took a sip of his wine. "He did sign a few people here and there, but none of them could hold a candle to Felicity." He stopped for a moment and stared, lost in thought. "Until Vanessa."

Alex shifted in his seat, and Gigi remained still and silent, not wanting to break his train of thought. He seemed to have forgotten she was there.

"The faster Vanessa's star ascended, the faster Felicity's descended. Poor Don." He laughed. "He was being pulled in two different directions. He wisely decided that Vanessa was the way to go and somehow managed to talk her into an affair." Alex rubbed his chin. "Although I'm sure there was something in it for Vanessa as well. That girl doesn't do anything that doesn't benefit her in one way or another."

"But he still represented Felicity?" Gigi put her wineglass down. She needed to keep a clear head.

Alex nodded. "He wasn't going to give up until the bitter end." He looked momentarily startled, as if he'd suddenly realized what he'd said. "But his heart wasn't in it. Personally, I thought he got Felicity a bum deal with this last contract. She still had a strong fan base; he could certainly have done much better by her."

"Did Felicity realize that?"

"Hell, yes." Alex sat bolt upright. "She was furious with him and threatened to fire him." He shook his head. "I don't know how he convinced her not to. Maybe she looked around and realized the pickings were slim. She's not . . . I mean she wasn't the star she used to be."

Gigi thought about that for a moment. Maybe Don had felt the only solution was to murder Felicity and cash in on that policy?

Gigi suspected she'd gotten about all she was going to get out of Alex and looked around for a way to gracefully end the evening. Alex was permanently settled on her sofa, his long legs stretched out, his posture completely relaxed, his wineglass still half full.

Gigi feigned a yawn. "Sorry, it's been a long day."

Alex looked startled. "Of course, you're absolutely right."

Gigi breathed a sigh of relief that her not-so-subtle hint had hit its mark.

"What you need is a back rub." Alex sat up straight and put down his wineglass. "Turn around," he commanded.

Gigi wanted to protest, but some part of her, probably the part that went to Catholic school and was used to taking orders, obeyed without her consent and she found herself receiving a back rub from soap star Alex Goulet. It was a position many women would give their all to be in. Unfortunately, Gigi wasn't one of them.

It did feel good, though. She found it hard not to relax under his strong but soothing touch. She allowed herself to enjoy it for another minute before squirming away.

"It is getting late," she said as firmly as she could.

"True." Alex winked, and Gigi watched in alarm as he slid out of his jacket and untied his ascot.

"What are you doing?"

"Don't you think it's time you slipped into something more comfortable?"

"What!" Gigi was surprised to find Alex echoing the very words that had run through her mind earlier. "No!"

"Surely you know how these scenes play out."

"What do you mean?"

Reg must have recognized the tone of Gigi's voice because he gave a low, serious growl.

"It's like this, darling." Alex put his hands on Gigi's shoulders. "We smooch for a few minutes, and then we walk arm-in-arm toward your bedroom . . ." He glanced around as if trying to ascertain where that was. "And then the camera focuses in on our two wineglasses sitting companionably side-by-side on the table, and then"—he made a circular motion with his finger—"fade to black."

"Unfortunately this isn't a movie or a television episode," Gigi said as she wiggled away from his embrace. "It's real life."

Alex lunged toward Gigi, and she couldn't help it, she let out a scream. That set Reg barking in earnest, and he managed to knock over a lamp just as the front doorbell rang.

Alex and Gigi stared at each other for a moment. Alex shot his cuffs and picked up his jacket and ascot. "I guess I'll be going," he said stiffly as he followed Gigi to the front door.

She yanked it open to find Detective Mertz standing on her doorstep.

He and Alex stared at each other for a very long minute, then Alex sidled past Mertz and hotfooted it down the path to his waiting sports car.

Mertz watched him go, then turned on his heel and took the same path—only he headed toward the spotless Crown Vic parked neatly at the curb.

Gigi stood at the door until both cars had departed, kicking up dust in their haste down the street. Then she slammed the door so hard that the picture of Nauset Beach on her foyer wall jumped off the nail and crashed to the ground.

Gigi spent another fitful night and woke with dark circles under her eyes and a headachy feeling that might have been from the wine, but she suspected it was more from tossing and turning all night long.

She made herself a good breakfast that left very little cleanup—a ziplock-bag omelet loaded with chopped onions, mushrooms, peppers and shredded low-fat cheese. Everything, along with two eggs, went into the bag, which she then sealed carefully and plunged into boiling water. By the time she was out of the shower, it was ready, and she rolled a delicious-looking omelet onto her plate. She had put together a second batch—this time in a bag especially created for use in the microwave—which she would deliver to Madeline at her office. All Madeline would have to do would be to put it in the microwave for a mere two minutes, and she would have hot, fresh eggs for her breakfast.

Gigi had another, singularly unpleasant task ahead of her this morning: letting Winchel know that his check had bounced and needed to be replaced.

She thought about it as she dropped off Madeline's breakfast and then turned the car toward Felicity's house. She didn't relish the upcoming confrontation. She was a little afraid of Jack Winchel. He had that effect on people, and she was quite certain he worked hard to cultivate it. She remembered reading about him in the gossip columns when he first started dating Felicity. He'd been burned by his first wife's desertion, and speculation was that he wanted a trophy wife spectacular enough to wipe the smirks off his competitors' faces. He'd certainly found that in Felicity. She'd been younger then, and even more beautiful, and she was a well-known actress to boot. At one time or another, almost everyone had seen at least one episode of *For Better or For Worse*.

Gigi passed the Book Nook, and her thoughts turned to Sienna. She and Sienna were the same age—they'd been roommates in college and had stuck together all four years since neither had elected to join a sorority. Gigi couldn't afford it, and Sienna was too independent. If Sienna was considered a dinosaur when it came to maternity, then Gigi was from the same era. And she didn't even have a man on the horizon. Well, actually, she had two. But one had already announced himself as being after nothing more than a good time, and while the other seemed more the marrying type, Gigi still had no idea how he felt about her. Which left her back at square one with her biological clock ticking and no appropriate man in sight.

Gigi turned into Felicity's driveway and pulled up in front of the house. Anja answered her knock. She gave Gigi a timid smile and stood aside as Gigi entered.

"What are you doing here?" Anja said.

"I need to speak to Mr. Winchel," Gigi said as she pulled off her gloves.

Anja raised an eyebrow. "He is on the phone," she whispered. "I would suggest you wait in the kitchen. He does not like to be disturbed when he is making important calls."

How did Anja know it was an important call? Gigi wondered as she headed down the hall. She supposed all of Winchel's calls were important.

At first she thought the room was empty, but then she noticed that Vanessa, Felicity's costar, was behind the open refrigerator door. Her hands were full, and she pushed the door shut with her hip.

"Good heavens," Gigi exclaimed. "What are you making?"

"A protein shake," Vanessa answered succinctly. She carried her load to the kitchen island and dropped it somewhat unceremoniously. A bright red Gala apple rolled down the counter and stopped short of the edge.

The top was off the blender, and Vanessa had obviously already added some sort of powder to the container. Gigi assumed it was protein powder.

Gigi hoped Alex was safely out of the house somewhere. She couldn't imagine why he didn't go back to New York and his own apartment. Had Mertz forbidden them to leave?

Gigi was at the kitchen table when Don burst into the kitchen.

"I knew you were here!" he exclaimed. "I recognized that little car of yours in the driveway." Don stood squarely in front of Gigi, his feet slightly apart, arms at his side, fists clenched. He was wearing a pair of gray slacks, a cream-colored turtleneck and a sport coat. The ensemble went a long way toward hiding the spare tire around his middle, and Gigi wondered if he had chosen it for that reason. His rather fleshy face was bright red, and beads of sweat stood out on his forehead.

He was toe-to-toe with Gigi. She backed up, but he took another step forward. The absurd tango continued until her back was against the Aga, which was throwing off an uncomfortable amount of warmth.

"You had to go around asking questions about me, didn't you?" Don asked, his face inches from Gigi's.

"What?" She temporized, trying to inch away from Don's bulk.

"Alex told me," he sneered. "I'm sure you thought your lover boy wouldn't rat you out, but he did." Don wiped a hand across his beet red forehead. "If you want to know the truth, I had nothing, *nothing*, to do with Felicity's death. Do you read me?"

Gigi nodded her head.

"I have an alibi, do you understand?"

Again, Gigi nodded affirmatively. Obviously Alex had decided to tell Don about Gigi's questions—probably to get back at her for spurning his advances.

Don backed away slightly and ran his hand through his black hair, leaving tracks through the gel he'd used to plaster it down.

Gigi took a deep breath. *In for a penny, in for a pound*, she recalled her Irish grandmother, Mary Elizabeth, saying to her. She drew herself up to her full five feet, five inches and threw her head back. "An alibi?" She arched an eyebrow challengingly at Don. "And what might your alibi be?"

He looked as if someone had slapped him across the face. He got even redder and sputtered like an old car trying to start up in the cold. "Alibi?" His nostrils flared broadly. "I don't need to tell you"—he nearly spit the word at Gigi—"what my alibi is."

And, as they say in the theater, he promptly exited stage left.

Gigi looked at Vanessa, startled.

She shrugged and pressed the button on the blender. "Don't bother asking me what that was about," she shouted over the roar of the machine, "because I ain't telling. Don would kill me."

Chapter 13

Gigi was still feeling slightly shaken by her encounter with Don when Anja came into the kitchen to announce that Winchel was off the phone and would see her in the library. Gigi gathered up her things and followed Anja down the hall.

Winchel was behind the huge partner's desk that dominated the book-lined room. The faint aroma of cigar smoke hung in the air and mingled with the scent of leather-bound volumes.

Winchel gave a practiced smile as Gigi entered and took a seat in the club chair opposite his desk.

He leaned forward, his fingers steepled under his chin. "So tell me, what can I do for you?"

Gigi suddenly found that her normal voice had been kidnapped by aliens and all that came out was a pathetic squeak. She tried again. "My bank informed me that the check you gave me . . ." She paused and cleared her throat. "Bounced."

Winchel's smile broadened. "I do apologize," he said, sounding anything but apologetic. "A problem with the checks. We'd switched over to a new account, and my accountant forgot to apprise me of the fact." He opened a slender drawer in the top right of the desk. "But that's easily fixed." He pulled a black leather-covered ledger from the drawer, opened it, and with a brisk flourish, plucked a fountain pen from the holder on his desk. The pen hovered over the open checkbook.

"The name again . . . ?"

"You can make it out to my company. Gigi's Gourmet De-Lite."

He wrote the check quickly, tore it from the book and handed it to Gigi with a smile. "It's been a pleasure, Miss . . ."

"Fitzgerald."

"Ah, yes. Fitzgerald. Of course." He leaned back in his dark green leather executive desk chair. "If I should need your services again . . ."

"I think you have my card, but just in case"—Gigi dug in her purse and pulled out her wallet—"here is another." She handed it across the vast expanse of desk to Winchel.

He took the card and was starting to rise when the door burst open. Anja rushed into the room, her blond hair coming out of its accustomed ponytail, and her normally pale cheeks flushed pink.

Winchel stared at her with a sharply annoyed look on his face. "What is it?" he demanded.

"It's Madam's Emmy! It's gone. I went to dust it, but it's gone." Anja's words tumbled over each other in her haste to get them out and ended in a long, drawn-out shriek.

Winchel looked bored. "That old thing? Who cares?"

Anja looked so shocked that even Winchel found it necessary to temper his statement.

"It's really only worth something to Felicity. The statue isn't made out of precious metal."

Anja looked ever so slightly mollified but continued to mutter under her breath as Gigi followed her out to the kitchen.

"We should call the police, no?" she said eagerly, turning to Gigi as soon as the swinging door to the kitchen shut.

"I suppose."

Anja narrowed her eyes. "I am certain it is that wretched boy again. He stole from Madam all the time—money from her purse, little trinkets from her dressing table. But this time he has gone too far." Anja balled one fist and slammed it into the open palm of the other hand, a very mulelike look of determination settled on her features. "Madam's Emmy is special. She cherished it. And now it's . . . gone. And so is Madam!" She dissolved into tears.

Gigi groaned. She knew what she had to do to appease Anja—call the police. Surely they would send a patrolman and not . . . Detective Mertz. More than once she wished that Woodstone was big enough to warrant two detectives, then she'd at least have a fifty-fifty chance of avoiding certain embarrassment.

Gigi was relieved when Alice answered the phone at the station. She hadn't wanted to call 9-1-1 since the horse, so to speak, had already left the barn, and this was hardly an emergency. Alice promised to send a patrolman out as soon as one of them got back to the station.

Gigi hung up the phone with a feeling of relief. She was anxious to get out of Felicity's house and back to her cottage, but she agreed to wait with Anja until the police arrived.

Gigi sat in the kitchen and tried to make small talk with Anja. She thought they were both relieved when a knock sounded on the door.

Anja jumped up and headed down the hall.

Gigi heard Anja's voice and the low murmur of masculine tones, but she couldn't tell who it was. She didn't think it was Mertz, and she fervently prayed that it wasn't.

Anja's voice became louder as she approached the kitchen. Nonetheless, Gigi jumped when the door to the kitchen swung open.

Her heart sank. Mertz stood there looking more formidable than ever, his shoes polished to a high shine, his hair parted with scientific precision, his posture as unyielding as ever. He smiled when he saw Gigi. Though he looked as if the smile were actually painful. He had his notebook in one hand and a pencil in the other.

"Please tell him about the statue," Anja pleaded. "Madam's Emmy."

"I don't know anything about it," Gigi protested.

"Where was it kept?" Mertz held his pencil poised over the pad.

"On the mantel in the formal living room." Gigi looked to Anja for confirmation.

"And it's not there now." Anja abruptly folded her arms over her chest.

Mertz's head swiveled back toward Gigi, and she shrugged.

"I haven't been in there recently."

She wondered if she ought to tell him about Derek and the theft from Felicity's jewelry box. She didn't want to go into it with Anja present. She tried to signal to Mertz with her eyes that she had more to tell.

He obviously caught the hint. "I'd like to talk to Miss Fitzgerald alone now." He nodded dismissal at Anja.

"I got the impression you wanted to tell me something," Mertz said as soon as Anja was safely out the door.

"It's about Derek."

"Derek? Who is Derek?" Mertz began paging through his notes.

"Felicity's stepson."

"Ah." Mertz made a note on his pad.

"I saw him in Felicity's bedroom one day going through her jewelry box."

Mertz looked startled. "Was this after she died . . . ?"

Gigi nodded.

Mertz slapped his notebook shut. "There's not too much we can do, but I'll alert the local pawnshops and if anyone tries to sell it, we'll get wind of it." He pursed his lips. "It's an odd choice for something to steal. I doubt a fence would touch it. Besides, who knows if it's even worth anything."

Gigi had a thought. "Maybe the person who stole it took it because it was something very important to Felicity. As a sort of revenge."

"It's possible. What was the relationship like between the stepson and Miss Davenport?"

"Felicity complained about Derek's stealing cash from her purse, but she liked him enough to leave him a substantial chunk of her estate."

Mertz's eyebrows shot up like rockets being launched. "What do you mean?"

Gigi felt a blast of heat that she knew was turning her face roughly the same shade as a persimmon. She tried to ignore the sensation as she answered. "I happened to hear . . ."

Mertz's eyebrows lowered abruptly. "You happened to hear?"

Gigi fiddled with the buttons on her sweater. "One of my clients works for Simpson and West," she said as if that explained everything.

Apparently it was enough because Mertz nodded, then shook his head in disbelief. "So you're still meddling—"

"I am not." Now Gigi was really steamed. Especially since she knew Mertz was right.

Mertz smiled. A real smile this time. "I stopped by your house last night to ask you something. But you were obviously busy."

Gigi opened her mouth in a rush to explain.

"I gather that poor Mr. Goulet's advances weren't particularly welcome. At least judging by the look on your face." Mertz actually laughed.

Gigi's shoulders inched back down, and she unclenched her fists. Then she, too, laughed. "Was it that obvious?"

"Absolutely. I assume you were planning on pumping him for information, but he had other ideas."

Gigi hung her head.

"I would have stuck around to make sure he didn't cause you any further trouble, but I heard the radio in the car squawk, and it turned out to be important. Besides, it sounded as if Reg had things under control."

"How is Whiskers doing? Is he settling in okay?"

Mertz smiled. "Whiskers is doing great. But he's a she. I took her to the vet to make sure everything was okay, and apparently it's a her not a him." He shook his head. "I can't believe how much time I can waste just playing with her. I picked up a bunch of toys for her. She especially loves the stuffed mice." Mertz looked down at his spit-shined black shoes. "You must think me a complete idiot going on and on about a kitten."

"Not at all."

Mertz smiled. "Before I forget, there's something I want to ask you. Will you have dinner with me?" He spread his hands out. "No interruptions this time. I promise."

Gigi was flummoxed. It was the last thing she'd expected.

Mertz looked away. "It's okay if you don't want to, I'll—"

"No," Gigi burst out. "I mean yes, I'd love to have dinner with you."

Gigi noticed, much to her satisfaction, that this time it was Mertz's face that got all red.

Gigi was slipping on her coat when Winchel came into the kitchen looking as if he were entering some remote, foreign territory.

"Look, Miss . . ."

"Fitzgerald." Once again Gigi filled in the blank for him.

"Sorry, Fitzgerald, that's right," he said, failing to look even remotely apologetic. "Look, I have some very important people coming for dinner tonight, and I'd appreciate it if you could stay on and prepare the meal. It seems Anja has taken to her bed over this whole affair . . ." He glanced at his watch and scowled. "As a matter of fact, if you wouldn't mind stepping in for the rest of the week, that would prove very helpful."

Gigi hesitated. Winchel had already handed her one bad check. Did she want to risk putting in more time and possibly not getting paid? But his explanation for the bounced check made sense. There was no reason to think he wouldn't make good on it, no matter what Oliver had discovered. Those people on Wall Street had a very different idea of what "having no money" actually meant. He probably still had millions and millions.

Gigi decided she had nothing to lose. Before she could actually say yes, Winchel was headed out of the room, obviously having taken her silence for assent.

Vanessa breezed into the kitchen in his wake bringing

with her the heavy scents of perfume and makeup. She was obviously headed out, dressed in the kind of jeans that fit to perfection and cost hundreds of dollars, a cashmere V-neck sweater that almost matched her eyes, a long scarf around her neck and a butter-soft black leather jacket. She had on long leather gloves, and it was impossible to miss the stunning diamond tennis bracelet she had fastened over one of them.

She looked every inch the leading lady, and once again Gigi wondered what impact Felicity's death would have on the show. Would the writers expand Vanessa's character or find someone to take Felicity's place?

Vanessa must have caught Gigi staring at the bracelet. She held her wrist up to the light. "Like it?" she said in a tone that oh, so clearly said *You'll never have one like it.*

"It's beautiful," Gigi said truthfully, enjoying the way the diamonds picked up the light and refracted it into colored prisms.

Gigi wondered if Don had already cashed in his insurance policy and run out to buy his lady love another expensive trinket.

"Will you be back for dinner?" Gigi asked as Vanessa hesitated in the doorway.

"Yes." She nodded briskly before heading down the hall.

Gigi listened as the clack of her heels retreated toward the foyer, then sat at the kitchen table noodling on a menu for that evening. She had been developing a chicken tikka masala using low-fat Greek yogurt and eliminating most of the butter and oil and all of the cream. It would be delicious served with brown basmati rice mixed with a handful of toasted pine nuts. She thought Winchel and his guests would like it. Meanwhile, she'd have to make a quick dash to the Shop and Save for the ingredients.

An hour before dinner, Anja was still in bed, having taken some herbal remedy she claimed would calm her nerves but which also had succeeded in knocking her out. Gigi had had a brief conversation with Winchel, and they agreed she would put the dishes on the sideboard and serve them buffet style.

Gigi began work on dinner, taking a couple of onions from the bag in the pantry and chopping them. She pushed them to one side of her cutting board, placed three generously sized garlic cloves on her work surface and pressed down on them with the side of a large knife blade to loosen the skins.

She was about to turn on the stove to heat some olive oil in her skillet when she heard the melodic tinkle of a feminine laugh coming from the direction of Winchel's library. Curious, she edged down the hall, the thick Oriental carpets muffling the sound of her footsteps. The clinking of ice against crystal mingled with the continuing sounds of low murmurs and throaty conversation. Obviously, there was a woman in the room with Winchel. Gigi wondered who it was. They sounded very intimate.

She sidled closer to the door, which was partially cracked. She wondered if she dared put her eye to the opening and peer inside. The woman's voice trilled in laughter again, and Gigi paused, listening. She knew that voice—she'd definitely heard it before. She waited, hoping the woman would say something. She finally did, and although Gigi couldn't make out the words, she definitely recognized the speaker.

She inched closer to the gap in the door and carefully peered around the edge. Vanessa was on the sofa with Winchel. She must have just come back. Her belted trench coat was tossed over one of the chairs. Her blond hair tumbled around her plunging neckline, and Gigi saw the diamonds in her tennis bracelet flash in the lamplight.

They were both holding champagne flutes, and an open bottle stood on the coffee table in front of them. Vanessa had one leg draped casually over one of Winchel's, and his arm was splayed along the back of the sofa, the fingers of his right hand buried in her hair.

It looked to Gigi as if Vanessa was working on getting ahead in more ways than one.

Chapter 14

Gigi's phone rang early the next morning. She recognized Mertz's number right away. Was there something new on the case?

"Hello?" She held the phone with her shoulder as she poured a mug of coffee.

Mertz cleared his throat twice before speaking. "I know it's short notice but . . ."

Was he about to ask her out? Gigi put down her cup and gripped the phone hard. "Yes?"

"I was wondering if you'd like to have dinner with me tonight."

Gigi said yes immediately.

Mertz sounded relieved. "Great, I'll get us a reservation for seven at the Auberge Rouge." He was silent for a moment. "What?"

Gigi realized he wasn't talking to her.

.

"Look, I'm afraid I've got to go. I'll see you tonight. I look forward to it," he added shyly and quickly ended the call.

Gigi drifted in a fog toward her bedroom and stood in front of her open closet door. She groaned. Reggie cocked his head at her.

"I don't have a thing to wear," she told him.

He raised his shaggy brows and proceeded to settle down with his rawhide bone.

"Just like a male," Gigi muttered as she went through the hangers one by one.

Since moving to Woodstone, she hadn't had much need for fancy clothes beyond the occasional opening at the Silver Lining. She spent most of her day cooking in jeans and a T-shirt. She did enjoy dressing up from time to time, but it hadn't been in the cards lately.

She thought about Abigail's Dress Shop on High Street and all the delicious items in the window. Unfortunately the prices were stratospheric, and even though Deirdre, the saleswoman, was always willing to give her a deal, she really couldn't afford to shop there.

But it wouldn't hurt to look, a little voice whispered in her ear.

The Auberge Rouge had opened only recently but had already been favorably reviewed by the *New York Times*. If Mertz was trying to impress her, it was working. Gigi stared in disgust at the things in her closet. None of them would quite do for Auberge Rouge.

She would check out Abigail's later that afternoon. She sighed. If she didn't find anything she could afford, she supposed she could wear her old standby black dress. But maybe she would treat herself to a pin to freshen it up.

* * *

It was noon by the time Gigi drove down High Street toward Abigail's, thinking about dinner at Auberge Rouge and the gorgeous outfit she would wear to really make Mertz sit up and take notice. Then she remembered her budget, and her spirits plummeted to below sea level. She would have to depend on nothing but her native attractiveness. Which she knew from experience wasn't going to get her very far.

Gigi dropped off a Gourmet De-Lite container of lunch for Madeline. For dinner, Madeline had a company function she couldn't skip, and Gigi had advised her on smart food choices she could make in such situations to keep her on track. Gigi pulled the MINI into the lot between Declan's and Gibson's Hardware, averting her head as she drove past the large white sign that warned *Parking for Patrons of Declan's Grille and Gibson's Hardware ONLY*. If anyone said anything, she would claim that she was coming back to pick up some nails or screws.

But first . . . Abigail's. She crossed her fingers that Deirdre would have something wonderful for her—in stock and on sale.

She was locking the doors of her MINI when she heard someone call her name. She froze. Was she busted already? Her parking excuse rose to her lips and then died when she turned around and saw who it was.

"Declan."

"Hey." He had a large plastic bag in one hand and was headed toward the Dumpster at the back of the restaurant. "I've been meaning to call you."

Gigi froze. She swore her blood actually stopped flowing in her veins. Declan had meant to call *her*? He smiled the sort of crooked half smile that made women swoon.

"I'm developing a new menu for the upcoming season, and I hoped you'd give me some input."

Gigi fumbled with her car keys, trying to stuff them into her purse without upending the contents all over the macadam. So Declan hadn't meant to *call* her in the usual sense. Disappointment nibbled at her innards. But then her Irish and Italian genes stood at attention and whispered in her ear, *He's only after a good time. Don't waste your energy on him unless you're sure you can handle that.*

"I'd be happy to help you." She tried to inject the right amount of warmth into the sentence—enough to let him know she was flattered but nothing more.

Declan gestured toward the restaurant. "The lunch crowd has gone, and I have a few minutes." He raised an eyebrow in question.

"Sure." Gigi devoutly wished she'd taken more time with her hair—done anything at all with it for that matter. It was flying around her face in untamed curls. She was wearing clean jeans at least, and her black turtleneck sweater was a great backdrop for her fair skin and auburn hair.

The restaurant was dim and quiet, the air permeated with earthy smells of roasted meats, pungent cheeses and yeasty ales. Declan immediately went behind the bar, and Gigi couldn't help but eye his lean, muscular frame—more like that of a soccer player than a football player.

He grabbed two glasses off the shelf and held them toward Gigi. "Drink?"

"I don't usually drink during the day," Gigi stammered.

"Just a sip then?" Declan popped the cap off a bottle of beer. He held it toward Gigi. "Bitter and Twisted. A rather unappetizing name, but it's very smooth with a nice lemon finish. Try it?"

"Okay."

Declan poured some for Gigi and slightly more for himself. "Cheers." He held his glass up to be tapped.

Gigi took a sip and wondered what on earth she was doing, drinking beer in the middle of the day, alone, with Declan McQuaid. The fact that it excited her more than scared her made her even more nervous.

"What do you think?" Declan tipped his glass toward the beer in Gigi's hand.

Gigi licked the froth off the top of her lip. "It's very good."

Declan leaned in close. "Can you taste the lemon?"

Gigi rolled the liquid around and around in her mouth before swallowing. She frowned. "Yes. Yes, I can. It's quite good," she said with surprise.

"I import it myself. I like to be able to offer my customers something a little different." His elbows were on the counter, and he leaned toward Gigi.

Gigi's eyes met his, and she looked away quickly. "You mentioned developing a new menu?" she said to cover her awkwardness.

Declan tossed back a sizeable quaff of his beer and wiped a hand across his mouth. "I can't compete with your American Thanksgiving, so I plan to embrace it. There's a turkey farm not far from here for some fresh birds." He stared into his beer for a moment, stirring the foam with his index finger. He looked up at Gigi with a strange expression on his face. "You know people come in here talking about how they wish Al Forno was still here."

Gigi was startled. Declan's parking lot was full whenever she went past, and the few times she'd been there, there had been a decent-size crowd.

"People don't like change," Gigi said. She had firsthand experience with that herself—she'd resisted moving on after

Ted's desertion until Sienna had dragged her kicking and screaming to her new life in Connecticut.

"I suppose you're right." Declan gave a sad approximation of a smile. "I will have to wow them with my food and the homey atmosphere and hope they forget that this wasn't always Declan's Grille."

Gigi nodded. "People need to get to know you as a person. For instance, Emilio was involved in the local theater." Gigi felt a lump rising in her throat and hastily swallowed it away.

"Can't see myself doing that." Declan gave his crooked smile again. "I'm a terrible actor." He spread both hands out on the counter. "But I did have this idea . . ."

He ducked his head.

"Yes?"

"You know that fellow who fell off his ladder while painting his house . . . Joe something-or-other?"

Gigi nodded. "Yes, Joe Flanagan. His mother-in-law, Alice, is a friend of mine."

"I saw it in the paper." Declan gestured toward a folded issue of the *Woodstone Times* tucked next to the cash register. "About how he can't work because of his injuries, and the family is getting into debt."

"Alice is very worried about them." Gigi often wondered if some of the money from Alice's second job was going to help Joe and Stacy. "I gather Joe is on disability, but he's used to taking on extra work to make ends meet, like providing security at parties, sporting events and the like."

"Here's my plan, then." Declan took a big swig of his beer. "I'm going to do a whole American Thanksgiving dinner—turkey, stuffing, all the trimmings. And"—he leveled a finger at Gigi, his eyes sparkling—"I'm going to donate all the profits to help out Joe and his family."

Gigi was speechless. She felt tears spring into her eyes at the thought of how relieved Alice would be when she heard.

"It's brilliant, don't you think?"

"Yes," Gigi stammered. "Absolutely brilliant."

"I'm going to need some help, though." Declan's voice lowered to a dangerously seductive level.

Gigi inched slightly backward, in full-on self-protection mode. "I'll do anything I can . . ."

"I'll need some advice with the menu—not being a native myself." Declan reached for another bottle of beer, uncapped it and held it over Gigi's glass.

She shook her head, which was already swirling more than enough.

Declan poured himself another glass. "For instance . . ." He paused to take a sip. "Do you traditionally serve jacket potatoes or mash?" Gigi must have looked confused because Declan laughed and went on to explain. "We call them jacket potatoes, but I think you call them baked potatoes."

"Oh, mashed, definitely." Gigi's mouth watered at the thought. "And lots of stuffing and gravy. And creamed onions and cranberry sauce."

Declan smiled. "I knew you would be able to help me."

Gigi left the restaurant with her head spinning from Declan's presence as well as from the beer. She realized, as she hurried down the street toward Abigail's, that she'd forgotten all about her evening dinner date with Mertz. She felt guilty as she pulled open the door to the boutique.

A blast of richly perfumed air greeted Gigi as she entered. The shop was hushed and appeared empty, although Gigi heard someone moving around in the back. The beaded curtains were pushed to one side and Deirdre came out. Her dark hair was pulled off her face into a tight bun, and she was wearing an amber-colored sheath with her gold name tag pinned to the bodice.

She smiled when she saw Gigi. "I just got in the perfect dress for you!"

Gigi made a sad face. "I probably won't be able to afford it." Did she want to torture herself by having a look? Or worse, trying it on?

"You must see it." Deirdre went to one of the racks and clicked through the hangers. She pulled out an item and held it in front of Gigi.

It was an exquisite dress, beautifully constructed and not too fancy. The blue-green would be perfect with Gigi's coloring. She tried not to look at it too closely. She knew she couldn't afford it. She couldn't even afford to think about it. Or look at it. Or try it on.

Gigi departed Abigail's with a bright, shiny, new shopping bag on her arm and a huge dent in her bank account. Deirdre had given her a very good price for the dress, but it had still been extremely expensive—especially for someone who spent most of her time in jeans and T-shirts and a stained apron. Gigi didn't know what had come over her. Why did she feel such a need to impress Mertz tonight? Was it the deafening sound of her biological clock ticking double time, or was she feeling guilty because of her attraction to Declan?

She glanced at her watch and realized she'd have to hurry. She threw the dress in the backseat of the MINI and dashed out of the parking lot, bumping up and down over the curb in her haste.

She felt a burning sense of shame over her spontaneous purchase that had her stomping on the gas and speeding down High Street in her irritation with herself.

She arrived at Felicity's house, parked her car and headed quickly for the kitchen.

She put together a simple boeuf bourguignon, browning the meat and onions carefully for maximum flavor. Anja was feeling slightly better and thought she would be up to doing the final preparations and the serving. Gigi put the stew in the oven and wiped down the counters. Almost time to go home and primp for her date with Mertz.

Date. The word hit her over the head with the force of a rogue rolling pin. She and Mertz were actually going on a date. She hadn't been on a date in years. A few well-meaning friends had tried to fix her up after Ted left, but the evenings had been disasters. The men were all wrong, and Gigi hadn't been ready. This date, however, had possibilities. And that thought scared Gigi half to death.

Gigi was alternately dreaming about and feeling guilty over the new dress waiting in the bag from Abigail's. It would take some digging, but she knew she had the perfect pair of shoes somewhere in the depths of her closet—left over from her New York days. High-heeled, black suede peep-toes. They didn't make them much more "come hither" than that.

Gigi had gone to the Auberge Rouge Web site and checked out their menu. She didn't want to be distracted by Mertz's presence as she tried to decide what to order. So far she'd narrowed it down to the osso bucco—a wonderful dish that took many hours to prepare—or the duck with wild rice and lingonberries. Duck wasn't something she generally made for herself, and she hadn't had it since that French restaurant Ted had taken her to for their last anniversary, ten days before he announced he was leaving. She'd had a strange aversion to duck for several years afterward, but it had finally passed.

Gigi was tossing her soiled apron into the laundry when she heard a peculiar noise.

She stopped for a moment and listened. The noise became louder and clearer. Gigi dashed into the hallway where she nearly collided with Anja, who had half run, half fallen down the stairs. Her mouth was open in another scream, but she managed to stifle it when she saw Gigi.

"What is it?" Gigi grabbed her by the shoulders.

Anja's mouth moved, but nothing came out.

Gigi gave her a gentle shake. "What's wrong?"

"Derek," Anja bleated.

"Is he ill?"

Anja shook her head, and her blond hair spun wildly around her face. "No."

"What is it, then?" Gigi demanded.

"He's dead."

Chapter 15

Gigi felt the blood drain from her face and rush south toward her feet. For one moment, she thought she might faint, but she took a deep, restorative breath and steadied herself.

Perhaps Anja was mistaken. She *had* to be mistaken. Maybe Derek had been experimenting with drugs and had taken something that had put him in a coma-like state?

Gigi mounted the stairs slowly, not looking forward to what she was going to find. Anja was uttering little cries of anguish under her breath and twisting a handkerchief around and around in her fingers. Gigi wanted to scream at her to stop.

Derek's bedroom was that of a young man in transition between childhood and adulthood. A pinup of some scantily clad celebrity jostled for space on a wall crowded with Harry Potter posters. One shelf on the bookcase was given over to model cars while the others were crammed with textbooks, popular magazines and the latest thrillers.

Derek looked as if he were sleeping, but when Gigi dared to get close enough to check, she realized he wasn't breathing. She stifled the scream that rose in her throat.

"We'd better call nine-one-one."

Anja didn't move, and Gigi had to take her by the arm and lead her back into the hallway.

"You stay here." She shepherded Anja to a padded velvet bench at the top of the stairs. "And make sure no one goes in there." Gigi already had one foot on the top stair. "I'll get my cell phone and call the police."

Gigi gave a doubtful backward glance at Anja as she headed down the stairs. The woman was dreadfully pale, and Gigi prayed she wouldn't faint. Maybe she should have told her to put her head down?

She nearly fell down the last steps and ran directly into Winchel.

"Oh."

"In a hurry?"

Gigi took a deep breath. She didn't want to tell him about Derek until she'd already called the police. "I left something on the stove," she fibbed, feeling the usual stab of guilt that was a relic from her Catholic school days. Even white lies, told to protect someone's feelings, caused her a pang of remorse.

Fortunately Winchel merely nodded and continued down the hall toward the library.

Gigi dug her cell phone out of her jacket pocket and, with shaking fingers, punched in 9-1-1. Then she walked down the seemingly endless hall to the library to break the news to Winchel.

Winchel heard her out, his face etched in stoic lines, only the clenching of his jaw betraying the slightest hint of emotion.

"Can I get you a drink?" Gigi asked.

"Thanks." Winchel put his head in his hands, and Gigi thought she heard him groan.

She fixed him a scotch and water that was more scotch than water and put it on the desk. He didn't look up as she tiptoed from the room. Hopefully he would have a few moments of peace before the police arrived.

Five minutes later, Gigi heard the front door open and then Winchel's deep voice. The police had obviously arrived. She waited in the kitchen, listening to the sound of footsteps overhead punctuated by the occasional shouted command. She thought perhaps she ought to make some tea. It would do her and Anja good, if nothing else.

Gigi was pouring out hot water when a quiet knock at the back door startled her. A few drops of boiling water landed on the top of her hand, and she winced. She pulled open the door, wondering if one of the policemen had gone around back.

Alice was standing on the doorstep, her gray hair caught by the wind and tossed around her face.

"I heard the news at the station, and I hoped that you'd be here." She was breathless.

Gigi opened the door wider. "I'm making some tea. You look as if you could use a good, hot cup."

"It is getting cold out there." Alice threw her jacket over one of the kitchen chairs. She sat down at the table opposite Gigi and cupped her hands around the mug of warm tea Gigi handed her. "Terrible about that young man. Even if he did strike me as rather useless." Alice took a sip of her tea and looked up at Gigi. "It looks as if our chief suspect is now dead."

"I know." Gigi's shoulders slumped. She sighed.

"How is Winchel taking it?"

"Stoically, of course."

Alice nodded. "Just as you'd expect."

"How is Stacy?"

Alice frowned. "You can imagine. Now that Joe can't work, she's even more unhappy. They've got that huge mortgage on that big house. Why she talked him into it, I'll never know. She might have to get a job herself, and she's not at all happy about it. Most of her friends are staying home, but they have children to care for." Alice stared into her tea. "She knows I've always worked. Even when her father was alive, I did something part-time to help out. If we wanted things, we knew we had to earn the money for them. Kids!" She threw her hands in the air. "They want everything handed to them today."

Gigi thought about Declan's fund-raising plans and nearly opened her mouth but clamped it shut quickly. It wasn't up to her to tell Alice about it.

Gigi glanced at her watch and was startled when she saw the time. She had to get home and start getting ready for her dinner with Mertz. She was about to retrieve her new dress from the coat closet to show Alice when she heard someone walking down the corridor toward the kitchen, their sharp footsteps striking the wood floor with the sound of authority.

Gigi looked up to find Mertz framed in the doorway, a very apologetic look on his face.

"I'm really sorry about tonight. I'll make it up to you, okay?" He gave a sketchy salute and turned on his heel.

Gigi sat slumped over her now empty cup of tea. "It hadn't occurred to me that we'd have to cancel tonight."

Alice patted her hand. "I can understand how disappointed you are, but he did say he'd make it up to you. You guys will go out another night."

Gigi sighed. "I guess I'd gotten myself all worked up that

it was going to be today." She wiped a corner of her eye with her napkin. "The way things have been going with us, who knows if there will be a next time." She struggled to smile. "I guess I'll go home and rustle up something to eat from the fridge."

"You could go out and eat some worms."

For a moment, Gigi was startled, but then, in spite of herself, she began to laugh remembering the childhood ditty they used to sing.

Her laugh was cut short when Mertz reappeared in the doorway. "Can I speak with you?"

"I've got to be going." Alice jumped up from her seat and grabbed her jacket off the back of the chair.

Mertz stood silently and watched her go, not saying anything until the kitchen door had closed behind Alice.

"I'm really beat." He sat down in the chair Alice had vacated and ran a hand across his forehead.

Gigi was startled. She'd never seen Mertz unbend an inch let alone admit defeat. "You need a cup of coffee." She pushed off from her chair and began to rummage in the pantry for the bag of Sumatra blend she'd brought to Felicity's.

Mertz didn't object but sat at the table with his head in his hands.

Now Gigi was really worried. She placed a scoop of coffee into the fancy coffee machine that made only one cup at a time. She added water and stood back as it gurgled and spit a cup of java into the mug she'd placed under it.

She slid the cup in front of Mertz.

Mertz ran a hand through his closely cropped hair, and Gigi thought she heard him groan as he took a sip of the bracing brew.

She slid into the seat opposite and waited for him to speak.

"The mayor's all over this." Mertz took a second draft and closed his eyes in appreciation. "Winchel's a real big shot in town. And Felicity put the town on the map. Everyone's screaming for an arrest." He looked up at Gigi.

"There are plenty of leads," Gigi declared authoritatively. "Derek Winchel stood to receive a substantial inheritance from Felicity, so he was at the top of my list." She glanced down into her empty cup. "We'll have to scratch that one, I guess. But there's still Don, Felicity's manager, and Vanessa." She frowned. "Even Winchel himself."

Mertz looked up, an eyebrow raised.

"Winchel stands to inherit a fair amount of Felicity's money as well." Gigi couldn't believe Mertz was actually talking about the case to her. She felt encouraged to continue. "And Don cashed in on a policy he took out on Felicity right before she died."

Mertz's head snapped up. "He did, did he?"

"And he got very touchy when he discovered I'd been asking questions about him."

Mertz gave a tired smile. "I'll bet."

"Even Vanessa has a motive of sorts. With Felicity out of the way, she stands to take the lead in *For Better or For Worse*. Vanessa is sporting some really spectacular jewelry all of a sudden. I'm thinking Don might have bought it for her with some of the proceeds of that insurance policy."

Mertz looked at Gigi over the rim of his coffee cup. He wiped a hand across his face as if he were trying to wipe something away. "Unfortunately there's no real, hard evidence to connect *any* of those people to Felicity's death." He smiled at Gigi, but it was a tired, sad smile.

"We'll have to find evidence. We'll—"

Mertz held up a hand and opened his mouth but then shut it again.

A strange feeling began to form in the pit of Gigi's stomach. She had a feeling that Mertz was about to say something she wouldn't like hearing. Something really bad.

"What?" she demanded.

Mertz shook his head as if trying to clear it. "You know the prescription pill bottle you found in Derek's bedroom?"

Gigi nodded, and the feeling in her stomach intensified. She felt as if she were going to be sick.

"What?" she said again.

Mertz looked down at his coffee cup as if seeking guidance from its depths. "We found prints on it. Other than Felicity's."

"Yes?" Gigi's heart was pounding so hard she was sure Mertz could see it.

"The prints belonged to your friend."

"Friend?"

Mertz nodded and managed to look even sadder. "Yes. Sienna Paisley."

Gigi stood in the kitchen and chopped furiously at a red onion for the salad. If anyone asked, she would say she wasn't crying—it was the onion making her eyes tear. She closed them for a moment. She'd been so excited about today. A real dinner date with an attractive man. And a new dress. It didn't get any better than that. But everything had disintegrated into a pile of ash. And she was facing the fact that the police still thought her best friend was responsible for a murder. She desperately wanted to go home, but Anja was a mess, and Gigi had promised Winchel she would stay. She wished she'd brought Reg with her—he always cheered her up—but the young girl next door was going to take him out and give him his dinner in her absence.

As soon as everything was ready, Gigi had decided, she would leave and go to Sienna's. She had to make Sienna tell her where she'd been the afternoon Felicity died. And with this new evidence, Gigi had no doubt that Sienna would realize how serious things had become.

The boeuf bourguignon in the oven was almost ready. Gigi had brought some of her Gourmet De-Lite containers with her, and she would fill one for her own dinner. She opened the kitchen door to go out to her car, and the wind immediately grabbed it and tried to wrest it from her. She managed to close it behind her amidst a hail of brightly colored autumn leaves. She glanced up at the sky. The clouds were dark, and rain was clearly threatening. She thought she felt a drop as she hurried toward her MINI.

She was closing her car door behind her when she noticed a flurry of activity at the front of the house. The door was open and several policemen and technicians were exiting. Gigi turned her head. She didn't want to see them carrying Derek's body out. She hadn't much cared for the young man, but it still made her dreadfully sad that his life had been cut short so young.

Gigi took her container inside and opened it up on the counter. She filled it with a half cup of noodles, and ladled some of the beef on top. It smelled delicious, and she was tempted to eat it right then and there, but her stomach was in turmoil, and she didn't want to get a tummy ache.

Suddenly the door to the kitchen swung open and Mertz entered. Gigi was struck by how terrible he looked. He didn't even attempt to smile but sat at the table and put his head in his hands. Gigi slid into the seat opposite him, her own hands clenched in her lap.

After several moments, Mertz finally looked up. "It's always hard when it's someone so young."

Gigi had to resist the urge to put her hand over his.

Mertz swallowed hard. Gigi saw his Adam's apple bob up and down.

"We found something in Derek's room." Mertz looked up. "Something that indicates we're looking at another murder here."

"Yes?" Gigi tensed.

"An insulin syringe. I've talked with Winchel, and Derek wasn't diabetic, nor had he been prescribed insulin for any reason."

For a moment, it didn't register with Gigi. Then she remembered. Sienna. Pregnancy-induced diabetes. Insulin. Needles.

She knew she ought to tell Mertz, but she clamped her mouth shut and didn't say a word.

Chapter 16

Gigi jumped into her MINI and backed ferociously out of the driveway. She swiped a hand across her face, wiping the moisture from her eyes. It couldn't be. Sienna couldn't possibly have murdered Felicity and Derek. Someone must have planted that syringe to try to make Sienna look guilty. And Gigi was sure there was a completely logical reason why they'd found Sienna's fingerprints on Felicity's bottle of prescription tranquilizers.

Even with Derek's death she didn't lack for suspects. She had to find a way to link the killer with the crime. She raised her chin slightly. Much as she hated doing it, she would have to ask more questions and probe into more lives. She'd do it for Sienna.

The streetlights were coming on as Gigi drove down High Street. It wasn't raining, but drops continued to fall from the trees and splatter onto her windshield. She turned on the wipers to clear the glass, and two curling red maple leaves, caught under the blades, swished back and forth across her windshield.

Mertz obviously didn't know that Sienna had contracted gestational diabetes and been prescribed insulin, but it wouldn't take him long to find out. Gigi had to talk to Sienna first and warn her. Sienna had what could be considered a strong motive—having been made a fool of by Felicity and the "leaked" picture and story of Oliver. There didn't seem to be anything to link her with Derek, but Gigi had no doubt that the police would come up with something.

The light was on over Sienna's front door, and Gigi hoped that meant she was home. Gigi crossed her fingers as she rang Sienna's doorbell.

Sienna was already in her robe and pajamas when she opened the door. Her long hair was pulled into a braid that hung down her back. She looked startled when she saw Gigi standing on her doorstep.

"Come in." She pulled the door wider. "Is it raining?"

"Yes." Gigi took off her coat and handed it to Sienna.

"What's up? Has something happened?"

Gigi nodded. "I'm sorry it's so late"—she gestured at Sienna's robe—"but we need to talk."

Sienna frowned. "You look terrible. Has something happened?"

Gigi nodded as she followed Sienna into the great room that served as both family room and living room. It was filled with comfy, overstuffed furniture. A fire was going in the stone fireplace, and the room smelled of delicious wood smoke. Gigi was sorry that she was going to have to ruin the peaceful scene.

Sienna curled up on the sofa, and Gigi collapsed into one of the chairs.

Sienna gave a wry smile. "I'm the type who likes to rip the Band-Aid off in one fell swoop, so out with it. Tell me what's happened."

Gigi sighed. "Derek is dead."

"Oh." Sienna's hand flew to her mouth. "I'm so sorry to hear that. So young." She was quiet for a moment. "What happened?"

"They don't really know yet. But two things have been found in his room."

Sienna raised her eyebrows.

Well, here it goes, Gigi thought. "You know that bottle of tranquilizers that belonged to Felicity?"

Sienna nodded.

Gigi gulped and took a deep breath. "The police apparently found your fingerprints on the bottle."

Sienna half rose from her seat. "You don't think I—"

Gigi shook her head vehemently. "No, of course not. But Mertz will certainly think you had something to do with it. Can you remember how your fingerprints would have gotten on the container?"

Sienna frowned and rubbed her forehead. "It was a while back, but I seem to remember that Felicity had a prescription pill bottle that she couldn't get open. She asked me if I could help." Sienna smiled. "Yes, I remember now. She'd had her nails touched up, and she didn't want to ruin them. She asked me to do it for her."

"Was it a vial of tranquilizers?"

"I don't know. I didn't look at the label. But it must have been. My fingerprints wouldn't be on any other pill bottles."

Sienna leaned back against the cushions, a look of relief on her face. Gigi rubbed a hand across the back of her neck. She had a giant knot on the right side. She knew what she was going to say next was going to upset Sienna, and she hated doing it. But it was better than having Sienna be blindsided by Mertz when he figured things out.

"You don't look convinced. Is there something you're not telling me?" Sienna leaned forward and stared intently at Gigi.

"There's more."

Sienna grabbed one of the throw pillows and clutched it to her chest. "Why do I have the feeling that I'm not going to like this?"

"I'm sorry. But I don't want you finding out from Mertz."

"Finding out what?"

"They found something else in Derek's room." Gigi closed her eyes. "An insulin syringe."

Sienna gasped. "No."

"Mertz checked. Derek hasn't been prescribed insulin."

"Someone is trying to implicate me." Sienna clutched the pillow tighter.

"It looks like it."

"What are we going to do?"

Sienna clutched the pillow even tighter, and Gigi saw her knuckles turning white. Gigi leaned forward and put a hand over Sienna's. "Don't worry," she said with more confidence than she felt, "between us, we'll find the real culprit and present him to the police."

Reg was beside himself when Gigi finally got home. She knelt down to let him lick her face. His tail slapped against her coat, making a thwacking sound, and he positively wriggled in his excitement to see her.

Gigi felt the usual peace settle over her that being in her cottage always brought. She wandered from room to room, turning on a light here and there and enjoying the pride of ownership that came over her every time she walked through the door. Finally, with Reg at her heels, she headed toward the kitchen.

"This is what you're after, I'm sure." She retrieved a dog biscuit from the cookie jar on the counter. She held it over Reg's head, and he danced on his back paws, licking his lips in anticipation. Gigi gave it a small toss, and Reg jumped and grabbed it from the air. He took it to his dog bed in the corner where he settled in for his snack.

Gigi put some hot water on the stove. She hoped a cup of chamomile tea would help her settle down. Her nerves felt as taut as violin strings. She couldn't even face the container of beef stew she'd brought home, although earlier her stomach had been growling fiercely. She sat at the table, her head in her hands, her eyes drooping closed. The shriek from the teakettle startled her, and she jumped up, barking her knee against the table. Tears of frustration flooded her eyes. Today had really been a no good, horrible, terrible, really bad day. She was ready to put on her pajamas, crawl into bed and put it behind her.

Gigi brushed her teeth, washed her face and slid between the covers. She pulled up the down comforter and sighed. Her bed felt delicious—warm and cozy and safe. The tea had soothed her frazzled nerves, and she found her eyes quickly closing.

The shrill ring of the telephone sent her heart into high gear. Her bare feet slapped against the floor as she lunged for the receiver on her nightstand.

"Hello?"

"It's Alice."

The weakness in Alice's voice alarmed Gigi. "What's the matter?" She heard Alice groan.

"I've fallen down the stairs. I think my arm is broken. I'm sorry to call so late, but Stacy isn't answering her cell phone. I don't want to call an ambulance and wake up all my neighbors. I'm terribly sorry . . ." Alice's voice drifted to a whisper.

"I'll be there as fast as I can."

Gigi had already begun to shimmy out of her pajama bottoms. She grabbed her jeans off the chair where she'd tossed them and pulled them on. They smelled like sautéed onions and garlic, but she didn't want to take the time to dig for a clean pair. Her T-shirt wasn't any fresher, but it would have to do. She grabbed her fleece from the closet and she was ready to go.

Reggie had already been home alone all day, so Gigi decided to let him tag along. He rode shotgun while she traversed the darkened streets of a sleeping Woodstone. Alice had sounded as if she were in pain. Gigi hoped she wasn't going into shock. She tried to remember what first aid she'd learned in Girl Scouts a million years ago. She knew she needed to keep Alice warm—she'd grab a blanket to wrap around her as they drove to the hospital.

Alice's house was dark except for the light over the front door, as Gigi pulled into the driveway. Alice was waiting, and flipped off the light as she opened the door to Gigi.

"No use keeping this on and burning up electricity."

"We might need it when we return. You don't want to trip coming up the stairs and hurt yourself further."

"True." Alice flipped the switch back to the on position.

She looked better than Gigi had feared, but she was pale and obviously in pain. "Do you have a throw or blanket handy? It's gotten rather bitter out."

"There's one on the sofa." Alice gestured behind her.

Gigi felt her way through the darkness toward the bulky shadow she assumed was the couch. She felt along the arms until her hands closed on what she assumed was a knitted afghan. She tucked it under her arm and helped Alice down the steps toward her waiting MINI.

She shooed Reg into the back, tucked Alice into the front passenger seat and carefully covered her with the quilt. Fortunately, the hospital was barely two miles away. The roads were deserted, and Gigi felt justified in ignoring the speed limit.

Bright yellow light from the emergency room entrance spilled across the drive. Gigi pulled into one of the designated parking spots and helped Alice to the door. The nurse behind the desk spied them coming and rushed toward them with a wheelchair. Alice settled into it gratefully.

"I'll try to fit you in as soon as possible," the dark-haired nurse said as she wheeled Alice toward the triage area. "We had a five-car pileup on the highway. I gather the roads are rather slippery tonight. And the usual chest pains, small children with fevers, and a woman whose hand swelled and now she can't get her wedding ring off."

The waiting room was crowded with adults and small children, half of them staring blankly at the wall-mounted television. A cop show was on, and someone had turned up the volume so the sounds of cars screeching and guns firing echoed off the walls. A young man in a baseball cap was shaking the vending machine, which had apparently failed to release the bag of stale cookies or chips he'd selected. Gigi took a seat and picked up one of the magazines, but she was too jumpy to make any sense of the words or pictures on its pages. She replaced it and got up to go in search of a water fountain.

A large wad of orange-colored gum floated in the small puddle of water in the basin of the drinking fountain. The paper-cup dispenser was empty, and Gigi decided against having a drink. She thought there was a half-full bottle of water in her car if she became desperate. At least the trip to the water fountain took up a couple of minutes, Gigi was pleased to note. She knew she was in for a wait—X-rays would have to be taken, and Alice's arm might need to be set. And who knew where she would fall in the queue already waiting for treatment. She began to envy Reg asleep in the backseat of the car.

Gigi had fallen asleep, her head propped up with her right hand, when she felt a tap on her shoulder. She woke to find a very good-looking young doctor standing in front of her.

He smiled. "You can come join your friend now, if you'd like."

Gigi jumped to her feet and straightened her shirt and jacket. Just her luck to run into such a good-looking man when she looked like someone who had been pulled through the bushes backward. She followed him through the automatic door behind the nurse's station and down the hall toward the last cubicle. All the rooms were occupied, and gurneys were lined up in the hallway.

"It's a busy night," the doctor said, giving a nod toward one of the waiting patients. "Fortunately none of the injuries are life-threatening. Still"—he sighed—"it will probably be morning before we treat everyone."

Gigi hoped she wouldn't have to be there until morning. She was already aching with fatigue.

The doctor pushed aside the brightly colored curtain and ushered her into a tiny room, crowded with medical equipment. Alice lay on the bed, an IV pumping fluid into her arm and a blood pressure cuff alternately inflating and deflating as it took her vitals.

"The doctor is waiting for the X-rays to come back." Alice struggled to sit up.

"Don't," Gigi said. "I can boost the bed up for you if you'd like."

Alice nodded.

Gigi fiddled around in back of the bed until she found the appropriate button. She was half-afraid of sending Alice flying through the doorway, but she managed to raise the bed to a modest level without causing any catastrophes.

"Do you want anything? Some water?"

Alice shook her head. "I'm fine. They're giving me something for the pain." She gestured toward the IV stand. "Why don't you sit down? You look all done in yourself."

Gigi slid into the orange plastic chair next to the bed. "They're busy out there tonight."

The curtain to Alice's cubicle bulged inward, and a nurse poked her head around the edge. "Sorry about that. Full house tonight. We'll try not to disturb you."

Alice and Gigi could hear her talking to someone outside the curtain. The voice sounded familiar to Gigi, but she couldn't place it. The nurse was obviously taking someone's medical history. The man complained of chest pains and shortness of breath. His voice was still tantalizingly familiar. Gigi glanced at Alice.

"Who is that?" Alice whispered. "I know the voice, but I can't place it."

"Any recent medical procedures?" they heard the nurse ask.

The man gave an embarrassed laugh. "Not really. Unless Botox counts," he said, his voice dipping lower.

"When?"

"Let me think. It was last Friday. Around four o'clock with Dr. Hollywood."

"Hollywood?" the nurse asked, her skepticism clear in her voice.

"Yes. He's over on Fairmount, near the corner of Cambridge."

Alice's eyes suddenly popped wide open. She hissed at Gigi.

"What?"

"I know who that is!" Alice leaned forward, her arm momentarily forgotten. "It's that fellow who is . . . was . . . Felicity's manager."

"I think you're right!" Gigi jumped up in excitement. "It certainly sounds like Don."

"Take a peek through the curtain."

Gigi carefully moved the curtain aside an inch and peered out. She pulled her head back in quickly. "You're right!"

Alice started to giggle. "Botox! Imagine."

Yes, indeed, Gigi thought. She did some quick calculations in her head. If Don was visiting Dr. Hollywood for cosmetic procedures on Friday circa four o'clock, then he definitely wasn't the person who'd locked Felicity in the sauna that same afternoon.

Gigi felt her stomach plummet as their list of suspects once again diminished by one.

Chapter 17

By the time Alice's arm was set and immobilized in plaster, it was almost one o'clock in the morning. Gigi had long since drifted asleep in the uncomfortable plastic chair, and the doctor ended up waking both of them when he arrived with Alice's discharge instructions.

Gigi tucked Alice into the front seat and tried to make her as comfortable as possible under the circumstances. Reg awoke long enough from his slumber to assess the situation before heading off into the land of nod again, his head resting on his two front paws.

High Street was slick with rain and patterned with dark shadows when they finally left the hospital parking lot.

"I'm so glad I took the short-term disability they offered at work," Alice said, somewhat groggily, her words slurring together and over each other. "With this arm, I don't know how I'm going to be able to work. It's the extra that's not covered."

"Extra?" Gigi glanced at Alice out of the corner of her eye.

"You know, the little jobs I do here and there—like helping you out. With Joe out of work, he and Stacy are going to need some help making ends meet."

Gigi remembered her conversation with Declan and was about to open her mouth when she again thought better of it. Perhaps he hadn't mentioned his plan to Joe or Stacy yet, and perhaps Alice didn't know about it at all.

They drove past Abigail's, and Gigi felt a pang for the dress hanging, unworn, in her closet. Would she and Mertz ever get another chance to go out? Perhaps she ought to return it. It had been an impulse purchase she could ill afford.

The dark street was punctuated by the glow from the streetlights, and Gigi noticed a stronger light up ahead. Several lights were still burning at Declan's, which was odd. She knew they stopped serving dinner at nine o'clock on weeknights, and even the most diehard drinkers ought to be home in bed by now.

She slowed as they passed the front of the tavern, and Gigi completely took her foot off the gas when she noticed the front door opening. Declan stood in the pool of light created by the lit sign over the front of the building. He was holding the door, and someone was exiting. They stood close together and appeared to speak a few words before the woman turned and walked toward the parking lot.

Gigi couldn't linger much longer, but she managed to slow enough to see who the woman was.

She glanced at Alice, and judging by the look on her face, Alice had seen, too.

Alice gasped. "It's my Stacy!" She turned to look at Gigi. "What on earth is she doing at Declan's at this time of night?"

Gigi didn't want to say anything. It was perfectly obvious

to her. No wonder Declan was so anxious to help Stacy out! She supposed Stacy was willing to play by Declan's rules— a good time but with no strings attached.

They drove the rest of the way to Alice's house in silence. Alice was clearly distraught, and Gigi was loathe to leave her alone, but Alice insisted she would be fine.

Gigi drove back to her cottage, waited while Reg ran off to lift his leg on one of the bushes, then went inside and locked the door. She shed her clothes as she headed toward the bedroom and didn't even bother with pajamas but crawled immediately under the down comforter.

Tonight had been the perfect end to her no good, horrible, terrible, really bad day, and she was ready to put it behind her.

"We still have plenty of suspects," Sienna said after Gigi explained about overhearing Don in the emergency room.

They were at the Book Nook, in what had become known as the coffee corner. The sofa and chairs were worn and enveloping, and a coffee machine gurgled steadily on the sideboard. Gigi noticed that now that Sienna's stomach was so big, she moved awkwardly in the small space.

"True." Gigi rested her head against the back cushions. In addition to the late night, she hadn't slept well. "And they all had access to Derek's room. The police have asked them to stay nearby for the interim."

"Winchel has been very hospitable letting them stay at the house so long." Sienna handed Gigi a mug of coffee.

"My guess is he's doing it to hide the fact that he and Vanessa have become an item. The gossip papers would be all over that one!"

"True." Sienna cradled her mug of tea in her hands.

"They'd have a field day with it. 'Soap Star Felicity Davenport Barely Cold in Her Grave When Husband Takes Up with Younger Costar . . .'"

Gigi laughed, although she didn't doubt that's exactly what would happen. "Meanwhile, everyone is being fooled into thinking Vanessa and Don are the couple."

"Even Don?" Sienna sipped her tea.

Gigi shrugged. "I don't know. Vanessa seems to be doing a good job so far." She looked down at the cup of freshly brewed coffee Sienna had handed her, and inhaled deeply. She needed a caffeine fix, stat! "Since Don has an alibi, perhaps Vanessa is the one who did the deed. Felicity's death put money in Don's pocket, and it sure looks like it put one heck of a diamond bracelet on Vanessa's wrist."

Sienna gave a small smile. "I gather your dinner with Mertz didn't happen."

Gigi shook her head. "No, not after Derek's body was discovered. He was busy all night."

"Another time?"

Gigi shrugged. "I don't know. He hasn't said anything about a rain check."

"He will. Give him time."

Gigi glanced at her watch. "I'd better get up to Winchel's and begin working on dinner. I'm trying another recipe I plan to use for Branston Foods. And I'm going to take Alice some so she doesn't have to cook."

"Poor Alice."

Gigi shuddered. "I can't imagine being incapacitated like that." She had a momentary thought—perhaps she ought to look into disability insurance. Her entire livelihood depended on her being able to use her arms and hands. What would happen if she fell down the stairs like Alice?

* * *

The driveway at Winchel's house was full when Gigi pulled in. She noticed Winchel's Escalade, Don's bright red Porsche Boxster, and Vanessa's black Mitsubishi Spyder. Even Anja's bicycle was leaning against the corner of the garage. It looked like she'd have a full house for dinner.

Gigi tied on an apron and got to work. Dinner was going to be a casual affair since none of Winchel's guests had been able to commit to a specific time for the meal. Gigi chopped onions and garlic and browned them in a smidge of hot olive oil. She added diced tomatoes, a can of green chilies, chicken broth and cut-up chicken. When the mixture had cooked and the flavors had melded, she would add black beans, corn and a flour-and-water slurry to thicken the mixture. Strips of corn tortilla baked to a crisp in the oven would go on top of the soup. And, for those who weren't calorie conscious, she would put out toppings of sour cream and grated cheddar cheese.

"That smells very good." Anja gave the ghost of a smile as she bustled into the kitchen.

"I'm going to leave the pot on the stove, and everyone can help themselves. Mr. Winchel wanted things to be casual tonight."

"I don't know what kind of appetite the poor man will have, having lost his son like that." Anja tut-tutted as she put out bowls, napkins and silverware. "Another tragedy." She turned toward Gigi, her face serious. "You know what they say?"

Gigi looked up from the tortillas she was cutting into strips with a pair of kitchen shears. "What."

"Well, in my country they believe things happen in threes. Good things, bad things, it doesn't matter."

"A lot of people here believe that, too."

Anja stared at Gigi. "Really? I thought it was just in my country. Do you?"

"Do I what?" Gigi looked away from Anja's gaze.

"Believe that things happen in threes?"

Gigi shivered but said firmly, "No. That's an old wives' tale." She hoped. She made the sign her Italian grandmother believed warded off the evil eye or *malocchio*—index finger and pinkie outstretched—and hoped for the best.

"Will there be dessert?" Anja paused in front of the glass-fronted cabinet filled with Felicity's collection of china.

"Yes." Gigi dusted flour off her hands. "Baked apples with caramel brandy sauce." It wasn't exactly low-calorie fare, but since most of the guests weren't dieting, Gigi felt a little extra comfort food was in order.

Anja got out the requisite number of dessert plates and placed them on the sideboard in the kitchen.

Gigi retrieved a bag of apples from the refrigerator and began to prepare them. Then she got whipping cream and butter from the fridge and brown sugar from the pantry.

"Is there any brandy?" Gigi turned toward Anja. She wasn't anxious to go into the library to look in the liquor cabinet herself. She didn't want to intrude on Winchel or any of his guests. Or, worse yet, Winchel and Vanessa in a clutch on the sofa.

"There is a supply of liquor stored in the cellar. It's cooler down there." Anja turned toward the door. "I will get a bottle for you."

"That's okay, I can get it myself."

"The shelves are on the right-hand side when you get to the bottom of the stairs."

Gigi opened the door to the cellar and felt for the light switch. She flipped it but nothing happened.

"What is it?" Anja had come up behind her and looked over Gigi's shoulder.

"The light seems to be burned out." Gigi peered down the dark, narrow stairs.

"Let me go. I know the way better than you." Anja started to step in front of Gigi. "There is another light at the bottom of the stairs, but it's a pull cord, and it helps if you know where it is."

"That's okay. I can manage. You finish setting out the dishes." Gigi started down the stairs before Anja could protest any further.

The air got colder and the light grew dimmer the closer she got to the bottom of the stairs. By the time she reached the landing, Gigi was feeling with her toes for the floor and regretting that she hadn't sent Anja on this errand instead. She waved a hand in front of her face, feeling for the pull cord Anja had mentioned, but she grasped nothing but air.

After a moment, her eyes began to adjust and she could make out the skeletal shape of the storage shelving unit. Gigi was heading toward it when her foot caught in something and she went flying. Her outstretched hands hit the cement floor first, and she felt the roughness scrape the heels of her hands. Gigi closed her eyes against the onslaught of tears that rushed to her eyes from the sharp, stinging pain.

Her knees connected with the floor next, and she was glad she was wearing jeans to protect them. Her foot twisted, and a sharp pain tore through her ankle. She jerked her leg, but her foot appeared to be stuck. She maneuvered to a sitting position and felt around with her fingertips. Her foot was lodged in an indentation in the floor—probably a drainage hole of some sort. Gigi yanked and her foot came free. She rotated her ankle, and the resulting pain made her cringe. It was sprained, or, at the very least, strained.

She sat on the floor for a moment. The cold from the cement seeped through her jeans, and she began to shiver. She had to get back upstairs. Anja could retrieve the brandy. Hopefully a few tablets of ibuprofen and she'd be able to finish the baked apples with brandy caramel sauce before heading to the emergency room.

Gigi stood up slowly and very carefully put some experimental pressure on her ankle. It wasn't as bad as she had feared. She managed to hobble toward the foot of the stairs. She was about to begin ascending when the cellar door slammed shut.

"Hey!"

There was no answer.

Gigi yelled again and again, but there was no response. She started to feel her way up the stairs, making her way one leg at a time like a child. The darkness felt thick and menacing, but she was too mad to be scared. She was going to give Anja a piece of her mind. What did she mean by shutting the door?

Gigi finally got to the top and swept her hands across the door until she found the handle. She turned and pushed.

Nothing.

She twisted the handle, and it turned easily enough. The door must be stuck. She had noticed that it was often left slightly ajar. The frame must have swelled. She put both fists against it and shoved. She thought she felt it give the slightest bit. She put up her hands and shoved again, this time yelling as loudly as she could.

Suddenly the door gave way, and Gigi flew forward into the kitchen and landed on her knees.

"Oh."

"Sorry about that." Vanessa smiled and took a sip from

the cocktail glass in her hand. "I saw the door was open, and I shut it. I didn't realize anyone was down there."

Gigi dusted herself off. "Couldn't you hear me yelling?" She hobbled to the counter, wincing with each step. She had some ibuprofen in her purse. She'd take it right away.

"What were you doing down there anyway?"

"I needed some brandy for the dessert."

Vanessa raised a perfectly shaped eyebrow. "I'll get you some from the library."

Gigi heard Vanessa's heels tapping down the hallway, and she reappeared in the kitchen a few moments later holding a bottle of Rémy Martin. "Will this do?"

"That's fine." Gigi took the bottle and plunked it down on the counter. She had the momentary urge to twist off the cap and take a big swig. She couldn't believe Vanessa hadn't heard her calling from the basement.

Vanessa trailed off, and Gigi got to work on the brandy caramel sauce for the apples. She really needed to get her ankle looked at. It had started to swell and was throbbing in spite of the painkillers she'd taken. She managed to hobble around the kitchen, stuffing the apples with brown sugar and butter and popping them into the oven to bake. Then she poured the container of heavy cream into a saucepan and brought it to a boil on top of the stove. She added the sugar and then after a few minutes, removed it from the heat and stirred in the brandy, vanilla and butter. She would let it cool, and Anja could reheat it later when the guests were ready for dessert.

Gigi paused for a moment and leaned her arms on the counter. How could she have injured herself? She had several new clients starting in a few days, and she would have to be completely on her game. She stared at her ankle, which looked like an overstuffed sausage with streaks of color the shade of an eggplant. How long before she was running around as usual? Was this the third bit of bad luck Anja had alluded to?

Gigi grabbed the bottle of brandy by the neck to return it to the library where it belonged.

She made her painful way down the hall, favoring her good leg heavily. The door to the library was half-closed, and a splash of light illuminated the jewel tones of the Oriental throw rug in the hall.

Gigi heard voices—male and female. She recognized the woman's voice as Vanessa's, but the man's, she wasn't so sure. It didn't sound like Winchel. The voice became louder, and Gigi stopped short just shy of the door. Obviously an argument was in progress, and she didn't want to interrupt.

Her ankle was really throbbing now, and she leaned against the wall to rest. The man raised his voice even more, and Gigi realized it was Don. She held her breath as she listened. Had Don found out about Vanessa and Winchel?

Vanessa's voice rose to match his and came clearly through the partially open door. "That part was mine."

It sounded as if she stamped her foot for emphasis. What a performance, Gigi thought.

Don's tone was wheedling. "I'm sorry, pet, but there was nothing I could do. The network had their heart set on bringing in Graciela for the lead. It's already in rewrites. They'll be bringing her on as Felicity's long-lost twin sister."

Vanessa groaned. "I deserve the lead, you know that. And now this!"

Gigi peered around the edge of the door. Vanessa's face was red and blotchy. Anger certainly didn't become her. Don rose from the sofa and put a hand on her arm, but she shook it off.

"You're my manager. Can't you do something?"

Don held up his hands in surrender. "There's nothing I can do. The decision has been made. They wanted a name for the part."

"A name?" Vanessa exploded. "What am I? Chopped liver? I've been on the show for three years. I have legions of fans. Legions!"

Vanessa paced in front of the sofa, her fists clenched, face tight. She whirled around to confront Don. "I would think you would be a little more interested," she said softly, her face inches from Don's. "After all, you know what I did to get this part."

There was a noise behind Gigi, and she moved as quickly as she could away from the door. But she had heard enough.

She was now more convinced than ever that Vanessa had killed Felicity.

Chapter 18

Gigi's ankle was slightly less swollen on Sunday morning, and she was pleased to be able to put more pressure on it. The doctor in the emergency room had confirmed that it was merely strained and nothing more serious. She was relieved to know that she'd be walking normally again in a day or two. Winchel had asked her to help prepare the luncheon after Derek's funeral on Monday, and she was still working on the meals for Branston Foods. She would spend the day with her foot up and hopefully all would soon be well.

Gigi felt fortunate that it was her left ankle that had sustained the strain, making it possible for her to still drive. Monday morning, she bundled Reg into the car with her—Tabitha had been moping about the house since Felicity's death, and Gigi hoped that some canine companionship would cheer her up.

A strong wind had swept the sky clear of clouds and

added an icy edge to the atmosphere. Gigi shivered as she got behind the wheel, and she cranked up the heat in the MINI. Reg took his accustomed seat and immediately pressed his nose to the glass, watching the passing scenery, his ears up and alert.

Gigi had the dress she'd bought at Abigail's hanging in the backseat. There was no point in keeping it. Mertz hadn't said anything about another date for dinner, so she had decided to return it.

First, though, she needed some supplies from Bon Appétit. Gigi drove slowly through downtown Woodstone, slamming on her brakes when she noticed the tail lights of a dark blue Volvo wagon go on, followed by the left-turn signal. Gigi waited patiently as a blond-haired woman with two children strapped into the backseat maneuvered her car out of the space.

Gigi made the sign of the cross and pulled up parallel to the opening in the long row of cars. If that woman had been able to park her wagon in the space, Gigi certainly ought to be able to shoehorn the MINI into it. She crossed her fingers and began turning the wheel, but almost immediately she realized she was coming in at the wrong angle. Reg's head spun around to look at her when they bumped the curb.

Gigi pulled out and tried a second time. She was closer, but the front of the car stuck out at an embarrassing angle. She couldn't possibly leave it that way. She was pulling out for the third time when she noticed a shadow out of the corner of her left eye. Someone had come up to the car and was blocking the reflection from the sun.

For a moment Gigi had the absurd thought that if she didn't look, the person would go away. But she knew that wasn't going to happen. She felt her face burning as she turned her head to see who it was.

"Oh," Gigi said out loud. She fought the urge to sink down into her seat, out of view. Instead, she rolled down her window, put on her most insouciant face and gave her biggest smile.

Mertz leaned an arm on the car and bent down to the level of Gigi's window. "It looks like you could use some help."

Gigi smiled back with grim determination. "No, thank you. I can handle it."

Mertz peered at the space and appeared to be assessing the angle of the car. "I learned this from my father. Unfortunately I blew a stop sign and failed my driving test anyway." He scowled. "I had to take the bus when everyone else was driving to school." He shook his head at the memory and smiled. "Somehow I survived. But it was the longest six weeks of my life until I was able to take the test again." He pointed toward the curb. "The key is to aim toward the rear corner of the space."

Gigi glanced into her rearview mirror. Check. She was aiming in the right direction.

"Now here's the trick. When your front seat aligns with the rear bumper of the car in front of you, stop and turn the steering wheel one revolution to the left. That will straighten your tires. Then keep backing until your right fender clears the fender of the car in front of you."

Gigi swallowed her tongue and her pride and did as he suggested. The MINI slid as easily into the spot as Cinderella's foot had into the glass slipper.

"That's all there is to it."

Gigi's mind was whirling. She was trying to memorize what Mertz had told her for future reference, all the while attempting to suppress her feelings of triumph.

"Thank you. That seems to have done the trick. I'll make

a note to remember it." Gigi was all briskness as she exited the car.

There was only one problem. Mertz continued to block her way.

"Excuse me." She gave him her most winning smile. "I'm going over there." She pointed across the street to the red, white and green sign of Bon Appétit.

Mertz took a deep breath and momentarily closed his eyes. "I'm so sorry about the other night. But in detective work, dead bodies trump dinner dates every time. I'd like to make it up to you. Tomorrow night? Please?"

Gigi felt as if the breath had been sucked from her body. She nodded yes.

Mertz nodded back and continued down the sidewalk toward the brick façade of the Woodstone Police Department.

Gigi glanced briefly into the backseat, then looked at Reg. "Guess I'll be keeping that dress after all."

Reg grinned at her, Westie style, his pink tongue bobbing up and down with each breath.

After a brief discussion with Winchel, Gigi had decided a buffet was the easiest way to serve the crowd that would descend on the house after Derek's funeral. There would be platters of cold meats—Gigi had already baked the ham, a turkey breast and the roast beef—along with a selection of salads, cheeses, rolls and breads. She had decided on a warm potato salad garnished with chopped bacon; a beet, goat cheese and arugula salad; and a quinoa salad that could double as a vegetarian main course.

Anja was setting up the dining room when Gigi arrived. Gigi unclipped Reg's leash, and he made a beeline for the hallway where Tabitha was stretched out in a sunbeam.

Together they raced the length of the hall several times before skidding into the kitchen for a big gulp of water from Tabitha's metal bowl. Gigi expected them to resume their race, but instead they both curled up on the rug in front of the kitchen fireplace.

By the time Gigi had peeled her tenth potato, she was wishing that Alice was still available to help. Fortunately, she had plenty of time before the guests arrived. And dessert was coming from the Take the Cake Bakery—a selection of bite-size confections.

The slamming of a car door heralded the arrival of the first guests. Gigi whisked off her apron and made a half-hearted stab at neatening her hair. Anja was already stationed by the front door, holding it open for the man and woman in black suits who were coming up the walk.

Within twenty minutes the dining room was crowded with people. Winchel was walled off in the corner by two grave-looking men in expensively tailored charcoal suits. *More business associates?* Gigi wondered. Couldn't they let him be even at his own son's funeral?

Vanessa hovered nearby, but as far as Gigi could tell, she hadn't managed to get any closer to Winchel than that. Alex and Don were on the other side of the room talking, but Gigi noticed Don's glance stray toward Vanessa every couple of minutes.

Several other members of the cast and crew of *For Better or For Worse* had made a second trip to Connecticut for the funeral. Gigi edged her way through them with a fresh platter of meats. She set it on the sideboard and removed the spent platter to take back to the kitchen. Technically, Anja was supposed to manage the serving herself, but Gigi didn't have any problems with lending her a hand. Her ankle was still a little sore but considerably better than it had been.

Gigi was backing through the swinging door into the butler's pantry when a young, blond woman approached her. She looked like a less-polished version of Vanessa and was about the same age. Gigi thought she remembered seeing her at Felicity's funeral.

"Excuse me?" she said in a broad southern accent.

Gigi paused, one hip against the door.

"Can you tell me where the powder room is?"

"There's one in the hall—"

The blonde made a face. "Someone is in there and has been for ages already. Isn't there someplace else . . ."

"There is one up on the third floor. You can take the back stairs."

"Great."

She followed Gigi down the hallway toward the kitchen.

"It's so much cooler in here." The blonde fanned her flushed face with her hand. "It must be over a hundred in the living room." She was wearing a knitted black dress with a pair of over-the-knee suede platform boots and had a fake fur boa wound around her neck.

The woman stopped and looked around the kitchen unabashedly. "This is some place." She turned to Gigi and stuck out her hand. "I'm Tammy, by the way."

"Gigi." They shook hands. "Are you here with—"

"The soap people? Yes." Tammy pursed her lips in displeasure. Her head swiveled as she looked all around the kitchen. "Vanessa and me, we go way back. Of course, she wasn't Vanessa Huff then."

"Oh?" Gigi's ears perked up.

"Just plain old Mary Jane Huffmeister. We grew up together. Down in Tennessee."

"Really?"

The blonde nodded as she examined her cuticles. She

picked at one of them and frowned. "We came north together
to the city. Looking for fame and fortune like in one of those
old movies." She flung the end of her boa over her shoulder.
"Of course, Mary Jane *had* to leave Ashland on account of
what happened."

Gigi waited, wondering if she ought to prompt her. But
Tammy was like a ship in full sail and didn't need any
prompting.

"Of course, we all did it back then, but Mary Jane . . . I
mean Vanessa . . . was different. The other girls and I would
shoplift a magazine or a pack of gum or something cheap
like that, you know? It was nothing but a game." She looked
at Gigi as if she expected her to understand. Gigi managed
to nod encouragingly, although her Catholic-school soul was
shocked to its very core.

"We didn't steal stuff we needed, but Vanessa had it real
hard at home." Tammy lowered her voice and leaned her
head toward Gigi's. "Sometimes I think her parents put her
up to it." Tammy snapped her gum loudly. "Her father was
out of work, and her mother cleaned for a couple people in
town. They had this trailer, a single-wide, which they were
desperate to hang on to." She paused for thought. "I think
they owned the trailer itself. It was a piece of junk to be
honest with you, but they still had to pay the park to rent
the lot."

"Really?"

Tammy nodded. "One afternoon we went into Taylor's
Jewelry Store. That's where we were supposed to go to get
our class rings. I sure as heck didn't have the money for one,
and I'm pretty sure Vanessa didn't either. But she kept insist-
ing, so I agreed. Next thing I know, she's yelling *Run!* and
she's through the front door so fast I near broke my neck
trying to keep up. She'd grabbed this bracelet—a whole

bunch of diamonds strung together with gold. Must have been worth a fortune."

Gigi's mind flashed to the diamond tennis bracelet Vanessa had recently begun wearing—*diamonds strung together with gold* as Tammy had described it.

"The owner was willing to drop the charges as long as he got his bracelet back. What a creep." Tammy shivered. "Thought he could take advantage of the situation, but Tammy's dad came after him with a baseball bat, and that sure changed his mind."

Gigi nodded encouragingly.

"Vanessa and I had to get out of town . . . fast. We decided to head north and ended up in New York City." Tammy shuddered, making her silver chandelier earrings bob to and fro. "I learned my lesson. No more taking what isn't mine." She was quiet for a moment. "But I'm not so sure about Mary Jane—I mean Vanessa. It's like she's driven, know what I mean?" She looked up at Gigi. "She'd do anything to get ahead."

"What part do you play on the soap? I'm afraid I'm not much of a television watcher."

Tammy made a face. "I'm not on the show. I do makeup. Vanessa did, too, until—"

The swinging door to the kitchen flew open, and Anja entered with an empty platter in each hand. Gigi wanted to swear but had to content herself with clenching her fists at her sides.

"Anywho, I really need to use the loo?" Tammy said inquiringly.

Gigi glanced at Anja, who was arranging slices of ham and turkey on one of the empty platters.

"Come on." Gigi cocked her head at Tammy. "I'll show you where it is."

They started up the back stairs.

"Vanessa certainly got ahead quickly in New York," Gigi remarked as casually as she could.

Tammy snorted. "She sure did. We were both up for that part, but she . . ." She paused. "Let's say there were some things I wasn't willing to do to get what I wanted no matter how much I wanted it. I'm not that kind of girl."

Chapter 19

When Gigi looked out the window the next morning, frost had tipped the ends of the grass with white. She shivered. Time to start dressing more warmly. She dug in her drawer and pulled out a black knit turtleneck and a pair of warm socks to go with the ubiquitous jeans.

Reg followed her down to the end of the walk where she retrieved the daily *Woodstone Times* from her box while he lifted his leg on a nearby laurel bush. He trotted obediently behind Gigi as she went through the back door to the kitchen and settled at the table. She unfolded the paper next to her mug of coffee.

According to the headline, Woodstone High had won Sunday night's football game. Gigi remembered hearing the horns blaring as students rode through town afterward. Woodstone was also considering a more stringent pooper-scooper law. Gigi glanced at Reg, who was now snoring softly in a sunbeam. There was also an interview with the mayor about crime in Woodstone. He was calling for immediate action in the death of Felicity Davenport and her stepson, Derek Winchel. He called the delay in an arrest "scandalous" and vowed that "heads would roll." The reporter closed with a quote from Mertz that the police would "do everything in their power to close the case within the next few days."

Gigi wondered what that meant. She hoped he wasn't going to jump to the wrong conclusions.

By the time Gigi had her coat on, Reg was waiting at the door. "Sorry, buddy, but I can't take you this time. I'm having lunch out, and restaurants frown on pets, although I can't imagine why."

Gigi had her keys in one hand and a Gourmet De-Lite container in the other. She'd made Madeline a low-calorie turkey burger stuffed with shredded zucchini and crumbled feta. She included a small container of low-fat tzatziki sauce and a Greek salad.

Now that most of her work for Winchel was finished, she was relieved that several new clients would be starting shortly. She'd enjoyed the brief foray into catering, but she was anxious to get back to her Gourmet De-Lite business.

Gigi stopped by Simpson and West where an exuberant Madeline greeted her with the news that she'd lost two pounds. She was wearing a new cranberry wool dress and high-heeled black suede boots and looked every inch the high-salaried executive she aspired to be.

Gigi was meeting Alice for lunch at the Woodstone Diner. Alice had wanted to go to Declan's, but Gigi had managed to steer her away from that idea. She didn't feel like facing Declan herself, and heaven forbid they would run into Stacy there.

Alice was already perusing the menu when Gigi arrived. She tossed the plastic-coated sheet down on the table. "Can you believe they still do a diet plate here of a hamburger patty, cottage cheese and a peach half?" She smiled at Gigi. "Is tonight your big night with the very handsome Detective Mertz?"

Gigi nodded.

"He's a nice guy, even if he does sometimes jump to the wrong conclusions."

The waitress buzzed by their table. "Something to drink?" she asked.

"A Diet Coke, please."

"Me, too," Alice said.

The waitress pulled a pad from her pocket and made a note. "Ready to order?" Her pencil was poised above the page.

"A turkey burger," Alice said, pushing the menu away from her.

"Same for me.

"I have some interesting news for Mertz," Gigi said as the waitress walked away.

"I met a colleague of Vanessa Huff's at Derek's funeral lunch. She seems to think that Vanessa would do absolutely anything to get ahead."

"Including murder?" Alice unfurled her napkin as the waitress approached with their drinks.

"So it would seem. I think Mertz should look into her alibi."

"He's not going to like you telling him how to run his business."

"I hope to be a little more subtle than that." Gigi took a bite of her turkey burger.

"I could easily imagine Vanessa killing Felicity. But Derek? What reason could she possibly have?" Alice asked around a mouthful of coleslaw.

"I'm not sure. Perhaps he saw her sneaking upstairs to lock Felicity in the sauna and threatened to tell the police?"

Alice lowered gray brows over her faded blue eyes. "Derek was more the type to go after something that would benefit him. Like a spot of blackmail, perhaps."

Gigi paused as the waitress slid their tea in front of them. "You're right. That's definitely more Derek's style. I wonder if I could get into Vanessa's room. Maybe there's a blackmail note or something like that . . . ?"

"Be careful." Alice lifted her spoon and pointed it at Gigi. "If the killer feels threatened, who knows what they might do next."

Reggie watched with seeming amusement as Gigi beat a path between her bathroom, bedroom and closet. She wondered if Mertz was spending even half as much time getting ready—most likely not. His biggest concern was probably whether or not he needed a second shave to get by.

Gigi, meanwhile, had shaved virtually every inch of herself, spread on half a bottle of lotion, washed and dried her hair with the diffuser on her blow-dryer—something she'd never done before. It had taken her twenty minutes alone to find the attachment.

Finally the big moment was at hand—donning her new dress. She felt a frisson of excitement as she slipped the fabric over her head. As usual, Deirdre was spot on. The color burnished the copper in her hair and brought out the green in her eyes. She wondered if Mertz would notice. Her stomach did a complete somersault at the thought.

Gigi was ready when Mertz rang her front bell at seven o'clock. He looked especially handsome in a navy blazer, open-necked blue shirt and gray slacks. And instead of the police-issue Crown Vic, he was driving a sporty Nissan.

Gigi tried to relax as they wound their way through Woodstone and into the next town. Mertz appeared nervous, too, which made her feel slightly better.

The Auberge Rouge was crowded when Gigi and Mertz arrived, and a tidal wave of voices washed over them as soon as they opened the door. The maitre d' rushed forward to check their names against his list and then led them to a plush-covered bench to wait while he checked on their table.

"I'm sorry." He smiled at Gigi. "Not sure what the point is in making a reservation if the table's not ready when you arrive." Mertz glanced pointedly at his watch.

"I don't mind," Gigi reassured him, and she noticed his shoulders relax. She was drinking in the atmosphere—the delicious smells, sights and sounds. It had been a long time since she'd been in such a restaurant. The women were all quite fashionably dressed—she couldn't help but admire the pair of short, black suede booties one of them was wearing. She was glad she'd splurged on her new dress. She felt perfectly at home in the sophisticated crowd.

Finally, the maitre d' led them to their table—tucked into a corner where, Gigi was delighted to note, she had a good view of the entire room.

"At last," Mertz said as they settled into their seats. "I've been wanting to do this for a long time now."

"Oh?" Gigi fiddled with her menu. It was odd being on

a date with anyone, let alone with Mertz. So far their relationship had been at times hostile, suspicious, conflicting and borderline cordial.

"What would you like to drink?" Mertz smiled at Gigi as the waiter approached their table.

Gigi froze. What was the cool thing to order these days? She used to enjoy a kir, but that was a long time ago. A glass of wine seemed so pedestrian. A cosmopolitan? Were they still considered *in*? She remembered a movie where they ordered dirty martinis, but she had no idea what that was. And she definitely didn't like the sound of it.

Mertz must have sensed her hesitation. "I'm having a Manhattan."

The waiter smiled. "Ah, the classics are classic for a reason."

Gigi remembered her grandmother drinking Manhattans. Surely she'd be able to handle one. She looked up with a smile. "I'll have one of those as well."

Mertz put his hand on the table, and Gigi pointed at it. "What happened? What's that?"

"Oh." Mertz laughed. "Whiskers and I were playing, and she scratched me. It's nothing, but I'm thinking maybe I should consider having her declawed."

"That's probably not a bad idea. Especially if she's going to be an indoor cat." Gigi picked up her menu.

Mertz did the same. "Some interesting stuff here. But I have to admit I don't know much about fancy food."

Gigi smiled. "I'm a fairly accomplished cook, so perhaps I can be of assistance." She began to read the entries. She glanced up at Mertz. "Any major dislikes? Likes?"

He smiled. "I'm not a huge fan of beets or Brussels sprouts, to be honest."

"There are plenty of choices, then." Gigi scanned the

menu for things that Mertz, a self-confessed "meat and pota-toes" kind of guy, would like.

"You'd probably enjoy the dry-aged New York steak and the fingerling potatoes."

"The three words I recognize are *steak*, *New York* and *potatoes*, but I'll take your word for it." Mertz put down his menu. "What on earth does dry-aged mean?"

"The meat is placed in a special cooler, ironically known as a hot box," Gigi said. She'd once done a piece for *Wedding Splendor* magazine on a well-known steak house in Brook-lyn, and the owner had insisted on explaining the process to her. "There's a lot of shrinkage and the whole process makes the steak cost more, but the meat is supposed to be extremely tender and flavorful."

The waiter placed their drinks on the table and discreetly withdrew.

"What's the alternative?" Mertz took a sip of his Manhat-tan, and Gigi thought she noticed his face actually relax.

"Appropriately enough, it's called wet aging. Virtually all the beef you find in supermarkets is placed in a vacuum-sealed bag and wet aged. There's less loss of moisture, there-fore less weight loss."

"I guess no one wants to start out with a pound of steak and end up with three-quarters."

"Yes, and dry aging can take up to a month."

"So this is going to be special." Mertz rubbed his chin. "I'm guessing I shouldn't order it well done."

Gigi was about to say something when she realized he was joking. She smiled as she told him, "Medium rare at the most."

Mertz picked up his menu again. "What would go well with that for starters."

Gigi glanced over the appetizers. She certainly didn't

want to recommend the oysters. She felt her face getting warm at the thought. "How about lobster bisque?"

"Ah. A sort of sequential surf-and-turf dinner. Excellent idea." Mertz put his menu down again. "What about you? What are you having?"

It was a tough decision. Gigi didn't dine at places like the Auberge Rouge every day, and she wanted to make the most of the experience. She could have steak anytime, even if it wasn't dry aged.

"I think I'll have the duck consommé with the foie gras dumplings. Followed by the duck with lingonberries.

"That sounds like something my grandparents would have made, only they would have shot the duck themselves and picked the berries from their own garden."

Gigi felt herself relaxing as the conversation ebbed and flowed naturally and seamlessly. By the time the waiter approached with their main course, she realized she was actually enjoying herself. Mertz, too, had let down his guard, although his impeccable posture hadn't slipped a notch in the process.

"The duck for mademoiselle." The waiter grabbed the plate from his tray.

Just as he did so, a man at the table in back of Gigi and Mertz jumped to his feet. His elbow jostled the waiter's arm, and the plate tilted, tilted, tilted until the duck breast Gigi had been so looking forward to slid right off and into her lap.

The waiter turned as white as his shirt.

For a moment Gigi could do nothing but sit and stare at the piece of meat reclining in her lap. The stain from the sauce was spreading in an ever widening circle. All over her brand new dress. Which had cost a fortune she could hardly afford.

Gigi closed her eyes in disbelief. Would the cleaner's be

able to get that mess out? It would probably be best if she went and sponged it with cold water in the interim.

Meanwhile, the waiter had commandeered a whole host of other waiters and busboys, who waved various bits of cloth and bottles of solution at Gigi.

"The dinner is on the house," Gigi overheard the waiter whisper to Mertz. Mertz looked relatively amused by the entire spectacle.

Finally, Gigi decided she needed to be alone to deal with things, excused herself from the table and bolted for the ladies' room.

The ladies' room was enormous, with two dark blue velvet chaises and a crystal chandelier, but Gigi hardly noticed the décor. She looked at her ruined dress in the beveled mirror and felt like crying. The cleaner's might be able to get the stain out, but there was no guarantee, and she knew from experience that grease was the worst possible offender.

And until now, the evening had been going so well. Gigi thought of her Uncle Frank on her mother's side. His answer to everything was *What are you going to do?* Always said with a quirk of a smile and a shrug of his massive shoulders. Indeed, Gigi said to herself, *What are you going to do? Let a simple accident ruin your evening?*

Gigi squared her own shoulders, took out her compact and powdered her nose. She was about to push open the swinging door when she felt her phone vibrate from the depths of her clutch. She glanced at the number and saw that it was Sienna's.

"Hello?"

"Gigi?" Gigi was startled to hear Oliver's voice, not Sienna's.

"Oliver?"

"I'm using Sienna's cell. I knew your number would be programmed in."

His voice sounded strange—very strained and almost panicky. Gigi felt panic rise in her own throat. "What is it?" *Oh please don't let something be wrong with the baby*, she prayed fervently.

"It's Sienna." Oliver swallowed a sob.

"What is it? What's happened?"

"The police." Oliver stopped and took a deep breath. When he went on, his voice was stronger and more assured. "The police have taken her in for questioning."

Chapter 20

"What's wrong?" Mertz jumped up as Gigi approached the table. He glanced at Gigi's dress. "I'm sure the restaurant will make good for the—"

"It's not that!" Gigi was so mad she felt like upending the whole table full of food all over him.

Mertz slid back into his seat but without taking his eyes off Gigi. "Do you want to tell me what it is, then?"

That only made Gigi madder. He knew perfectly well that the police were picking up Sienna tonight and taking her to the station. He probably planned to head there right after their dinner. And yet he calmly sat there, made small talk and ate and drank with Sienna's best friend. The nerve!

A knowing look came over Mertz's face. "Oh," was all he said.

Oh, indeed, Gigi thought. She sat opposite him, her arms crossed over her chest, food forgotten.

"It's that friend of yours, right?" Mertz pushed his steak aside.

Gigi nodded.

Mertz rubbed his face with his hands. "I'm sorry. I really am. We had no choice. The mayor is breathing down our necks. When the chief heard about the latest development, he insisted we bring her in for questioning. I asked him if we couldn't possibly avoid it, but he was insistent. One murder in Woodstone was bad enough, but now with two . . . he's playing it strictly by the book."

Gigi still hadn't touched the fresh plate of food the waiter had brought. She thought she would choke if she tried to eat anything.

"But why Sienna? There are plenty of other suspects."

"The chief insisted." Mertz rubbed his face again. "Listen, if you really want to help your friend, then get her to tell us where she was the afternoon Felicity was killed. She claims to have an alibi but refuses to divulge what it is."

Gigi barely slept a wink, worried about Sienna and imagining her giving birth behind bars. She stared at the window waiting for the barest hint of dawn, for once taking scarce comfort in the delightful warmth and comfort of her cozy bed. At the first glimpse of light, she slipped her feet over the side and felt around for her slippers.

Reg opened one eye and stared at her, confused.

"It's early. Go back to sleep."

But he got up anyway and followed her out to the kitchen.

Gigi brewed a cup of coffee and poured it into her lucky mug—the one with the picture of President Kennedy on it. Her parents had purchased it during his campaign, and, although plenty of other bits of crockery had been broken or lost, it had remained. She reached into the refrigerator for the carton of milk and noticed the foam container with last night's dinner. The waiter had insisted on packaging it up for her along with a large slice of chocolate amaretto pie, on the house. Frankly, Gigi would be more than happy if she never heard of the Auberge Rouge again.

She finished her coffee and checked the clock. It was still only six A.M. Definitely too early to call Oliver and find out about Sienna. Instead, she grabbed a frying pan from the overhead pot rack and plunked it down on the stove. She was making Madeline a breakfast of whole wheat blueberry pancakes and turkey sausage. It wasn't the lowest-calorie breakfast imaginable, but if one practiced portion control, it was still something a dieter could enjoy. And Gigi was providing the portion control. Madeline couldn't eat what she didn't have.

Once the pancakes were done, Gigi took a quick shower and pulled on her favorite jeans and the sweater that had started life as waist length but over time had stretched to tunic length. It was her "blankie" for when times were really bad. She'd worn it relentlessly after her breakup with Ted, but it hadn't been out of the closet in months.

She grabbed the containers with Madeline's breakfast and jumped into the MINI.

The streetlamps were still on in downtown Woodstone when Gigi got there, and the shops were closed with their windows shuttered, but a steady stream of men and women carrying briefcases was already hurrying silently toward the Woodstone train station.

Gigi stopped quickly in front of Simpson and West to deliver Madeline's meal, then continued on toward Sienna's house. As she pulled into the long driveway, she realized she was clenching both her teeth and her hands on the steering wheel. She pulled up to the front door and sat for a moment, wiggling her fingers and her jaw, trying against the odds to relax.

A light was burning toward the back of the house. Gigi picked her way through the brittle red leaves that littered the path leading to the kitchen door. She peered through the window. Sienna was seated at the kitchen table, her head in her hands. Gigi tapped lightly on the door.

"Gigi!" Sienna jumped up and rushed to pull the door open. "I am so glad to see you. It's been horrible." She buried her face in her hands.

Gigi threw her arms around Sienna and gave her a fierce hug. "Thank goodness, the police let you go."

Sienna nodded. "They just took me in for questioning. That was bad enough. I think they were trying to . . . scare me."

"It's going to be okay. Why don't you sit down while I make you a cup of tea?"

Sienna allowed Gigi to lead her toward a kitchen chair. "I don't know what to do." She looked up at Gigi with tears in her eyes.

"For starters, you can tell the police where you were the afternoon Felicity was killed. Right now they seem to think you snuck into the house using your key, crept up the back stairs and doctored her glass of water with a handful of tranquilizers."

Sienna shook her head so fiercely that her hair whipped back and forth across her face. "But I didn't!"

Gigi pressed on. "And then you waited until she was in the sauna, and you blocked the door knowing that she would be too woozy to get herself out." She gulped. "And you raised the heat as high as it would go."

Gigi glanced at Sienna. She sat with one hand on her

belly, which protruded through the opening in her robe. Gigi felt terrible. She didn't want to upset Sienna, but she could see no other way. Sienna *had* to tell the police where she was that afternoon!

Gigi knelt by Sienna's chair and took Sienna's hands in her own. They were frigid. She rubbed them gently. "The only way out is to tell the police the truth, don't you see?"

Sienna turned her head away. "I can't."

"Why not?" Gigi gave her hands an encouraging squeeze. "You can tell me if you like, and I'll give the information to Mertz. You won't even have to talk to him."

"I can't." Sienna gave a loud sniff.

"Why not?" Gigi asked again, trying to keep the exasperation out of her voice. She couldn't begin to imagine what could be so bad that Sienna didn't want to reveal it.

"It was horrible." Sienna sniffed again and swiped a sleeve across her nose. "They made me sit in this stuffy little room without even a glass of water, until your horrible Detective Mertz got there."

"He's not *my* Detective Mertz," Gigi said, thinking of the previous evening. So Mertz had gone straight from dropping Gigi off to the station to question Sienna. "It will only get worse if you don't tell them what they want to know."

"It's so embarrassing." Sienna turned to look at Gigi.

"Embarrassing?" Gigi squeaked. "Embarrassing is when you leave the restroom and don't realize you have toilet paper stuck to your shoe. Embarrassing is when you call someone by the wrong name. Embarrassing is not knowing you have spinach caught between your teeth."

Sienna's expression turned sheepish. She twiddled with the ends of her bathrobe tie, rubbing them between her fingers and turning them this way and that.

Gigi grabbed Sienna's hands and forced Sienna to look

her in the face. "What could be worse," she said slowly and carefully, "than going to jail for a crime you didn't commit."

"You're right." Sienna bit her lip and looked away for a moment. "Besides, Mertz knows I'm taking insulin."

Gigi sat up straighter. "He does?"

Sienna bowed her head, and her hair formed a curtain across her face. Gigi couldn't see her expression. "He asked me whether Oliver or I had access to insulin. I couldn't lie." She looked up. "He only had to ask my doctor to find out."

"Then all the more reason to tell them what you know."

"It's about Oliver," she said so softly that Gigi could barely hear her.

For a moment Gigi wondered if Oliver was having an affair. Perhaps he really *had* been seeing Felicity, and the story wasn't made up? Somehow she couldn't believe it. Oliver was devoted to Sienna, especially now with the baby coming. It had to be something else.

"Tell me what it is. Just dump it all out. Remember what you said about how it hurts less if you pull the bandage off quickly?"

Sienna nodded. She put her hand over her mouth and mumbled something.

"What?"

"I followed him."

"Oliver?"

Sienna nodded. "I had to see where he was going."

"Why?"

"Because he's been going . . . somewhere . . . lately." Sienna clenched her eyes shut tightly. "And money's been missing from our joint account." She grabbed a napkin off the table and began twisting it between her fingers. "I thought . . . maybe . . . the two were related. So I followed him."

"And?"

"It was the afternoon of Felicity's murder." Sienna gave an exaggerated shiver. "The wind was biting, and a light rain had started. He . . . Oliver . . . was driving toward New Haven, and I followed. About ten miles from the city, the rain really picked up, and it was hard to see. But I managed to keep him in sight." She looked at Gigi. "I couldn't imagine where on earth he was going."

Gigi was quiet and let Sienna talk.

"He was heading for some place I'd never been before. I didn't know what to expect. He pulled into this parking lot. There was a sign at the entrance, but I was so busy keeping my eye on Oliver's car that I missed it. He got out and so did I." She closed her eyes for a moment. "It was pouring, and I got soaked. I remember thinking that all this had better lead to something."

"Did it?"

Sienna nodded. "I followed him, discreetly of course, to the door of this rather elaborate building. Finally I was able to read the sign."

"What was it?" Gigi realized she was holding her breath.

"A casino," Sienna responded, her laugh catching in her throat. "The Riverwoods Casino. He's been gambling," she said flatly.

If Gigi hadn't promised Sienna to talk to Mertz, there was no way on the face of the earth that she would be headed toward the Woodstone Police Station that morning. She was still mad at Mertz for not telling her that they were bringing Sienna in for questioning last night, but she realized she had been rather rude about the whole thing. He was just doing his job, and he *had* taken her out for a nice dinner, or at least tried to.

Gigi found herself slowing down as she approached the police station. She wished she'd worn something . . . nicer . . . and had done more with her hair than run her hands through it. But it couldn't be helped. If she didn't do this now, she might lose her nerve.

She was as surprised as Sienna to discover that Oliver was gambling. It wasn't like him. Sienna said he'd never gotten involved in it before, and they'd been married for over ten years. Oliver hadn't noticed her following him, but Sienna planned to broach the topic when the time was right.

Gigi pulled into the police station lot and parked. She gave a quick glance into the rearview mirror, but there wasn't much she could do with her appearance. She'd left her purse at home, taking only her keys and her license along to Sienna's, and didn't have her compact, a lipstick or even a comb.

Gigi sat for a minute, rehearsing what she would say to Mertz, then got out, locked the MINI and walked up the path to the front door of the station. The lobby was quiet, and the woman behind the desk was drinking coffee and reading the newspaper. Gigi went up and tapped on the bulletproof glass that protected the front-desk personnel from anyone crazy enough to carry a gun into a police station.

"Hello?"

The woman stopped with her sugar-and-cinnamon donut halfway to her mouth. "Yes?"

"I'd like to see Detective Mertz, please."

"Not here," the woman mumbled around a mouthful of pastry.

A sense of relief washed over Gigi so abruptly that her knees almost buckled.

"Fine. I'll come back another time."

Gigi had to stop herself from running out of the building.

She yanked open the front door and bolted for the sidewalk where she walked briskly toward the parking lot next to Declan's Grille. She was almost to where she had parked the MINI when she sensed someone behind her. She glanced over her shoulder.

"Hey."

Gigi stopped.

"You look like someone who could use a good cup of coffee."

It was Declan McQuaid acting dreadfully chipper for so early in the morning. He was headed toward the back door of his restaurant, his keys in his hands.

"We don't open until noon, but I've already got a pot of coffee going. Let me give you a cup."

"That would be great." Gigi silently vowed for the one millionth and hopefully final time that she was never leaving the house again without combing her hair and at least putting on some lipstick.

Declan fell into step beside her as they headed toward his restaurant. The sign was unlit, and the grate was still pulled down over the front window. Declan fished a wad of keys from his pocket, selected one and opened the front door.

The interior smelled of freshly brewed coffee along with the residual scents of rich food and the tangy aroma of slightly stale beer. Gigi found it oddly comforting. She perched on a bar stool as Declan retrieved thick white mugs and filled them with freshly brewed coffee.

"I've got the timer set so that when I arrive in the morning, the coffee is ready." Declan grinned, and Gigi noticed the laugh lines around his eyes and the darker flecks in his blue eyes. She thought he noticed her looking, and she quickly took a sip of her coffee to cover her confusion.

"Mmm, this is delicious."

"Glad you like it. To my mind, a good cup of coffee is one of the most important things in life."

Declan continued to grin, and Gigi again noticed those attractive laugh lines. Warmth rose up her neck and spread, and she quickly hid her face in her mug.

Declan went behind the bar and scrambled through a stack of papers. He came back brandishing one of them. "I think I've got the menu for my Thanksgiving Day dinner hammered out."

He took the stool next to Gigi and spread the paper out on the bar. His shoulders were wide, and they nearly touched Gigi's as they sat side-by-side. He ran a finger down the list, and Gigi tried to concentrate.

"I do know that Thanksgiving is all about the bird." Declan gestured toward the first item on his list. "I found a farm a few miles from here where they raise turkeys, and I've ordered fresh ones for the day. I'll be able to pick them up two days before, and that's about as fresh as you're going to get."

Gigi nodded agreement. For one moment, she could smell the bird roasting in the oven, the creamed onions simmering on the stove and the pumpkin pie cooling on the counter. Thanksgiving was her favorite holiday for a reason.

"What else do you have there?" Gigi ran an eye down the neat column of menu items. "Stuffing, gravy, mashed potatoes, creamed onions and peas."

"What do you think?"

"There's one thing missing."

"What's that?" Declan made a sad face, and Gigi laughed.

"Sweet potatoes. You absolutely have to have sweet potatoes."

Declan felt around in the pocket of his flannel shirt, pulled out a stubby pencil and carefully wrote in *sweet potatoes* on the piece of paper.

"Do you have any good recipes?"

Gigi was suddenly conscious of how close together they were. She felt a trickle of sweat make its way down her back.

"I have lots of good recipes. My favorite is the casserole with the miniature marshmallows on top."

Declan wrinkled his nose. "That sounds heinous."

Gigi laughed. "It's quite good, actually, if terribly sweet."

"Let's do that one, then, shall we?" Declan turned so that he and Gigi were face-to-face, their knees touching, eyes locked.

Gigi took a deep breath to steady herself. Declan had made it very clear he was only out for a good time. Gigi was looking for something more.

"I'll send you the recipe," she said as she slid off the bar stool. She feigned looking at her watch. "Sorry, but I've got to get going."

Declan gave an amused smile, and Gigi suspected that she wasn't the first female to bolt from his attractiveness only to be reeled in later like a hapless pike caught on the hook. Gigi had the impression that he was willing to bide his time to get what he wanted.

She practically bolted out the door and onto the sidewalk, running full tilt into a pedestrian.

"Sorry," she said as she glanced up.

Right into the cold, uncompromising stare of Detective Mertz.

Chapter 21

Gigi had heard other women talk about the so-called walk of shame—leaving your boyfriend's apartment first thing in the morning wearing the clothes from the night before. And that's exactly how she felt as Mertz glanced pointedly toward the closed and shuttered front of Declan's. Well, she had absolutely nothing to be ashamed of! Absolutely nothing!

Mertz merely looked deflated. Gigi was shocked to see his shoulders slump. She wanted to tell him that nothing had happened between her and Declan, but the words refused to form. Mertz looked as if he cared . . . but what if he didn't? She'd make a fool of herself.

"I need to talk to you," she said, smiling, hoping he could read the message in her eyes. "I have some information on your murder case you might be interested in hearing."

"Really?" Mertz's voice was glum. "We can go to my

office, then." He gestured toward the police station down the street.

It felt like the longest walk of Gigi's life. They were both silent. Several times she tried to say something, but the words still refused to come. Finally, they were at the station and walking down the hall toward his office.

Mertz led Gigi into his office where she perched on the edge of the wooden chair meant for visitors. Mertz dropped into his desk chair, sending it rolling backward. It caught on the edge of the carpet and stopped. He pulled himself closer and leaned his elbows on the desk.

He smiled at Gigi. "Okay, shoot. What is it you wanted to tell me?"

Gigi's mouth had gone dry suddenly. "Sienna has an alibi," she finally blurted out.

Mertz's eyebrows shot upward. "That's great. Let's hear it."

Gigi looked at him askance. Was he teasing her? "Sienna wasn't anywhere near Felicity's house the afternoon Felicity was murdered. She was following Oliver."

Mertz's eyebrows shot up again. "Following Oliver?"

Gigi stared at a spot just above Mertz's right ear. "Yes. She was concerned about . . . something . . . and she followed him."

"Where did he go?" A faint smile hovered around Mertz's mouth.

"To a casino. Just outside of New Haven." Gigi felt as if she were giving out someone else's secrets, and she could feel her face getting hot.

"What did he say?"

"What do you mean?" Gigi twisted the fringe on her scarf into a braid.

"Well, when Sienna confronted Oliver, what did he say?

He must have been pretty upset to have been caught out like that."

"I don't know," Gigi mumbled. "She didn't actually talk to him."

"She didn't actually *talk* to him?" Mertz repeated.

Gigi felt her cheeks burning. "No. But she definitely saw him."

"But she didn't speak to him, and he didn't see her."

"That's right."

Mertz leaned his elbows on the desk and steepled his fingers. When he answered, his voice was gentle.

"Frankly, Gigi, this just doesn't ring true to me. Don't you think it sounds like your friend Sienna is trying to give both of them an alibi?"

Gigi's breath caught in her throat. She realized that in trying to be helpful, she had pushed Sienna from the proverbial frying pan into the fire.

How was she going to break it to her?

Gigi's newest client, Bea Dennis, lived at the other end of Woodstone, in a new development that had sprung up between it and the next town. She had recently opened a jewelry store in downtown Woodstone—the sort of place where one could get a gold bracelet to celebrate a graduation, a silver teething ring to commemorate a birth or a strand of pearls to mark a wedding or anniversary.

Gigi had spent the day immersing herself in cooking—trying not to think about Declan, trying to forget Mertz and trying to put off talking to Sienna. She'd chopped and diced and minced and pureed, but still the thoughts swirled in her head. How was she going to convince Mertz that neither

Sienna nor Oliver had had anything to do with Felicity's death?

Gigi packed up the chicken rollatini she'd made for Bea and stowed it in the back of the MINI. It should be a quick trip, so she let Reggie tag along. He sat happily in his accustomed seat, sniffing the air rushing in from the barely cracked window.

"Sorry, bud." Gigi zapped the window up the rest of the way and turned on the heat. "It's a little chilly for someone not sporting your thick fur coat."

Borne by a brisk wind, brown, curling leaves skidded across the road. Gigi glanced at the landscape rushing past the window. Some brightly colored leaves still clung here and there, but the skeletal branches of the trees were already visible. Autumn was almost over.

She found Bea's house easily enough. Bea had a skeleton dangling from the lamppost and a blow-up ghost on the front steps. The wind blew the ghost toward Gigi as she mounted the stairs. She jumped and then looked around quickly, hoping no one had noticed.

Bea answered the door almost immediately. She had on pink sweats with a large *B* embroidered on the zip-up top, and fuzzy black slippers.

"I just got home and couldn't wait to change. We were incredibly busy this afternoon. But that's good." She smiled at Gigi. "Come in, come in."

Gigi stepped into the foyer where a braided rug provided a splash of color against the pale wood floor.

"It smells delicious." Bea sniffed the container. "And I'm starved." She smiled almost apologetically. "Unfortunately, I had to skip lunch we were so busy. And it's not even Christmas yet."

Gigi nodded and was about to say good-bye when Bea took a breath and was off and running again.

"I heard all about your diet service when one of my customers told me that Felicity Davenport had hired you. That must have been so exciting."

Gigi opened her mouth, but Bea rushed on, her penciled brows rising toward her graying hairline.

"You could have knocked me over with a feather when that other actress from the soap walks into my shop. Vanessa Huff. I couldn't believe my eyes."

Gigi had been inching toward the open door, but that stopped her. "Vanessa Huff?"

Bea nodded. "She plays Daphne on *For Better or For Worse*."

"I know."

"She came in to buy herself a little treat. Said she owed it to herself on account of something that happened a long time ago."

"Really?" Gigi tried to provide encouragement, but fortunately, Bea needed virtually none in order to continue.

"I thought she was after a charm for a bracelet or perhaps a thin gold chain. You know, something like that. But no, she picked out our most expensive item—a diamond tennis bracelet."

"Really?" Gigi said, picturing the gorgeous string of diamonds that had so recently graced Vanessa's wrist.

"I didn't know if we'd ever sell that piece, it being so expensive, but she didn't hesitate for a minute. Tried it on and said she'd take it, just like that." Bea snapped her fingers.

"I wouldn't want that credit card bill," Gigi said, not so subtly digging for more information.

"Oh, she didn't charge it," Bea said, her eyes round. "She handed me a check." She shook her head. "I was a little reluctant at first on account of the check was from a third party. But then the third party was Cornelius Vandenberg, the well-known collector. I can't imagine he'd be writing bad checks, can you?"

Gigi reassured her that the check would most likely sail through the clearance process, and then made her way back down the stairs toward the MINI where Reg had his face pressed to the driver's side window, leaving a horizontal string of nose prints.

As Gigi unlocked the door, she mulled over what Bea had told her. How had Vanessa come by a check from Cornelius Vandenberg large enough to buy one of the most expensive items in Bea's jewelry store?

Vandenberg was a well-known collector specializing in pieces related to television, particularly its early days. His collection included the uniform Lucille Ball had worn in the famed chocolate factory episode of *I Love Lucy*, Rob Petrie's typewriter from *The Dick Van Dyke Show* and Fonzie's motorcycle from *Happy Days*. Had Vanessa sold him something?

She must have, or why else would he have given her a check? Gigi mulled this over as she drove down High Street. It was already getting dark, and the streetlamps cast an orange glow on the rain-slicked street.

Vandenberg ran a gallery in New York City where he bought and sold bits and pieces of his collection. Gigi made a mental note to pay the gallery a visit in the near future.

Chapter 22

By the time Gigi finished work and got home later that evening, she was unusually tired. Maybe she was coming down with something? She hoped not. She couldn't wait to kick off her shoes, don her sweats and spend at least ten minutes playing fetch with Reggie. Then she was going to crack open the bottle of inexpensive Chardonnay chilling in the fridge.

Gigi headed toward her bedroom and was reaching for her sweats when she changed her mind. Why bother? She would only be getting undressed again later. She pulled her most comfortable pair of flannel pajamas from the drawer— the ones with the reindeer on them that her mother had given her for Christmas when she was still in college. She was rushing the season slightly, but no one would see her. Besides, the flannel was worn and soft. They were the pajama equivalent of her comfort sweater.

Five minutes of fetch tired Reg out, and he retired to the rug in front of the back door. Gigi got the Chardonnay out of the fridge and had to wrestle with the cork. It came out partway, then broke off. She ended up shoving the cork back into the bottle and then straining the wine into her glass. No matter, it tasted just as satisfying.

She took her glass over to the comfy chair and ottoman in her tiny living room. She was too tired to even bother with dinner. She made herself a plate of cheese and crackers and a bowl of popcorn. She had a little of each and then a sip of her Chardonnay. Who knew white wine and popcorn were such a mellifluous pairing?

Gigi turned on the television and flipped through a number of channels before settling on some bridal show. She watched as women were submerged in enormous and intricate ball gowns. She thought about Vanessa. Was she hoping to become Mrs. Jack Winchel number three? Did she know about Winchel's financial troubles? If the rumors were even true. Winchel's second check to Gigi had cleared without a hitch.

Gigi's head dropped back against the chair cushion, and her eyes were closing when the doorbell rang. Gigi jumped and splashed Chardonnay on her pajama bottoms. Who could that be at this hour? Was it Sienna or Alice come for a visit?

Gigi cracked open the front door and peered around the edge. Standing on the step, silhouetted against the glare from the overhead light, was Detective Mertz.

Gigi glanced down at her attire and cursed the thought that had made her opt for her pj's instead of her sweats.

Too late now. Gigi pulled open the door and invited him in with as much aplomb as she could muster.

She thought she saw a smile cross Mertz's face, but it was impossible to be sure since it was gone as quickly as the flap of a bird's wings.

"Would you care for some wine?"

"Why not?" Mertz ran a hand across his face. "I'm off duty."

Gigi rummaged in the kitchen cabinet and returned with a second glass. She poured the Chardonnay and handed it to Mertz.

"I hope I'm not disturbing you." He gestured with the glass toward Gigi's nightclothes.

She shook her head. "No. Not all. I just wanted to be comfortable." Gigi thought Mertz's eyebrow rose a fraction of an inch, and she felt heat suffusing her face. "Please sit down." Gigi moved Reg's rather tattered-looking blanket from the sofa.

Mertz sat gingerly on the very edge, his hands knitted together in his lap. He looked very uncomfortable, and Gigi wondered why he had come.

He took a sip of his wine and cleared his throat. "I've come to . . . to . . ." A fit of coughing cut off the rest of his sentence.

Gigi didn't know whether she should pat him on the back or fetch him a glass of water. She sat on the sofa next to him and, deciding on the former, rather gingerly patted his back.

"Sorry about that." Mertz wiped away the tears that had sprung to his eyes. He ducked his head. "I wanted to say I was sorry for last night." He took a huge gulp of his wine, sputtered briefly and continued. "I should have warned you that we were bringing your friend in for questioning, but I didn't want to ruin our evening."

He looked glum. "I'm sorry. It only made things worse for you. I understand that now."

Gigi was floored. Mertz was actually . . . *apologizing*! She glanced at his sharp profile, and her stomach did a sudden flip-flop. He really was very handsome. She realized suddenly that their thighs were touching.

Mertz turned toward her, and now their faces were inches apart. Gigi's breath caught in her throat. She found herself focusing on Mertz's lips, and she had to force her gaze to meet his eyes. What she saw there made her heart nearly stop beating. He leaned toward her, closer and closer . . .

Gigi panicked. "Can I get you some more wine?"

Gigi bit her lip. What a fool she was! Why hadn't she let Mertz kiss her? She *wanted* him to kiss her—quite badly actually. She realized that the last time she'd kissed a man it had been Ted as he left for work the day that ended with his telling her he was leaving her. Hardly the most romantic experience. Too late now. She could only hope that Mertz would give it another try.

"I'm fine, thanks." Mertz gave a bemused smile. "By the way, we got the autopsy results in and they indicate that Derek was smothered, possibly by a pillow. The same tranquilizers that were found in Felicity's system were also found in his, although there's no way to determine if he took them himself or if he was doped. But what they didn't find were any needle marks or any indication that he'd been given insulin."

"That's wonderful news." Gigi was thoughtful for a moment. "Someone was trying to set Sienna up."

"Could be." Mertz agreed. "Anyway, I thought you'd want to know." He put his glass down and stood up. "I'd better be going." He glanced at his watch.

Gigi stood, too, and followed him to the front door. "Thanks for coming. I appreciate your taking the time to fill me in on things." She opened the door, and Mertz stepped onto the front steps. Gigi started to close the door.

"It's such a relief knowing that Sienna and Oliver aren't going to be bothered anymore by the police and can concentrate on the coming baby."

Mertz put his index finger against the door and pushed it open wider. He stuck his head around the edge. His mouth was set in a grim line. He hung his head briefly. "I don't even know how to tell you this."

"What?" Gigi's heart began to pound.

"The chief is zeroing in on Oliver as our prime suspect. We think he was having an affair with Felicity, and he was furious when she leaked that story to the newspapers and gossip columns." He hung his head again. "There's really nothing I can do about it. If he's innocent"—Mertz shrugged—"it will be proven soon enough."

He pulled the door closed in back of him, and Gigi stood stock-still in the middle of the living room for several moments. Then she threw one of the sofa cushions at the closed door.

She wondered if Mertz heard it hit.

Gigi lay in bed, acutely conscious of the fact that she'd set the alarm clock for an hour earlier than usual. She now had to prepare and deliver breakfast to both Madeline and Bea. Also, Winchel had asked her, begged her almost, to prepare a lunch for his board meeting. They were convening at his house, and he didn't want to have to take the time to go to a restaurant.

She knew the minute her head hit the pillow that it was going to take her an eternity to fall asleep. She couldn't get her conversation with Mertz out of her mind. Especially the part where she thought he was going to kiss her. And how she'd desperately wanted him to kiss her, but she'd blown it.

Gigi finally did fall asleep with Reg curled up snugly against the crook of her legs. In what seemed like only minutes, the alarm shrilled in the quiet morning, and she slapped it shut for another ten minutes. It rang again, and she slipped from bed, did a few rudimentary stretches that Reg watched with amusement, and slipped into her bathrobe.

Gigi dressed, prepared her clients' breakfasts, downing only a cup of coffee herself, and then packed the containers in the backseat of her MINI. Reg joined her in his accustomed spot in the front. His nose twitched, and for a moment it looked as if he were going to jump into the backseat to explore the Mexican egg tortillas Gigi had packed in her Gourmet De-Lite containers. Fortunately, a stern look and word from Gigi had him turning back around. He heaved a huge sigh and contented himself with looking out the window.

Gigi delivered the breakfasts as quickly as she could and headed toward Felicity's house. When she arrived, several cars were already parked in the driveway, including a long, black limousine whose driver was busying himself polishing the already immaculate hood with a cloth.

Gigi went in through the back door, hung her coat on one of the hooks in the mudroom and grabbed a clean apron from the stash in the cupboard. Reggie and Tabitha romped around each other in a circle until Gigi shooed them out of the way. They scattered to a place near the stove, and Gigi went into the butler's pantry. She was surveying the available serving platters when she heard raised voices coming from the direction of the library.

Gigi tiptoed toward the swinging door into the dining room and pushed it open a couple of inches. The voices were louder, but she still couldn't make out what they were saying. It was obvious, though, that a very heated argument was going on. Gigi wondered if it had to do with Winchel supposedly losing so much money.

Gigi peered around the edge of the door. The dining room was empty. Anja had already set the table, and there was an air of expectancy about the room. Gigi skirted the enormous table and tiptoed toward the doorway and into the hall.

The voices were even louder now and slightly clearer. Gigi caught the words *exposed us all*, and *if the Feds get wind of it*, before she heard footsteps on the stairs. She hastened back to the dining room where she was pretending to straighten a napkin when Anja came in.

Anja gave her a questioning look but didn't say anything. Gigi whistled tunelessly, trying to look innocent as she made her way back to the kitchen.

Gigi spent the morning peeling, chopping and dicing while thinking about what she'd heard. *Exposed us all.* And *if the Feds get wind of it*. She knew very little about finance, but the first thought that popped into her mind was insider trading. Was that what Winchel was up to? Was he desperately trying to make up for the money he'd lost? Felicity had a lot of money to leave—half to Derek and half to Winchel. Maybe Winchel had gotten greedy?

Gigi indicated to Anja that the meal was ready. Anja moved in and out of the room silently, filling platters with the food and delivering them to the dining room. Once again it was a buffet meal, elegantly displayed on the sideboard.

Gigi was finishing a cheese sauce when her mind went blank. Suddenly she couldn't remember the ingredients or the order of preparation. Sweat broke out around her hairline and under her arms. Was she having some kind of nervous breakdown? Things had been awfully stressful of late. Maybe she needed to find some way to relax—yoga, or jogging or meditation. Gigi wiped a hand across her sweaty brow, but the harder she tried to concentrate, the more elusive the information became, like wisps of gray smoke disappearing on the wind. She looked around the kitchen. Felicity had a stash of cookbooks neatly arranged in a large wooden breakfront.

Gigi scanned the titles quickly and reached for a tattered volume labeled *The Art of Cooking*. She knew she would find what she needed within its pages. She'd also find seriously esoteric directions on how to skin a squirrel and the correct temperature for cooking head cheese.

The volume flopped open to the index, and Gigi ran her finger down the list of *C*'s. Finally, she found what she was looking for. *Cheese sauce*.

As she began thumbing through the book, it yawned open at a crack in the binding. Gigi was about to start over when she noticed a newspaper clipping had been tucked between the pages. She eased it out carefully. It was yellowing but not yet brittle. The date at the top was from four years ago.

Gigi absentmindedly sat on one of the stools tucked under the kitchen island and began to read. Along with the article was a black-and-white photograph of a young woman with blond hair, and the headline read, "Maid Arrested for Stealing." Gigi skimmed the article. It appeared that this woman, Monica Tuomi, had been employed by Felicity, and Felicity had accused her of stealing. The woman in the picture looked vaguely familiar, but Gigi couldn't have met her because all this had happened before she moved to Woodstone. She wondered what had happened to the case. Perhaps Mertz would know.

It was a shame that Gigi had sworn to herself to never, ever talk to him again.

Chapter 23

Gigi wasn't sure why, but she carefully tucked the discolored clipping into the pocket of her jeans. Maybe she would ask someone else if they knew anything about it.

She finished plating the lunches, and Anja ferried the last dish out to the dining room. Gigi untied her apron and tossed it into the hamper in the mudroom. Reg and Tabitha had given up begging for treats and were snoozing under the kitchen table. Gigi started to run a hand through her hair but then stopped. What a mess she must look! She still had to drop off Madeline's and Bea's lunches—it might be best to tidy up before she went out in public.

She didn't want to use the first-floor powder room in case any of Winchel's guests might need it, but there was a bathroom on the third floor between the room that Sienna had used as an office and the one that had been given to Anja. She wouldn't disturb anyone up there.

Gigi headed up the back stairs and was rounding the

second-floor landing when Alex Goulet came out of his room.

"Alex." Gigi stopped him and pulled out the clipping she'd found in the cookbook. She held it out toward him.

He quirked an eyebrow inquiringly.

"I found this tucked in one of Felicity's cookbooks. I'm curious. Do you know anything about this?"

Alex didn't seem to find it strange that she was asking questions, and Gigi sighed with relief. She waited as Alex read through the newspaper article, his brows drawn together in concentration.

He tapped the clipping with a finger. "I remember this. Vaguely. But I do remember it." He thought for a moment. "It was a big brouhaha. Felicity thought her maid"—he tapped the clipping again—"was stealing from her. The police were called in, and the woman was arrested. I think it was Winchel who posted bail in the end. It wasn't much, but the poor girl had little more than the clothes on her back. She came from some Scandinavian country—Norway, Sweden? I don't remember." He handed the clipping back to Gigi.

"What happened after that?"

Alex closed his eyes for a moment. "If I recall correctly, there was this big drama." He lowered his voice and leaned closer to Gigi. "She bolted." He swept a hand through the air and snapped his fingers. "Somehow she found the means to buy a ticket back to wherever it was she had come from." His voice lowered even more, and he put a hand alongside his mouth. "Rumor was that she and Winchel were . . ." He raised his eyebrows up and down.

Gigi nodded understanding.

"It was probably Winchel who paid for the ticket. But just like that, *poof*, she went back to some country in Europe and the Woodstone Police were left holding their—" Alex cut off the sentence abruptly, but Gigi knew what he meant.

It was a good thing she hadn't asked Mertz about it. It was probably a very sensitive subject.

Alex handed the clipping back to Gigi, and she tucked it into her pocket. Alex gave her a chipper salute—he obviously wasn't holding a grudge about the other night—and Gigi continued up the stairs to the third floor.

The door to the bathroom was open. The bathroom was obviously meant for staff. The original claw-foot tub was still in place surrounded by a very utilitarian plain plastic shower curtain. The wooden medicine cabinet looked to be original to the house as well, and the mirror embedded in the door had a thin crack running down its length.

Gigi went in, closed the door and sank down onto the side of the tub. It had been a busy morning, and she was bushed. After a few minutes, she picked herself up and risked a glance in the mirror. She cringed at what she saw. A smear of chocolate ran from her left ear almost to the corner of her mouth, and something gooey had caused a clump of hair to stick together. She tackled the smear first, washing her face in extra-hot water.

Her hair was another matter. She hadn't thought to bring her brush with her. She did what she could by washing out the sticky stuff, and then used her hands to comb through her curls. She dug in the pocket of her jeans and triumphantly pulled out a hair elastic. She managed to subdue her mass of dark red locks into some semblance of a ponytail, after which, with her face clean, she looked reasonably presentable.

Gigi was about to turn out the light when she noticed a crumpled piece of paper half hidden by the shower curtain. She bent to pick it up. It looked as if someone might have been aiming for the dented metal wastebasket but missed.

She opened it up and smoothed out the wrinkles. There were only a few lines of text, printed boldly in pencil. The letters were regular and easy to read.

Gigi scanned the message, then slowed down and read it again.

I know you did it. I saw you. Pay up or I'll tell. Gigi turned the paper over, but that was it. No signature and no salutation. No clue as to who sent it or for whom it was meant. One thing was obvious, though: It was some kind of blackmail note.

For one chilling moment, Gigi realized that Sienna's office was only two doors down the hall. She probably used this bathroom and could have easily tossed that note herself. Sienna had an alibi, and Gigi believed her, but she doubted Mertz would.

Gigi squared her shoulders and gritted her teeth. She'd have to show the note to Mertz. It might turn out to be nothing—a mere prank—or it might turn out to be important evidence. She wondered if she could drop it off at the police station without having to encounter Mertz face-to-face.

Gigi turned out the light and opened the door. As she was stepping into the hall, she heard footsteps. Instinct made her tuck the crumpled blackmail note behind her back.

She looked up to see Anja coming toward her. Anja gave her a small smile, nodded and disappeared into the bathroom.

Gigi gave the counters one last swipe with a soapy sponge, then laid open two of her Gourmet De-Lite containers. She'd had a low-calorie pulled pork cooking in the slow cooker all morning to go over whole wheat buns that she'd toasted to a rich, golden brown. With it she would serve pepper slaw—a German version of coleslaw that included chopped green pepper and was dressed with a sugar and vinegar dressing. By substituting artificial sweetener for the sugar, Gigi had significantly lowered the calories. She'd rounded out the meal with a fresh fruit cup enlivened with a splash of orange juice.

Anja came through the swinging door from the butler's pantry. "They are still eating." She gestured toward the dining room, from which Gigi could hear the low murmur of voices. Fortunately, the shouting had stopped—at least for now. "I am going to run a quick errand." She eyed Gigi's containers open on the counter. "You are leaving?"

"Yes. As soon as I get these meals packed up."

Anja pursed her lips. "No matter. I will only be a few minutes." She grabbed a long, dark cape off a hook in the mudroom and went out the back door.

Gigi was rinsing out the slow cooker when she noticed Anja coming around the side of the house, wheeling her bicycle. She wondered if she ought to wait until Anja returned. But Bea and Madeline would be getting hungry, and it wasn't fair to keep them waiting. Winchel would have to manage on his own.

Gigi packed the meals into a large woven basket she'd bought for the purpose, grabbed her own jacket from the mudroom and slipped into it.

"Come on, Reg." Gigi held out his leash.

Reg uncurled himself from his spot under the table and did a quick stretch in each direction. Gigi clipped on his leash. She gave one last look around the kitchen. Everything was in order. She flipped out the lights and pulled open the back door.

The wind caught the door almost immediately and tried to tug it from Gigi's hand. Leaves swirled around her as she made her way around to the driveway where she'd left her car.

The fierce breeze made Reggie look as if his coat had been turned inside out, and Gigi laughed as he jumped into the front seat of the MINI. She got into the driver's seat and gratefully closed the door against the suffocating force of the wind.

Bunches of leaves and small twigs and branches were scattered over the road that led from Felicity's house to the main road. Gigi drove slowly, but even so she noticed how the wind rocked her small car from side to side. She held the wheel and eased up even further on the gas. A low-hanging branch from one of the trees had broken, and it hung over the narrow lane. Gigi jumped as it slapped against her windshield. She breathed a sigh of relief when she gained the main thoroughfare.

Gigi increased her speed slightly. The road was clearer, and the wind had abated slightly. The note she'd found was burning a hole right through her jeans' pocket. She really did have to show it to Mertz. She thought briefly about giving it to Alice to take to him—would that be too thoroughly cowardly of her?

The wind picked up again. Gigi felt the car rock, and she moved her foot toward the brake. But before she could slow down, the left front end of the car collapsed and began to pull hard in that direction. Gigi gripped the steering wheel and held on with all her strength. *What on earth is going on?*

The car began making a hideous grinding noise that was nearly deafening. Gigi glanced at Reg, and he was sitting very still, his coat puffing out the way it did when he was disturbed. Movement off the left side of the car caught Gigi's eye, and she watched in horror as her front tire bounced down the road and disappeared down an embankment. By now the car was crossing the left lane despite Gigi's effort to pull as hard as she could to the right. Fortunately, no one was coming in the opposite direction, although the car behind her had started to honk its horn.

Gigi gave a small sob as she fought to regain control of the car. She was edging off the macadam now and bumping across the grass verge. She closed her eyes as the car made a beeline for the guardrail.

The jolt wasn't as bad as Gigi expected. The trek across the grass had slowed the MINI considerably. She opened her eyes to discover that they had stopped, the front end of her precious MINI crumpled against the steel of the rail. Reg had slid off the seat and was cowering in the foot well. Gigi felt a surge of anger and then immediately burst into tears.

She was digging in her purse for a tissue when someone knocked on the driver's side window. Gigi looked up, startled. Right into Declan McQuaid's very blue, very concerned eyes.

His cell phone was already out, and he was speaking into it. Gigi buzzed down her window while motioning to him that she was fine, and there was no need to call 9-1-1.

Declan crouched beside the car, his eyes telegraphing his concern. "Don't worry, the police and an ambulance are on their way."

"I don't need an ambulance. I'm fine," Gigi protested.

"At least let them look you over. Some of these injuries can sneak up on you days or weeks later."

Gigi opened the door and got out of the car. She was shocked to discover how wobbly her legs felt. A wave of dizziness came over her, and she grabbed for the door frame.

"Whoa." Declan put an arm around her. "Maybe you'd better sit down. Don't want you fainting and landing face-first in the mud."

Gigi was about to protest when another wave of dizziness

convinced her that Declan was right. He led her to a tree stump, and she sank down gratefully.

"Reg—"

"I'll get him, don't worry. You stay here. Put your head down if you start feeling faint."

Gigi watched through a haze as Declan went around to the passenger side of the car and retrieved Reg. Reg stood by the car for a moment looking slightly dazed, but then he gave a vigorous shake and headed for the nearest tree to lift his leg.

Declan brought him over to where Gigi was sitting. She looked up at Declan.

"What happened? All of a sudden I couldn't control the car."

Declan gestured toward the MINI. "Your tire came off."

Gigi felt that wave of dizziness again. Thank goodness she hadn't been on the highway or going downhill when it happened.

"When was the last time you changed that tire?"

Gigi thought for a moment. "I had them rotated last month. I took the car to Smith's Garage over by the train station."

"I would go have a word with them if I were you. It looks as if someone didn't tighten the lug nuts properly."

Gigi shivered. She wasn't entirely sure what lug nuts were, but the fact that the whole tire came off . . . that was enough to frighten her silly.

Reg had been sniffing the ground energetically, but he suddenly stopped and sat, rotating his ears like a pair of receivers.

"What is it, Reg?" Gigi was scratching his ears when she heard it—the wail of a siren coming from the other side of town.

"Sounds like the police are on their way."

Gigi suddenly became very conscious of Declan's presence. She felt the blush she'd been cursed with coloring her face. "I'll be okay now. I don't want to keep you." The heat in her face intensified.

"I wouldn't forgive myself if I abandoned you now."

Gigi felt another rush of dizziness, but it had nothing to do with the accident. Just then the sirens got louder as a police car crested the hill and pulled to a stop several yards behind Gigi's MINI. Two officers got out. One skittered down the embankment toward where Gigi's tire had spun, and the other came toward her and Declan.

The officer, a tall, skinny fellow whose head looked too heavy for his body, pulled a notebook from his pocket and stood with his pencil poised above the page. "What happened here?" He scowled at Gigi as if the accident had been her fault.

Gigi felt Declan bristle and hastened to explain what had happened. The officer's face softened, and he looked over his shoulder. "Ambulance should be on its way."

Once again, Gigi insisted that she was fine, but she was quickly overruled by Declan and the officer. Meanwhile, the other officer had scrambled back up the embankment, wheeling the tire in front of him. He walked toward them, a grim expression on his face.

"All four lug nuts were off," he said as soon as he was within earshot. "Where did you have that tire put on?"

Gigi explained about going to Smith's for her tire rotation.

Both officers shook their heads. "People gotta learn to be more careful," the skinny one said. "If I were you, miss, I'd go have a word with the manager there." He jerked his head toward her car. "You could have been hurt. Badly hurt."

All of a sudden the seriousness of what had happened washed over Gigi like a rogue wave, and she began to shake.

"Hey, it's going to be okay. Fortunately, nothing really bad happened." Declan pulled her close and held her tightly.

Gigi leaned her head against him and shut her eyes. Her lower lip quivered, and tears built up behind her closed lids. She bit her lip. She couldn't cry. It would be too embarrassing. She was vaguely aware of another car pulling off the road, the slamming of a door and then the crunch of loose gravel as someone began walking toward them. She opened her eyes briefly and peered over Declan's shoulder.

Mertz was coming toward them, his face as black as a storm cloud.

Chapter 24

Gigi didn't know what to do, so she closed her eyes again, crossed her fingers and wished with all her might that some fairy godmother would transport her somewhere else—anywhere else. Antarctica in a blizzard would be preferable to seeing the hurt radiating from Mertz's eyes.

Mertz stopped shy of Gigi and Declan. "I heard someone in a red MINI had gone off the road. I thought it might be you." He sounded breathless, as if he'd been running, and Gigi could see the muscle jumping in his cheek. "If anything happened to—" He bit the words off abruptly.

Declan looked back and forth between the two of them. "It looks like you're in good hands. I've got to get back to the restaurant. I came out for some salt. Believe it or not, we ran out."

Both Gigi and Mertz were silent as they watched Declan make his way toward his SUV parked at an angle off the road behind Gigi's crumpled MINI.

Mertz sighed. "What happened? When I heard that some-one in a red MINI had been involved in an accident, I . . ." He wiped a hand across his eyes and took another deep breath. "Are you all right?"

Gigi nodded. "I'm fine." She gestured toward the ambu-lance, whose crew was hovering. "I don't think I'll be need-ing that."

"It would be a good idea to get checked over. You never know. Your neck, your back could be affected. Might not show up for days."

It was the same thing Declan had said, but Gigi didn't mention that. "Sure," she said to reassure Mertz. "I'll let them have a look."

Mertz nodded, satisfied. "I didn't mean to interrupt you and your . . . boyfriend." Mertz said the word as if it burned the inside of his mouth. "I apologize." He stared at his feet.

"He's . . . he's not my boyfriend. I hardly know him. He came along in back of me, and I guess . . . I guess I kind of lost it for a minute there."

"Oh." A smile lit Mertz's face.

Just then one of the EMTs came over. He had a stethoscope draped around his neck and a clipboard in his hand. "Sorry, miss, but we need to check you out before we take off."

Gigi succumbed to his ministrations and allowed him to take her blood pressure, temperature and pulse. He gently felt her neck and up and down her back. "I'd feel better if you let us take you in for an X-ray or a CAT scan."

Gigi looked imploringly at Mertz, but he shook his head in assent.

"Fine." Gigi allowed them to strap her to a gurney. "But what about my car? And what about Reg?" she said on a note of panic.

"Don't worry. I'll take care of the car, and if you'll give

me your keys, I'll drop Reg off at your place." Mertz squeezed her shoulder reassuringly. He glanced toward the spot where her cheerful red MINI was tangled with the guardrail. "It looks like there's damage to the fender, but I'm guessing it can be repaired. Of course, you might be riding a bike in the meantime." A broad grin cut a swath across his face. "At least it will be easy enough to park."

Gigi started to laugh but then realized that it hurt. Her ribs, in the area where her seat belt would have been, felt slightly bruised.

"If you're ready?" The EMT looked from Gigi to Mertz and then back again.

He was about to pick up the back end of the gurney when Mertz stopped him.

He leaned over Gigi. "If you wouldn't mind quickly telling me what happened. I gather you threw a tire?"

Gigi nodded. "I had them rotated last month at Smith's, and it looks like one of the workers forgot to tighten the lug nuts."

Mertz shook his head, grim-lipped. "Someone might have done this on purpose. To stop your investigating."

Gigi felt her breath catch in her chest. That had never occurred to her. What if the murderer had been rattled? And they'd decided to scare her off . . . or worse, do away with her? She shivered.

"Leave the investigating to me from now on, okay?"

"Okay," Gigi said, her voice coming out breathless and very tiny.

The EMT once again began to hoist the end of the gurney, but once again, Mertz stopped him. He leaned over Gigi for a moment and then quickly bent and kissed her cheek.

Mertz turned to the EMT. "Take care of her, okay?"

The EMT nodded and sketched a brief salute before loading Gigi into the ambulance.

* * *

It was midnight by the time Gigi was released from the Woodstone ER with a clean bill of health. She had a couple of bumps and bruises—or hematomas, in the parlance of the ER—but nothing more serious. Except for an overwhelming case of the heebie-jeebies. The idea that the murderer might have been trying to . . . kill . . . her, left her hyperventilating. She'd been thinking about nothing more than getting back home to her cozy cottage, and now the very thought scared her nearly half to death.

Oliver came to pick her up at the hospital. He offered to stay with her, but once Gigi saw her home, the windows lit with welcoming light, and heard Reg's bark carrying on the cold night air, she felt her fears dissipate. She reassured Oliver that she would be okay, and rather wearily made her way up the front steps and through the door.

Gigi didn't wash her face or even brush her teeth, but fell into bed and was immediately deep in sleep.

When Gigi awoke, light was already streaming through the windows. She didn't immediately recall the events of the day before, but turning over in bed brought everything rushing back. She groaned softly, and Reg sat up in alarm, his ears high and alert. Gigi reached out and scratched his head.

"It's all right, boy, I'm a bit sore. Nothing to worry about."

But life still had to go on. Gigi eased her way out of bed and immediately popped two ibuprofen. That, followed by a hot shower, had her feeling almost as good as new. She just had to be cautious about making any sudden moves.

She brewed a cup of coffee and began work on breakfast for Bea and Madeline. She was trying something new, and she hoped they would like it—quinoa cooked in low-fat milk topped with chopped apples, walnuts and the merest drizzle of maple syrup.

Gigi put the pan on the stove, poured in the milk and quinoa and turned on the burner. While that cooked, she put some walnuts in the oven to toast lightly and began peeling, coring and chopping the apples.

She was thinking over the events of the day before when she realized that Mertz had actually *kissed* her! It had been only a quick peck on the cheek, but then the way he'd told the EMT fellow to look after her . . . Gigi felt her face get warm from the memories.

Sienna was picking Gigi up to make her early morning deliveries, and then dropping her off at Alice's. Alice still wasn't able to drive, so she was loaning Gigi her car until the MINI was repaired. In exchange, Gigi was going to ferry Alice to and from the police station so she could continue her part-time job, albeit with one arm. Alice was positive she would be able to handle it, and Gigi knew how important the income was to her.

Gigi was looking out the window when Sienna arrived. Sienna struggled to get her stomach around the steering wheel and when she'd finally extricated herself, stood for a moment with her hand on her back. She was panting slightly.

Gigi had the door open before Sienna even mounted the steps. Her normally fair complexion was even paler than usual, and the circles under her eyes had deepened to a charcoal hue.

"Are you okay?" Gigi asked in concern.

"Sure." Sienna stopped on the top step to catch her breath. "Other than that I'm the size of an elephant and about as graceful. I can't breathe, I can't sleep, and I haven't seen my toes in a month."

It sounded horrendous, and Gigi was surprised to feel a pang of actual jealousy. Would she find her own Mr. Right soon enough to have a baby herself?

"Only a few more weeks to go, and I can't wait." Sienna tried to bend down to scratch Reg's head, but it was impossible. "I wish we didn't have this huge cloud over our heads. That's not making it any easier."

"I'm sure the police will find the killer soon, and you and Oliver can relax."

Sienna sighed. "I hope so." She looked at Gigi. "Ready to go?"

"Just a sec. Let me get my meals." Gigi looked down at Reg. "Sorry, bud, but you'll have to stay home this time. I'll be back before too long."

Alice's decade-old Taurus was parked in the driveway when Gigi got there. Gigi looked at it in dismay. How she missed her MINI! But the garage had assured her they would perform the repairs as quickly as possible.

Gigi turned and waved good-bye as Sienna backed out of the driveway, and then she started up the path to Alice's front door. Flowers on either side of the path had succumbed to the early frost and were lying gray and limp in the garden. Gigi knew Alice was an avid gardener, and it must be killing her to not be able to get out and put her precious plants to bed for the winter.

Alice was ready and waiting when Gigi rang the bell.

"How is Stacy?" Gigi asked tentatively. She didn't know if it would upset Alice more if she asked about Stacy . . . or if she didn't.

Alice shrugged and opened the hall coat closet. "I don't know." Her voice echoed strangely with her head halfway in the closet. "I've called over there a couple of times, and she's never home." Alice handed Gigi a tan, belted raincoat, and Gigi held it out for her. "Unless she sees it's me on the caller ID and doesn't pick up." Alice was slightly breathless from struggling into her coat.

Gigi held open the front door.

"I'm dying to get out of the house," Alice said as she handed Gigi the keys to the Taurus. "If I watch any more daytime television, my brain will rot. I did catch a couple of episodes of *For Better or For Worse*, though. Reruns. I'll be curious to see how they deal with Felicity's absence."

Gigi held the passenger door open for Alice.

Alice got in and grabbed for the seat belt and missed. "Oh, I hate being one-armed!"

Gigi stuck her head in the car and helped Alice fasten the belt. "I wonder if they're bringing someone else in to take over the part."

"Could be. I know Vanessa was hoping they would make her role bigger."

Gigi got behind the wheel, and Alice looked at her with concern. "How about you? How are you doing? I heard about your accident."

Gigi shrugged it off. "Nothing worse than a couple of bruises." She pulled out the newspaper clipping she'd found and had tucked in her purse. "Do you know anything about this?" She handed it to Alice.

Gigi waited as Alice read the short piece.

"I do remember that. At the time, a lot of people thought the maid"—she gestured toward the grainy black-and-white photo in the clipping—"had gotten a bum deal. It was just as likely that Derek was the one stealing the money from Felicity's handbag."

Gigi nodded slowly. She should have thought of that given Derek's history. "That woman looks so familiar, but I don't know why."

"You weren't here at the time, so you couldn't possibly have known her."

Traffic on High Street was fairly light, and before Gigi knew it, they were pulling up in front of the Woodstone Police Station. The geraniums the Woodstone Garden Club had planted out front were shriveled and wilted.

Alice tut-tutted when she saw them. "They should have swapped those out for some mums weeks ago. If I weren't being held hostage by this thing"—she gestured toward her casted arm—"I'd do it myself."

Gigi waited while Alice got her purse and lunch tote together and exited the car. She watched as Alice mounted the front steps. Suddenly the image of Sienna and the dark circles under her eyes flashed across Gigi's mind. She thought of the blackmail note she'd found but had yet to show to the police. She really should bring it to Mertz. Even though he would most likely pooh-pooh it. Unfortunately, now she was feeling peculiarly shy about seeing him. That kiss he'd given her . . . while only a peck, it had signaled . . . something.

She pulled away from the curb, drove the several dozen feet to the Woodstone Police Station parking lot and pulled in. Gigi found a space in the last row, parked and turned off the engine. She sat for a minute, giving herself a pep talk. She had no right withholding this evidence from Mertz if it could in any way help find Felicity's murderer. She would have to gather up all of her courage to go in and present it to him. He could dismiss its importance all he liked, but she would have done her duty.

Maybe he won't be in his office, Gigi hoped as she got out of the car and locked the doors.

Gigi approached the woman behind the bulletproof glass in reception. She dutifully dialed Mertz's extension, and they both waited while she listened to the buzzing of the telephone. Gigi crossed her fingers behind her back. She really hoped Mertz wasn't in. Really. It would be so much easier to leave the note for him to look at later, after she was gone. Long gone.

It was not to be. The woman led Gigi down the hall to Mertz's office. He was on the telephone but gestured with his chin toward the empty chair in front of his desk. Gigi perched on the edge. She wished she hadn't eaten breakfast—nerves were gnawing at her stomach.

She looked at Mertz out of the corner of her eye, and he looked nervous, too. That made her feel slightly better.

Mertz finally hung up the phone, and his normally serious face broke into a smile. "You're looking good. I mean . . ." The color Gigi suspected she'd seen in his face earlier deepened. "I mean, you look none the worse for wear . . . I mean . . . after the accident." He seemed to realize he was digging himself in deeper and suddenly became quiet.

The silence lengthened, and Gigi grabbed for her purse. She extricated the note she'd found in Felicity's bathroom and held it toward Mertz as if it were a sacred offering.

"What's this?" He frowned as he took the ragged piece of paper.

"I found that on the floor in Felicity Davenport's third-floor bathroom."

Mertz's eyebrows shot up.

"I wanted to freshen up, and I didn't want to use the first-floor powder room because Winchel had guests, and I knew there was a bathroom on the . . ." Gigi realized she was babbling and ground to a halt.

Mertz had his head down and was reading the neat, precisely printed words. He looked up, his eyebrows drawn down over his light blue eyes. "What is this?"

"I don't know. I thought maybe it was a blackmail note." Gigi fidgeted under Mertz's stern gaze.

"And you found this at our murder victim's house?"

Gigi nodded, unhappy with the turn the conversation had taken.

Mertz was quiet again, but it was a different type of silence this time. Gigi fidgeted, wishing he would say something, anything.

He finally did, and his teeth were clenched so tightly, Gigi could barely understand him.

"How can I convince you to stop poking your nose in where it doesn't belong? It's dangerous. It makes me nervous."

Gigi opened her mouth but then closed it again quickly as Mertz continued.

"Someone"—Mertz pointed a stern finger at Gigi—"loosened the lug nuts on your tires. Someone"—his voice got louder—"wanted your tire to come off. Someone"—he was practically shouting now, and a vein that ran across his forehead throbbed purple—"is trying to you kill you." He finished by pounding the top of his desk with his fist.

Gigi kept her mouth closed. Silence was probably her best defense.

Mertz closed his eyes and rubbed his forehead. "I told

you. If anything happened to you . . ." He looked at the note on his desk. "I don't suppose there will be any useful prints on this. . . ." He mumbled to himself. He looked up at Gigi. "Where did you find this again?"

"In the third-floor bathroom."

"What else is up on the third floor?"

"There's Anja's room and what looks like an exercise room of some sort—at least I noticed a treadmill and a couple of weights . . ."

"Go on," Mertz prompted. "There's something you don't want to tell me."

Gigi looked startled.

"You wouldn't be much of a poker player, you know."

"So I've been told."

"So, out with it." Mertz leaned back in his chair, and it creaked loudly.

"Sienna's office," Gigi admitted, the words sticking in her mouth like peanut butter. "Or, it used to be her office when she was working for Felicity."

"So the two people who were most likely to be up on that floor were Sienna and this Anja."

Gigi nodded unhappily.

"And Derek," she added. "He used the exercise room sometimes."

Mertz pursed his lips. "In truth, anyone in the house might have gone up there."

Gigi nodded eagerly.

"Of course, this might be some kind of prank." Mertz brandished the note. "There are no names on here. Nothing, really. Just a note taken out of context." He let out a gusty sigh. "But I'll do my best." He pointed his finger at her again. "On one condition."

"What's that?" Gigi asked in a very small voice.

"That you stop investigating this minute. Promise me you'll stop. Please."

"Okay," Gigi said.

She didn't tell him her fingers were crossed behind her back.

Chapter 25

Gigi was on the road delivering Bea's and Madeline's lunches when she had a phone call from Winchel. The board had convened an emergency session, not having finished their business the day before. Could she whip up a simple dinner for them?

Gigi couldn't afford to turn down business, although she had never intended the focus of her company to be on catering. But money was money. She drove home quickly to pick up Reg, and then turned Alice's ancient Taurus around and headed back to Felicity's.

The wind had picked up, and the skies were the sort of steely gray more common in late November than October. Gigi shivered and switched on the heat. A few colored leaves still clung to some of the trees, but the tops of the branches swayed like skeletal arms scratching the darkening sky.

Lights had already been turned on at Felicity's when Gigi got there, casting a warm glow into the gloom. She pulled into the lay-by at the top of the driveway, clipped on Reg's leash and walked toward the house.

Anja was in the kitchen when Gigi opened the back door to the mudroom. She glanced up when Gigi and Reg entered.

Gigi unclipped Reg's leash, and he took off with Tabitha, who had been dozing by the oven. They circled the kitchen table several times before dashing off into the hallway.

Gigi sat at the table and pulled a piece of paper and a pen from her handbag. She had to come up with a quick menu for Winchel and his guests. He'd indicated he wanted something simple, and Gigi was more than willing to give him that—a main course and something sweet for dessert. She went through the recipe file in her head. Something with boneless chicken breasts. She could bake them topped with naturally low-fat mozzarella cheese and a quick, homemade tomato sauce. A sprinkle of fresh herbs would serve to enhance the flavor. She began scribbling ingredients on her piece of paper.

She'd do a big, fresh green salad, and for those not watching their weight, she'd offer crusty bread to dip in olive oil perfumed with herbs. Dessert, for those wanting it, would be quick tiramisu sundaes—ice cream on top of vanilla cookies moistened with amaretto, served with chocolate sauce, fresh whipped cream and a cherry.

She'd noticed a couple of heads of lettuce in the refrigerator earlier—she could start washing them for the salad. Then she'd head out to the Shop and Save for the rest of her list.

Suddenly Reg came tearing through the pantry with Tabitha at his heels. The Oriental throw rug bunched and scattered behind them. Gigi jumped up, startled. Reg had a bone in his mouth—a veal shank by the looks of it.

"Give that back, Reg," Gigi yelled as she took off in pursuit of the canines.

The harder she chased, the faster they ran. Reg started up the back stairs, his short legs making hard work of the steep steps. Tabitha was right behind him, panting slightly.

Reg paused briefly on the second-floor landing, but with Tabitha so close behind, he didn't dare stop but kept on going up the stairs to the third floor. He dashed into the empty room that had been Sienna's office, but before Gigi could go after him, he turned on his heel and ran out again, Tabitha still in hot pursuit. Gigi cursed mildly under her breath, nearly losing her balance on the small rug the dogs had churned up in their wake.

Reg passed the bathroom and darted toward Anja's room. Gigi yelled at him to stop, but the marrow bone was too much of a temptation, and he dove under the bed and out of reach. Tabitha attempted to go after him, but she was too big and she got stuck, her more substantial rump wedged beneath the bed frame.

Gigi sighed in exasperation and looked around. The room was comfortable but impersonal. It reminded Gigi of a room in a budget hotel. Plain beige spread, plain beige curtains, serviceable furniture. Anja had added little of herself to the room. An alarm clock stood on the bedside table with a worn-looking paperback next to it. A pair of wool slippers peeked from under the bed skirt, and a dark cardigan sweater was draped over the single chair.

A single bottle of perfume stood on top of the dresser. The name was in a foreign language, but there was a picture of a single flower on the front. Next to it was a dark blue enamel frame. Gigi glanced at the picture and started to turn away, but then came to a sudden halt.

She wrested the newspaper clipping she'd found in Felicity's cookbook from her pocket and held it up to the picture of the girl in the frame. The photos were of the same girl.

Tucked into the corner of the frame was another clipping. Suddenly, the wind sent a thin tree branch raking across the window, like a skeletal hand rapping against the glass. Gigi jumped, her heart leaping into her throat.

She waited until her heartbeat slowed, then eased the clipping from its mooring and opened it up. The girl whose picture was in the frame stared back at her. The story was in a foreign language—Gigi thought it might be some Scandinavian language—but she could tell that it was an obituary. The girl's name was printed under the grainy black-and-white photograph, and under that were two dates—her birth and death. Gigi traced her finger along the unfamiliar words until she came to a list of what looked like names. In the center of the line was *Anja Lauri*.

Gigi tucked the clipping into the pocket of her jeans along with the other one, then got down on her hands and knees, collapsed onto her stomach and stuck her head under the bed. Reg had his treasure tucked between his two front paws. Gigi grabbed hold of his collar and dragged him out from under the bed. As soon as he'd cleared the frame, he took off again with Tabitha close behind.

Gigi brushed some dust balls off her sweater and blew a lock of hair out of her face. She was about to follow the dogs, but when she turned around she came face-to-face with Anja.

Anja gave Gigi a strange look, then issued a small smile that barely lifted the corners of her mouth. Gigi managed to smile back, although she was sure her eyes had given her away. She hadn't been able to resist glancing toward the dresser where the frame was missing its accompanying clipping. Gigi prayed that Anja wouldn't notice it was gone until Gigi had managed to flee the house.

Gigi started out of the room, fingers crossed that Anja

would follow her. She did, and Gigi breathed a huge sigh of relief. They retreated to the kitchen in mutual silence where the only sound was the grinding of Reg's teeth against the purloined bone.

Suddenly Reg dropped his bone and began to whine and scratch at the back door.

"I suspect that veal bone has given him a tummy ache," Anja said. "I always take peppermint tea when my tummy hurts, but I don't suppose you can give that to a dog."

"I doubt he would drink it." Gigi clipped on Reg's leash and retrieved her jacket from the hook in the mudroom. She felt in her pockets, but they were empty. She would need something with which to scoop should Reg decide to do his business on the lawn.

A sleeve stuffed with grocery bags to be recycled hung next to the refrigerator. Gigi grabbed two and shoved them into her pocket. She opened the back door, and a blast of cold air blew into the kitchen.

The wind immediately whipped her hair across her face, and she thought she felt the frigid touch of a snowflake against her cheek. She looked toward the sky where white flecks swirled down from above, melting on contact with the still warm ground.

Reg pulled her down the drive and toward the street, but before they got there, he stopped. Gigi waited until he was finished and then fished the heavier of the two plastic bags from her pocket. It had *Bon Appétit* printed across the front in black letters and reminded her of the day Anja had set out to purchase some of Evelyn's special tea for Felicity. The whole terrible ordeal of the murder came rushing back, and she shivered.

She pulled her collar up, then stuck her hand into the bag to invert it. A piece of paper was trapped inside. Gigi pulled it out. It appeared to be a receipt from Bon Appétit. She looked at it more closely. It was for $5.59 and *special diuretic tea blend* was noted on it in Evelyn's bold handwriting. She had also signed and dated it—Evelyn still liked to do things the old-fashioned way. Gigi folded the paper in half and carefully tucked it into her pocket. Anja must have missed it when she put the bag away and might need it for reimbursement later.

Gigi thought about the clipping as she drove home after finishing the dinner prep for Winchel. Maybe she could find someone to translate it.

The recollection that someone had tried to stop her from snooping altogether by loosening her tire brought her up short. She remembered her panic as she lost control of the car and felt it veering toward the left. Whoever had done that was serious. They'd meant to warn her off . . . or kill her. Gigi's mouth went dry, and she gulped. She looked around the interior of Alice's Taurus, but she'd forgotten to pack any bottles of water.

The snow had turned to pelting rain by the time Gigi got back to her cottage. She parked the car and ran for the door, pulling her jacket up over her head. She switched on the lights in the kitchen, then rummaged in the refrigerator for something to eat. She hadn't felt like eating earlier. She found the remains of some chicken, mushroom and wild rice soup and put the container in the microwave to heat.

Meanwhile, she booted up her computer and did a search for nearby community colleges. Hopefully they would have professors proficient in several languages. The closest was Brookcrest Community College, approximately twenty miles away. Gigi made a note of the telephone number, and by then the timer on the microwave had pinged.

Gigi ate her soup quickly, then dug her cell phone from

her purse. She dialed the number she'd jotted down for Brookcrest Community College. It only took being put on hold for a total of thirty minutes, being redirected to eight different extensions and four voice mails, and being forced to redial after one dropped call to discover that a professor by the name of Hendrik Nissen, who taught art history, also had an interest in Scandinavian languages.

Gigi arranged to meet with him and show him the clipping.

Chapter 26

At one time Gigi had been a passionate New Yorker who never wanted to leave the city, but somehow, after her move to Connecticut, she had managed to avoid going into the city even once. But if she was going to talk to the people at the Vandenberg Gallery about the check they'd given Vanessa Huff, she was going to have to take the bull by the horns. She checked the train schedule for the third time and decided that she would take the eight forty-five train into Grand Central Station.

The biggest problem was—what to wear? Gigi dove into her closet for the third time and emerged with her former go-to outfit: a black pantsuit. She blew the dust off the shoulders and pulled it off the hanger. She would wear her new blouse with the ruffles down the front and add a colorful scarf. Scarves were practically de rigueur for women in the city no matter what the weather or temperature. It would add a note of sophistication to an otherwise bland outfit.

She laid the suit, blouse and scarf on the chair in her bedroom along with her good high-heeled leather boots and a tote bag for reading material and a pair of tennis shoes in case her feet gave out. She pawed through her jewelry box and selected a pair of—real—gold earrings, a gold bangle her mother had given her for college graduation and a thin gold chain she'd bought herself when she'd landed her first job. She thought of the fantastic diamond tennis bracelet Vanessa had treated herself to and felt completely belittled. But there was nothing she could do about it. This was all she had to work with.

The eight forty-five pulled into Grand Central Station barely more than five minutes behind schedule. Gigi followed the dozen passengers out of the car and toward the steps leading to the main level.

Vandenberg's gallery was in a home built by his ancestors back when horses and carriages were the main means of transport up and down Fifth Avenue. It was located in the Murray Hill section of New York City—the area roughly bounded by Fortieth and Thirty-fourth Streets north and south, between Madison and Third Avenues. Gigi planned on walking the short distance from the train station. The rain had finally stopped, and it was a perfect fall day with a crisp breeze and blue skies.

Gigi stood on the sidewalk and took a deep breath. People rushed past her on all sides, and it took her a moment to get into the stream of pedestrian traffic. She started walking, feeling the return of her "city legs" with every step. She came to a traffic light and stood impatiently, waiting for it to turn to *Walk*. She had to remind herself not to flinch as the traffic went roaring past spewing exhaust and other noxious fumes.

Vandenberg House, as it was known, was visible from

several blocks away. A dark, brooding building, it dwarfed everything around it. Gigi stood on the sidewalk and stared up at the mullioned windows, rounded turrets and miniature gargoyles. There were multiple doors, and she had no idea which was which until she noticed a small, discreet sign announcing *Vandenberg House Gallery*.

Gigi pushed open the glass door. An ornate, antique desk was in the entryway, and the girl behind it was dressed all in black with gold chandelier earrings that brushed her shoulders when she moved her head.

Gigi felt her mouth dry up at the prospect of approaching her, and she had to remind herself that she was doing this to save Sienna from jail. The girl turned out to be very friendly—they didn't get many visitors since Mr. Vandenberg didn't approve of anything so crass as advertising. She invited Gigi to have a look around.

Gigi rounded the corner indicated by the receptionist and found herself in an enormous room lined with glass cases. She supposed it must have been the ballroom when the house was originally built. Between the cases she noticed fleur-de-lis wallpaper and gilt sconces dripping with crystals.

The cases contained all the television memorabilia Vandenberg had collected over the years—props, costumes, original scripts. Gigi made her way around the room marveling at the different items—everything from the kitchen table and chairs from the sparse set of *The Honeymooners* to one of the harem outfits worn on *I Dream of Jeannie*.

Gigi turned the corner and came face-to-face with a case housing a high table—it resembled an altar—on which a statue rested. She moved in for a closer look. It wasn't an ordinary statue—it was an Emmy award. Squinting, she was able to read the name on it: Felicity Davenport.

Gigi turned on her heel and headed back toward the reception desk.

"Excuse me."

The receptionist swiveled her chair from her computer monitor toward Gigi. "Yes?"

Gigi wet her lips nervously. "I noticed you have an Emmy that belongs . . . I mean . . . belonged to Felicity Davenport."

The receptionist smiled. "That's one of our latest additions. Mr. Vandenberg has been most anxious to secure one for his collection, but until recently, he hadn't been successful. When that one became available, he cleared out one of his displays—I believe it was the reins and bridle that belonged to Mr. Ed." She shrugged. "Never heard of the show myself."

Gigi sidled closer to the desk and wet her lips again. "How did Mr. Vandenberg come by Miss Davenport's Emmy? Did she give it to him for his collection?"

The blonde shook her head, and her long, dangly earrings whipped back and forth briskly. "Oh, no. He bought it from someone. She came in with it in an old Saks Fifth Avenue bag, and he bought it from her on the spot."

Gigi wondered if the blonde even realized that Felicity was dead. Did she even watch television? "You don't happen to know who that was, do you?"

She nodded briskly, sending the earrings spinning. "Yes. Mr. Vandenberg was dreadfully excited because the girl was on some famous soap opera." She rolled her eyes. "I can't imagine wasting time on them myself. It's not like they're real or anything."

Gigi guessed her typical television fare was the spate of reality shows that had sprung up in recent years. The soaps probably seemed tame and old-fashioned to her. "Did she just show up, or did she have an appointment?"

"Oh, Mr. Vandenberg doesn't see anyone without an appointment. He's a little peculiar, if you ask me." She made small circles around the side of her head with her finger. "He has very set hours and doesn't see anyone who hasn't called in advance."

"Even someone with an Emmy statue for sale?"

The girl shrugged. "I don't know about that, but this woman did call ahead for an appointment."

"Is there any way you can find out what day she came in with the Emmy?" Gigi wracked her brain for a reason to substantiate her question, but the girl wasn't in the least bit concerned.

"Everything is written down in the appointment book." She pulled a large, leather-bound ledger toward her. "Mr. Vandenberg won't let me keep track of things on the computer." She gestured toward the sleek monitor and hard drive on her desk. "His family has used books like these for like, centuries, and he insists on doing the same."

She opened the enormous ledger, and, tongue between her teeth, began to flip through the pages. Finally, she stopped at a page and ran her finger down the columns. She looked up at Gigi.

"I've got it all right here. Dates, times, everything."

She rattled off the information, and it took Gigi a moment to process it. "How long was the lady here?"

The blonde shrugged. "She came in the morning for the appointment, like I've got written here. Then Mr. Vandenberg took her out to lunch. He doesn't usually do that, but"—she shrugged again—"she was quite attractive, if you know what I mean."

Gigi nodded. "Yes, yes, I do know what you mean."

"They didn't get back here till nearly four o'clock, and Mr. Vandenberg called his chauffeur to bring the car around and drive the lady to the train station. I think she was headed for Grand Central, but I can't say for sure."

"Yes, that's probably right."

Gigi did a few calculations in her head.

If the blonde was right, Vanessa had spent the entire day in the city. It was the same day that Derek was found dead in his bed. She couldn't possibly have murdered him.

So . . . unless two separate murderers were loose in Woodstone, Vanessa most likely didn't murder Felicity either. Which left everyone back at square one.

Exhausted by her unaccustomed trip into New York City, Gigi spent the weekend sleeping late, playing with Reg and resting in front of the television. By Monday morning, the clouds that had been threatening snow had been blown away by a vigorous wind, and the pale blue sky above was revealed as Gigi drove toward Brookcrest Community College for her meeting with Professor Nissen.

Reggie obviously sensed they were going somewhere out of the ordinary, and he watched the passing scenery eagerly, his bright pink tongue lolling to one side. Gigi found the college easily enough. It wasn't very large—a handful of brick buildings around an open square crisscrossed with walking paths. Gigi followed the signs to the visitor parking lot and pulled in. She hated leaving Reg in the car, but she knew that before she was even out of sight, he would be curled up on the seat, dozing happily.

She locked the car, checked the address Professor Nissen had given her, and headed toward Wordsworth Hall. The classrooms were all empty and quiet. Gigi realized it must be the lunch break.

Gigi climbed a narrow iron staircase to the third floor

where she found herself facing a row of ancient oak doors with tarnished brass plates. A radiator at the end of the hall belched hot, moist air, and Gigi stopped to undo her coat.

She found Professor Nissen's office and knocked on the solid door. It was cracked open immediately, and Gigi found herself staring into the bluest eyes she had ever seen. Nissen was tall and thin, with a halo of fuzzy, washed-out blond hair.

He invited Gigi into his office where files were stacked against every wall and mounds of paper were lying along the windowsill.

"Sorry," he said as he removed papers and folders from a worn and scarred wooden chair. "Please." He gestured for Gigi to take a seat. He went behind the desk and collapsed into an ancient swivel chair with a tattered seatback. "What can I do for you?"

Gigi fished the clipping from her purse and handed it to Nissen. "I was hoping you could translate this for me. I think it must be one of the Scandinavian languages, and I gather you have some proficiency in them."

"That is true," Nissen said as he scanned the newspaper article. He put it down on his desk. "But this"—he poked a long, crooked index finger at the yellowing piece of paper—"is not one of the Scandinavian languages."

"No?" Gigi tried to keep the disappointment out of her voice.

"No," Nissen said decisively. "This is Finnish."

Gigi cleared her throat. Far be it from her to tell Nissen his business, but . . . "But isn't that Scandinavian?"

"No." Nissen shook his head vigorously, and his mop of fuzzy blond curls swayed back and forth. "A lot of people make that mistake. Finnish is one of the Uralic languages, much closer to Hungarian than it is to Swedish or Danish."

"Oh," Gigi said in a very small voice. "I don't imagine you can help me, then."

"On the contrary. My maternal grandmother was from Finland, and I have something of a working knowledge of the language." He peered at the clipping again.

It didn't take him long to decipher it.

It was an obituary as Gigi had suspected. And Anja was a relative of the woman pictured.

As a matter of fact, Anja was listed as her sister.

By the time Gigi got back to her car, she had a pounding headache from the close heat in Nissen's office as well as from all the information swirling around in her mind. She let Reg out of the car and walked him briefly around the small square, hoping the fresh air would clear her head.

Gigi headed back to Woodstone and High Street. Alice had called Gigi's cell to say that she was ready to be picked up. Gigi pulled over to the curb in front of the police station to wait for her. She was leaning back in her seat, with her head against the headrest, when someone tapped on her window.

Gigi jumped. It was Sienna. Gigi quickly rolled down her window.

"Waiting for Alice?" Sienna leaned an arm on the windowsill.

"Yes. She should be out any minute now."

They heard the clacking of heels against the pavement and both turned to see Alice rushing toward the car.

"Hi, girls," Alice said slightly breathlessly. "What say we all go down to Declan's and get a drink." She turned toward Sienna and gently tapped her stomach. "Nonalcoholic for you, of course."

Gigi was surprised. "I didn't think you'd want to . . ." She trailed off, hoping Alice would fill in the blanks.

Alice looked Gigi right in the eye. "I want to check things out for myself. Make him a little uncomfortable, you know? If he's seeing my Stacy, I'm not going to stay away and make it easy for him."

"Gotcha," Gigi said.

Far from looking uncomfortable when the three of them pushed open the door to his restaurant, Declan looked delighted to see them. He rushed forward to greet them.

"Ladies, what can I do for you? Are you here for dinner or just a drink?"

"Just a drink," Alice said, her tones as frosty as a north wind.

Declan either didn't notice Alice's frigid demeanor or decided to ignore it. He immediately showed them to a small, round table in front of a fire, which cast a mellow light onto the paneled walls. The table was ringed with comfortable, corduroy-covered club chairs. Gigi took a seat closest to the fire and held her hands out toward the warm flames.

Most of the tables were still empty—it was early for dinner—but a smattering of people perched on the tall stools around the bar, and the three other tables surrounded by club chairs were full. Gigi glanced around but didn't recognize anyone.

Declan himself came to take their order. Sienna opted for seltzer with lemon, Alice a Chardonnay, and Gigi a glass of Merlot.

"Can I tempt you ladies with dinner?" Declan gave a smile that Gigi thought was more tempting than anything that could possibly be on the menu. "I'm doing roast quail with fresh figs tonight."

They regretfully shook their heads, and Declan headed toward the bar with their order.

Alice watched him go. "He really is terribly good-looking. No wonder Stacy . . ." She sat up straighter and squared her shoulders. "Still. It isn't right."

A few minutes later, a waitress in an old-fashioned barmaid's uniform approached their table. She slipped glasses in front of each of them along with a dish of olives and a bowl of Marcona almonds. She smiled. "Anything else I can get you?" The ladies all shook their heads in response.

Alice watched as she walked away. "You won't believe what I just heard," she burst out as soon as the waitress was out of earshot.

"What?" Gigi and Sienna chorused.

"The police have arrested Vanessa Huff!" she exclaimed triumphantly. "At least she's been brought in for questioning, but I'm guessing an arrest is next."

"No!" Gigi and Sienna said in unison.

Alice nodded her head, setting her gray curls bobbing. She lowered her voice. "I don't know too much about it on account of Joe not being at the station at the moment, but one of the gals told me about it."

"Vanessa?" Gigi exclaimed, her glass of wine halfway to her mouth.

"You did say she was making a big play for Winchel." Sienna ran her finger around and around the ring of moisture her glass had left on the table. "Maybe they think she wanted to get Felicity out of the way."

"Unless we're dealing with two different murderers, it can't be Vanessa." Gigi explained about her trip into the city and how the girl at the Vandenberg Gallery had given Vanessa an alibi.

"Well, that does mean she didn't kill Derek, but I can definitely see her killing Felicity," Alice said. "She's ruthless. She wanted Felicity's man, and she wanted her part on the soap. Or"—Alice's face lit up with a sudden thought—"maybe she was in it with Don? Maybe she doesn't give a fig about Winchel but is just playing up to him to throw everyone off the scent, so to speak. Vanessa kills Felicity, and Don makes sure he has an alibi. Then when Derek becomes a problem, Don does the deed"—Alice ran her finger across her throat in a slicing gesture—"and Vanessa makes sure she's the one with the alibi."

"Have you told Mertz what you learned at the gallery?" Sienna rubbed her belly, which was pressed up against the cocktail table.

"I left a message, but I'll try him again." Gigi pulled her cell from her purse. She glanced at it and frowned. "No service. I'd better go outside."

"Vanessa can stew for a bit. Do her good, if you ask me. Besides, I imagine they'll hold her for theft of Felicity's Emmy if nothing else." Sienna put her hand on Gigi's arm. "You enjoy your drink."

"I have some news, too." Gigi looked around, but the people at the nearest tables were deep in conversation.

She explained about the clipping and how it appeared that the woman in the obituary was Anja's sister.

Sienna wrinkled her nose. "Don't you think it's rather odd that Anja would choose to work for the very woman who accused her sister of stealing? Assuming we're right, and Anja is this girl's sister."

"It's not odd at all." Gigi reached for an olive. "Not if Anja was planning on avenging her sister." She popped the olive into her mouth. "I think she got her revenge. I think she murdered Felicity."

Alice regarded Gigi with her mouth open in a round *O*.

Sienna took a sip of her lemon water. "Revenge is certainly a strong motive. Especially if the sisters were close."

Alice's face was creased in a deeply furrowed frown. Sienna turned toward her.

"What is it?"

"There's something we're forgetting." Alice worried her napkin between her fingers. "I can't get hold of it. Give me a minute." She furrowed her brow even more.

Suddenly she slapped the table with her hand. "I've got it now. Anja can't have done it. She wasn't there. Don't you remember? She went off into town on that bicycle of hers to fetch that special tea Felicity liked."

Gigi felt her face fall. She was surprised that her chin didn't actually hit the table. She was so positive that she'd solved Felicity's murder! She fiddled with the paper napkin under her drink.

"I suppose you're right," she said with a soupçon of ill humor.

"Cheer up! If it turns out Vanessa really didn't do it, we still have plenty of suspects." Alice reached for her purse. "I don't know about you, but I'd best be getting along home."

"Me, too." Sienna opened her purse, pulled out her wallet and put a credit card on the table.

Gigi pulled her wallet from her handbag with leaden fingers. She had been so sure she was right!

The waitress came by and swooped up the tabs. "I'll be right back with these."

She was as good as her word, and moments later they were headed toward the front door. Declan's had filled up, and many of the patrons looked as if they had come off the train from the city. Gigi supposed they were the ones who could afford Declan's prices for dishes like roast quail with figs.

The cold air outside made them all gasp, and Gigi pulled her collar up around her neck as they walked toward where she'd parked Alice's car.

"You look tired," Alice admonished Sienna when they reached Alice's Taurus. "You should go home and put your feet up."

"Oh, I will," Sienna assured her. "I just have to stop by Winchel's. I think I left my flash drive somewhere in the office I was using."

"Just be careful," Alice said with a dark look. "Terrible things have happened in that house."

"Don't be silly." Sienna gave Alice an affectionate squeeze. "Nothing is going to happen to me."

Gigi got behind the wheel, and after several false starts, the Taurus roared to life. She dropped Alice off at her house and gratefully turned the car toward home, breathing a sigh of relief as her cottage came into view. She pulled into the drive, and she and Reg got out.

The wind grabbed Gigi's scarf and slapped it playfully against her face. "Come on, Reg," she called to the Westie, who was busy sniffing a bush, "it's freezing out here."

Gigi closed her cottage door behind her, leaned against it and groaned with relief. It was good to be home! Reg ran through the living room and into the kitchen, sniffing furiously as if reacquainting himself with what were once old, familiar smells.

Gigi kicked off her shoes and padded out to the kitchen. Her stomach growled briefly, reminding her it was dinnertime. Fortunately, she had a container of homemade chicken soup in the freezer. She would heat that up and along with a piece of toast, she'd be more than satisfied.

She was pressing the defrost button on the microwave when Reg began mewling and scratching at the back door.

"All right, Mr. Whiny Pants, I'll take you out. Although I suspect what you really want to do is check out that bush you were sniffing earlier, a bit more thoroughly."

Gigi pulled her coat from the closet and put it on, Reg circling her legs the entire time. She stuck her hand into her pockets to retrieve her gloves. A piece of paper came out with them and fluttered to the floor.

She was tempted to leave it but instead bent and picked it up with a sigh. She glanced at it briefly and was about to put it on the table in the foyer when she did a double-take.

It was the receipt from Bon Appétit that she'd meant to give back to Anja. And the information on it made her knees weak and her hands tremble.

Chapter 27

"Come on, Reg," Gigi commanded as she opened the front door. "We've got to get over to Felicity's."

She had to drag him past the bush that had enticed him so, but he jumped into the car readily enough when Gigi opened the door.

Gigi had to resist the urge to speed on the way to Felicity's. She thought of calling Mertz, but by the time she explained the situation and convinced him she was right, it might be too late.

The receipt from Bon Appétit that she'd pulled from her pocket clearly showed that Anja had purchased Felicity's herbal tea three days before Felicity's murder. She had planned the whole thing in cold blood and had even given herself an alibi.

And Sienna was there, possibly alone, with a killer.

Gigi pressed down a little harder on the gas. Five miles over the limit ought to be safe enough. She rounded the corner, and nearly missed the turn into Felicity's driveway. She made the left on two wheels, cringing a bit at the squealing of her tires. The only car in the driveway was Sienna's. A light was on over the front door, but no other lights shone through the front windows.

Gigi parked behind Sienna's car. "You'll have to stay here," she said to Reg, who was ready to jump out as soon as she opened the door. "I'll be right back."

Gigi walked around toward the back of the house. A bright light was burning in the kitchen. It shone through the window and cast a pool of light on the shriveled herb garden outside. She tiptoed toward the back door and peered through the window. The room appeared to be empty, and there was a pair of black leather gloves sitting on the table alongside a purse that she thought she recognized as Anja's. She pressed her nose to the glass, attempting to see farther into the room, but it was in vain.

Gigi tried the back door handle and breathed a sigh of relief when it turned easily. She slipped into the kitchen and looked around. Everything was neat and tidy—all cleaned up and put to bed for the night. She wondered if Winchel was dining out. Certainly Anja had left no preparations for his evening meal.

There were no sounds from the hall, so Gigi cautiously inched out of the kitchen. The living room was dark except for a small lamp on top of the piano. The dining room was completely dark, and for once, there was no light coming from Winchel's library. Two battered-looking suitcases stood to the side of the front door. Gigi flipped the luggage tag over on one of them. Anja's name and a foreign address were printed in neat block letters. It looked as if Anja was ready to make a run for it.

Gigi began to creep up the staircase, staying to the side

where she knew the stairs wouldn't creak. She made the second-floor landing undisturbed. A wall sconce cast a dim splash of light across the carpet.

She rounded the bend in the staircase and started toward the third floor. She wanted to call out for Sienna, but didn't dare. If Winchel was home, he'd have every right to call the police and have her ejected. The thought of Mertz arriving to find her . . . her face burned like an overheated oven. She tiptoed even more quietly up the third flight of stairs toward Sienna's old office, and the room that had been Anja's.

A small lamp was lit in the hallway, but the rooms were dark. Gigi checked Sienna's office first, but no one was there. She wasn't surprised—why would Sienna be sitting there in the dark? She suppressed a nervous giggle at the thought and made her way toward the other end of the hall and Anja's room.

It, too, was cloaked in darkness. Gigi swept a hand along the wall until she found the light switch. The sudden glare from the overhead light nearly blinded her, and she closed her eyes quickly. When she was able to open them again, she could see that the room was empty. The picture frame was gone from the top of the dresser and so were the comb and brush and other little odds and ends Anja had kept there. She tiptoed farther into the room and slid open a drawer— also empty.

Gigi started down the back stairs, which would lead her directly to the kitchen. She paused every few steps to listen, but save for some creaks and groans, the old house was silent. She wondered where Anja had gone. Obviously her departure must be imminent if her bags were already packed and waiting by the door.

There was a noise, and Gigi nearly slid off the step. It was too faint to identify—it could have been coming from inside or out. Her heart beat so loudly in her ears that it was hard to hear, and she had to wait until the rhythm slowed. She had her foot on the last step when she heard the noise again. It was definitely coming from inside, and unless she was mistaken, it sounded like someone calling.

She peered into the kitchen, but Anja had not reappeared. She couldn't imagine where Sienna had gone—she couldn't be far away with her car still parked in the driveway. Gigi realized she hadn't checked the butler's pantry, although she couldn't imagine what on earth Sienna would be doing in there.

Just as Gigi pushed open the swinging door to the pantry, she heard the noise again. It was someone calling, and it sounded as if it were coming from the basement. She paused to listen and was caught off guard when someone shoved the pantry's swinging door hard against her.

Gigi stumbled backward and slipped on a throw rug. She went down hard, knocking her head against a cabinet door. She looked up to find Anja standing over her.

"Get up." Anja put out a hand, and Gigi had no choice but to grab it for support.

As soon as Gigi was on her feet, Anja transferred her grip to Gigi's upper arm.

"Ouch."

Anja snickered. "If you hadn't started sticking your nose into things." Anja gave a wicked smile. "Although it was very helpful when you discovered that I'd moved the chair away from the sauna after I was quite certain Madam was dead. I needed to know what your policeman knew to prepare myself." Anja threw her head back and laughed. "And then that idiot Vanessa taking Madam's Emmy. As if I cared." She snorted. "But at least it occupied the police for a while."

Anja had a viselike grip on Gigi, and although Gigi tried to pull away, Anja held fast.

"Let me go."

Anja shook her head, her lips set in a thin, determined line. "You're going to join your friend in the basement."

"Sienna?"

Anja nodded her head.

"You can't do that. She's pregnant. She's having the baby any day now."

"I do not care. It is her own fault."

By now, Anja had already hustled Gigi halfway to the basement door. The sounds she'd heard earlier were louder now, and she was fairly certain it was Sienna calling from the cellar. Gigi increased her struggles, but Anja increased her grip and marched her in lockstep even closer to the door.

Gigi's head throbbed, and she was fairly certain there would be a sizeable goose egg on her scalp. She gathered all her strength and tried to throw Anja off, but it was impossible. She grabbed the edge of the counter and held fast. Anja was momentarily stymied, but when she picked up a meat mallet and threatened to bring it down on Gigi's fingers, Gigi let go. She thought of grabbing for the mallet herself, but Anja blocked her before the idea had even completely formed.

Gigi thought she heard Reg barking from her car parked out front, and she panicked. What would Reg do without her? She renewed her efforts to break Anja's grip, but to no avail. She soon found herself face-to-face with the door to the basement. Sienna's cries were quite clear now. Her voice was choked with tears and that infuriated Gigi. She rounded on Anja with all her might, but Anja already had her hand on the doorknob and managed to yank the door open. She gave Gigi an almighty shove that sent her tumbling down the stairs head over heels.

Chapter 28

Gigi landed on the cold, stone floor with a thud. For a moment, she was too startled to understand where she was or what had happened, but it all came back as her head cleared. She looked up to find Sienna standing over her, her face collapsed in worry.

"Are you okay?" Sienna sniffed back tears.

"I'm not sure. I think so." Gigi moved both arms, then both legs. Nothing was broken, although she throbbed from her head to her toes. "Give me a hand." She held out her hand to Sienna and got rather unsteadily to her feet.

Gigi swayed slightly, and Sienna grabbed her quickly. "Maybe you'd better sit down."

"I'll be okay. Give me a minute." Gigi explored the back of her head. She was right—there was a huge goose egg forming. She winced and turned toward Sienna. "How are you? Is everything okay with the baby?"

Sienna put a hand on her protruding stomach. "I think so. It's kicking like mad, and that's a good sign."

"We have to get you out of here." Gigi looked around the basement. She'd been down there once before but hadn't paid much attention. Canned goods and other supplies were stacked on the rough wood shelving unit that lined one wall. A small window, caked with dirt, was high up on the other wall. Unfortunately, there were no ladders or even step stools that might have helped her reach it. She didn't doubt that Anja had already bolted the basement door, so there would be no escape that way.

"I guess we'll have to wait until Anja leaves and Winchel comes back." Sienna gave a brave smile. "We won't be down here forever." She brushed some dust off an overturned carton and sat down, a hand at her back.

"Are you sure you're okay?"

Sienna nodded. "A cramp. It's nothing." She closed her eyes and clenched her fists at her sides.

Gigi didn't believe her. Sienna was in labor. They were going to have to get out of there sooner rather than later.

"If I could reach that window," Gigi said when Sienna opened her eyes and looked up again.

"It's not worth it. Winchel is bound to come home eventually. We can wait till then. I don't want you to risk getting hurt."

Gigi bit down on her impatience. She didn't want to upset Sienna, so she spread out a plastic bag she found on one of the shelves and eased into a sitting position on the floor, her back against the shelving unit. She leaned her head back and closed her eyes. It was hard to think with her head throbbing so badly.

"What's that smell?" Sienna sniffed loudly.

Gigi's eyes flew back open. "What smell?"

"Maybe it's my imagination . . ." Sienna's brow furrowed as she took another deep breath.

Gigi closed her eyes and took a sniff. There was the hint of something in the air, but she couldn't place it. She inhaled deeply again.

Suddenly Sienna jumped to her feet. "It's gas! I smell gas."

Gigi shook her head. "No, I don't think . . ." She took a deeper breath and sputtered. "You're right. It's gas! Anja must have turned on all the burners and blew out the flames." She turned toward Sienna. "We have to get out of here now. If there's a spark . . ."

Sienna gave a sob and once again closed her eyes, both hands pressed hard against her back.

"If I could reach that window . . ." Gigi looked around the basement again, but nothing had materialized since her earlier perusal. The shelving unit caught her eye, and she went over to examine it. She gave it a good shake.

"This doesn't appear to be attached to the wall," she said excitedly. "If we can take everything off and move this over by the window, perhaps I can use it as a ladder."

"Are you sure? It's not very sturdy."

Gigi coughed. The smell was getting stronger. "We don't have any choice." She started shifting cans of diced tomatoes and chicken broth to the floor. "It's this or . . ." She didn't have to spell out the consequences to Sienna, who immediately began moving some of the lighter items.

By the time the shelves were emptied, Gigi was sweating and sneezing from the dust; however, the most difficult part of the task was still at hand—moving the unit itself. It was fairly light but very awkward. Gigi would have been tempted to give up except for the strengthening smell of gas and the thought that at any minute a spark could blow them both sky high.

With Sienna's help, she finally maneuvered the shelving under the sole basement window and the next step was at hand—climbing the thing. Gigi wasn't a huge fan of heights, but she could manage if she were careful not to look down or to think about it too much.

"If you can hold it here"—she indicated a place to Sienna—"then I think it will be steady enough." Gigi looked up at the pieces of wood nailed haphazardly together, and her stomach plummeted as if she were on the downward slope of a roller coaster. But she had to put on a brave face for Sienna. And, as the famous slogan put it, "just do it."

She grasped one of the upper shelves with a firm grip and stepped onto the first shelf. The whole construction wobbled a lot less than she'd anticipated, and emboldened, she took another step. This time, the unit swayed slightly, but she was able to hold fast. The wood was rough under her fingertips, and she winced as she felt a splinter slice through the skin of her thumb, but she didn't stop. The smell of gas increased with every passing second.

Gigi looked down to see Sienna staring up at her, her lip caught between her teeth and her face pinched with worry. Gigi gave her a reassuring smile and struck out for the next rung, or rather, shelf. She was now level with the window. Gigi felt a jolt of triumph, but it didn't last. The most difficult part was still ahead of her. She had to squeeze onto the shelf to actually reach the window. As soon as she tried to lever her whole body onto the wood slab, the unit swayed dangerously, as if a tropical storm had suddenly hit. Gigi held on for dear life as Sienna tried to steady the increasingly wobbly structure.

"Are you okay?" Sienna gasped, staring up at Gigi in horror.

"I'm fine," Gigi lied between gritted teeth. "If you can hold it steady for another minute, I think I can do this."

Sienna increased her grip, and Gigi slowly eased onto the shelf nearest the window. The shelf held, and the whole structure actually steadied. She took a moment to catch her breath and offer up a silent prayer of thanks.

The basement window looked even grimier up close, with dirt caked into all four corners and cobwebs crisscrossing the glass. Gigi prayed it would open easily enough. She didn't have much leverage in the position she was in. A tiny spider spun toward her face on a gossamer piece of web, and she forced herself not to scream or even move. She clamped her eyes shut, and when she opened them again, the spider was gone. The thought crossed her mind that it might now be entangled in her hair somewhere, and she forced herself to think about something else.

The window latch looked as if it hadn't been touched in decades, but it moved freely enough. Gigi let out her breath in a sigh of relief. She was one step closer to getting Sienna safely to the hospital.

Gigi gave the window a good shove, and it opened almost as easily as the latch had. It was a bit of a struggle getting through the space. She winced when she heard a loud rip as her jacket caught on something. She was glad she was wearing her old fleece and not the new leather one she'd treated herself to.

The window was barely above ground level, and Gigi found herself lying facedown in the pile of leaves that had collected alongside the house's foundation. She stumbled to her feet and brushed at the dirt and bits of twigs and leaves that clung to the front of her jacket and the knees of her jeans. She sensed a presence and looked up to find Anja staring at her with those frigid blue eyes of hers.

"Very clever. How did you manage it?"

Gigi's heart was still beating so loudly she barely heard Anja's words. She gestured toward the open window. "The shelving unit."

"As I said, very clever. But I'm afraid, not clever enough." Anja brought her right arm out from behind her back.

Gigi took a step backward when she saw the shovel in Anja's hand.

"One of the gardeners very conveniently left this lying against the side of the house instead of putting it away." Anja gave a hiss of annoyance, presumably at the employee's laziness.

Even before Anja raised the shovel over her head, Gigi was off and running. She ran as fast as she ever had, fairly certain she had to be setting some kind of record. She kept going even when her breath became so ragged it tore at her chest and she tasted blood in her mouth. Anja was never more than a few feet behind. Her breath sounded like a locomotive in Gigi's ears, and it spurred her on even after she nearly tripped and fell, and again after she twisted her ankle on the hidden roots of a tree.

She was at the bend in the driveway now, probably halfway down its length. She tried to think, but fear propelled her forward with no plan beyond outdistancing and outlasting Anja and the menacing iron shovel.

Gigi felt something catch at her jacket and glance off her shoulder. She bit her lip in pain. Anja was right behind her and swinging wildly. Tears blurred Gigi's vision, and she narrowly escaped colliding with a tree. She didn't know how much longer she could run. Anja must have superhuman powers because she kept coming and coming.

Another blow glancing off her right shoulder gave Gigi a shot of adrenaline, and she made a last-ditch effort to pick up speed. She heard the shovel slice through the air but felt nothing. Anja must have dropped back at last. Gigi was rounding the second bend in the driveway when she ran smack into something.

It wasn't a tree—it was quite hard but at the same time, softer and more yielding. She looked up to discover Detective Mertz towering over her. Suddenly several people in uniform rushed out of the shadows and whizzed past Gigi and Mertz. She heard scuffling and the sounds of a struggle. She turned around to see Anja handcuffed and subdued between two burly policemen.

She gave Gigi a venomous stare, her lips drawn back into an animal-like snarl. "I only wanted revenge for my sister. Is there something so wrong with that?" She tried to shake off the men gripping each of her arms.

"But murder?" Gigi squeaked.

"She deserved it." Anja spit furiously. "She accused my sister of stealing, and Monica was deported. She took her own life."

Gigi gasped.

"All along it was that useless stepson of hers, Derek, who was taking the money. He got his just deserts, that's for sure. Can you believe he tried to blackmail me?" she shouted after Gigi as the policemen hustled her into the waiting squad car, its lights throwing a whirling display of colors against the side of Felicity's house.

"What about Sienna?" Gigi turned to Mertz. "We have to get her out of there."

Mertz gestured toward the fire truck in front of the police cruiser. "The firemen have turned off the gas and opened all the windows. They'll have her out in a second."

"I think she's in labor."

Mertz turned around, startled. "Labor? Really?"

Gigi shook her head.

He reached through his open car door, grabbed his radio and barked orders at the person on the other end. He turned back to Gigi. "Ambulance will be here in a few."

"How did you—"

"Come to be here?" Mertz finished for her. "Your dog." He pointed toward Alice's Taurus where Reg was now curled up, asleep, on the back package shelf. "I guess he started barking, and it irritated the old geezer who lives down the road, and he called in a complaint. I was on my way out here anyway to ask Winchel a few more questions, so I agreed to check on it. When I saw Reg sitting in the car, barking his head off, I knew something had to be up. It's not like him to make a racket like that for no reason. Then, as I got closer to the house, I smelled the gas and called in the fire brigade. Next thing I know you're running smack into my arms."

"I didn't run into your arms." Gigi felt her face blossom with heat.

"In a manner of speaking, you most certainly did." The smile on Mertz's face made Gigi go all weak in the knees.

"Here she is!" Gigi heard someone shout. She peered through the trees and saw someone in uniform carrying Sienna down the driveway.

"Sienna!" Gigi, ran, panicked, toward her friend. "Are you okay?"

Sienna was very white, but her eyes fluttered open when she heard Gigi's voice. "I'll be fine," she whispered and closed her eyes again.

"Bus is here," someone called, and Gigi caught sight of headlights coming up the drive.

The ambulance pulled up behind the squad cars, adding

another rotating halo of light to the scene. A man and a woman jumped out, yanked out a gurney and within seconds had Sienna safely in place. They loaded her into the back, and Gigi could see them taking her vitals and starting an IV drip.

She fished her cell phone from her purse and dialed Oliver's number. Before Gigi even hung up, Oliver was in his car on the way to the hospital.

Mertz was busy commanding his troops, so Gigi waved and got into her own car. Reg lazily climbed down from the package shelf and came over to lick her face in greeting. She ruffled his fur and kissed the top of his head. "You're a hero, Reg. You saved me and Sienna."

Reg preened himself a bit and then settled into the passenger seat to continue his nap.

"We're off to the hospital, boy. Sienna is having her baby."

Chapter 29

Gigi was still shaking when she arrived at Woodstone Hospital. She'd thought about running Reg home—he'd already spent way too long sitting in the car—but he was napping peacefully on the passenger seat still, and she hoped he wouldn't mind waiting a bit longer. She wouldn't rest until she found out how Sienna was doing.

She recognized Oliver's BMW in the emergency parking lot and pulled into a space three cars down. The woman at the reception desk took forever, asking Gigi a million and one questions before finally issuing her a pass and directing her to room twelve. Gigi was almost dancing with impatience by the time she was ushered through the door.

She passed room ten, eleven and then came to the curtain blocking cubicle number twelve. "Hello?" she called out.

Oliver's reassuring baritone greeted her, and she pushed the curtain to one side. Sienna was sitting up in the hospital bed, an IV running into her arm and a pulse oximeter clipped to one of her fingers. She was pale but looked okay.

Oliver smiled when Gigi entered, and gave a thumbs-up. "We're on our way to the maternity ward. Looks like this baby is finally coming."

"Really!" Gigi gave Sienna a quick hug.

"It's the first, so it could be a while—then again . . . ?" Oliver shrugged.

"You'll let me know the minute—"

"Of course." Sienna smiled reassuringly.

"Well, I've left Reg alone in the car long enough. I think I'll go home and . . . wait."

"Hopefully not too long." Sienna grimaced slightly and put her hands on her belly.

Oliver leaned over her, stroking her forehead and smoothing her hair back.

Gigi backed out of the cubicle. They didn't need her there right now. She felt a pang of jealousy and wondered when she'd find someone to be there for her.

The thought that Mertz had shown up at just the moment she needed him crossed her mind, and she smiled to herself.

Gigi headed back to her car. Reg lifted his head briefly when she opened the door, but by the time they were out of the lot, he was back to sleep again.

Gigi was extremely grateful when she rounded the corner and her cottage came into view. She thought about soaking her aching bones in a nice, hot bath but decided that she'd probably crawl straight into bed instead.

The message light on her phone was blinking. Gigi hesitated with her finger over the flashing button. What could be so important that it couldn't wait till tomorrow? But maybe Oliver had called? Maybe the baby had arrived, jet propelled, while Gigi was on her way home?

She pushed play. A deep unfamiliar voice came through the speaker. It was Victor Branston. A chill swept Gigi from her head to her toes. Was this going to be good news or bad?

Branston Foods was located several miles outside of Woodstone in a small industrial park. The building was a long, low rectangle with a large parking lot in the rear. Gigi pulled Alice's Taurus into one of the spaces marked *Visitor* and got out.

Branston hadn't revealed much in his voice mail message—just that his secretary would be in touch about a meeting. Gigi had e-mailed him the set of recipes she'd created, and his test kitchen was going to assess their suitability for freezing. Gigi crossed her fingers. *Please let this be good news.*

The lobby of Branston Foods was spare, with floor-to-ceiling windows that looked out onto a patch of shriveled grass, a few small trees and a deserted-looking park bench. The furniture was utilitarian, and there was a coat rack behind the receptionist's desk.

Gigi gave her name and was told to wait. She eased onto a fake leather chair and tried to calm the butterflies in her stomach. Barely two minutes later, a door to the left opened, and a woman came out. She was wearing dark slacks and a turtleneck, and her gray-streaked brown hair was cut short.

"Gigi?" She smiled and held out her hand.

Gigi hoped her own hand wasn't sweating, and she was tempted to wipe it on her coat before extending it.

She followed the woman through the door and into a carpeted corridor lined with open doors. Various plaques hung from the walls, as did a large gold-framed picture of Victor Branston.

The woman led Gigi into a small anteroom with a desk, computer and what Gigi thought was transcription equipment. A large, fake ficus tree stood in the corner. Another framed portrait of Victor Branston dominated one wall. The woman tapped lightly on a door at the rear of the office, then cracked it open and stuck her head around the edge.

"Miss Fitzgerald is here."

"Send her in, then."

Gigi recognized the voice as Victor Branston's. She sent up a quick prayer and entered.

"Gigi!" Branston said warmly, coming out from behind his desk to shake Gigi's hand. He clapped her on the shoulder. "I appreciate your coming today." He led her toward two armchairs arranged around a low wooden table. "Please. Have a seat."

Gigi settled into one of the chairs. The seat was very deep, and she had to move forward a bit to avoid having her feet dangle off the floor. Branston sprawled in the other one, one leg crossed casually over the other, revealing a peek at his diamond-patterned socks. He had the look of a top executive—silver gray hair cut just so, expensively tailored suit, autocratic nose—but Gigi had always found him to be surprisingly warm despite his position.

She tried to gauge his thoughts from his expression, but like any good CEO, he kept them well hidden behind a noncommittal exterior.

"Well." Branston clapped his hands together and rubbed them briskly. "Our test kitchen has checked out all your delicious recipes, and if you're in agreement, we'd like to get going right away on a line of Gigi's Gourmet De-Lite frozen meals."

Gigi's heart, which felt as if it had stopped, started again with a giant *thud*. She felt the grin that broke out across her face. So much for playing her cards close to her vest.

"Wonderful," was all she could manage.

"Some of the recipes will have to be adapted, of course, for the freezing process." He held up a hand. "Nothing that would change the taste or quality, don't worry about that. Sometimes flavors have to be heightened in order to withstand being frozen."

Gigi nodded mutely. The rest of the room had retreated to a haze, and Branston's voice sounded as if it were coming at her through a long, hollow tube. She shook her head in an attempt to clear it.

"We're going to start with your excellent beef stew, the chicken tortilla soup, your low-fat Swedish meatballs and for our breakfast entry, the Mexican egg tortilla. How does that sound?"

Gigi still hadn't found her voice and settled for nodding yet again.

The rest of the meeting went quickly, and what seemed like only minutes later, Gigi was waving good-bye to the receptionist and heading toward where she'd parked the MINI.

She had to restrain herself from giving a small skip as she walked to the car. It was hard to believe that in several months' time, grocery stores all around the area would be carrying meals with *her* name on them. From *her* recipes.

She was overcome with a sense of lightness she hadn't felt in a long time.

The first dusting of snow arrived in Woodstone two weeks before Thanksgiving. It frosted the tree branches, twinkled on the grass and gave a festive, Christmas-card appearance to the whole town. It was the perfect setting for Declan McQuaid's pre-Thanksgiving dinner to benefit Joe and Stacy Flanagan. Sienna and Oliver were going, bringing along two-week-old Camille Paisley, whom Gigi, Oliver and Sienna all agreed was the most adorable, intelligent and charming baby girl ever born. Alice was going, of course, and Evelyn Fishko from Bon Appétit, virtually all the other shopkeepers and a good number of the townspeople as well. Even Mertz planned to be there, assuming there wasn't a crisis that required police presence.

Which was why Gigi was taking so much trouble with her outfit. Reg sat curled up on the braided rug in her bedroom watching as she slid into her new dress—the one she'd bought for her date with Mertz that had turned out so disastrously. The cleaner's had done an admirable job of getting the stains out from her spilled dinner. So what if Mertz had already seen it? No one else had, and she knew from experience that clothing wasn't the sort of thing men remembered—sports stats, maybe, but not fashion. Reg nodded his approval, or so Gigi imagined, as she twirled in front of the mirror.

Gigi refilled Reg's water dish, tidied a few things in the kitchen and got her coat from the closet—the good one she wore constantly in New York but had hardly looked at since moving to Woodstone.

"I'll be back soon," she reassured Reg as she closed and locked the front door.

Her MINI was waiting in the driveway, clean and polished and good as new. She was thrilled to have it back. She'd been grateful for the loan of Alice's car but had really missed her own.

The parking lot at Declan's was filled when Gigi got there.

She was pleased to see that he had such a great turnout. She drove past and found a spot on the street outside Bon Appétit. She pulled her collar closer around her neck, yanked her hat down over her ears and began to walk the block back toward the restaurant. A plume rose from Declan's chimney, and the delicious scent of wood smoke filled the air.

The mellow sounds of voices and tinkling glasses, along with the aroma of roast turkey and other delicious dishes, washed over Gigi as soon as she pulled open the door. She stood for a moment to take in the scene. Fires crackled in the fireplaces where groups of people gathered, the men in blazers and sweaters, the women in knit dresses and suede jackets. Once again, Gigi was glad she'd splurged on her new outfit. She looked good, and she knew it.

The tables were already set with pumpkin-colored napery and vases filled with autumn leaves. The silver shined, the glasses twinkled; it was magical. Declan had done a splendid job. Gigi noticed Joe Flanagan ensconced in a deep red velvet armchair, his leg propped on an ottoman. The small table at his side held a drink and a plate of hors d'oeuvres. He was being treated like royalty, and Gigi thought he looked like he was enjoying it thoroughly. She wondered how he'd feel if he knew that his wife and Declan were going around behind his back.

"Gigi!"

Gigi turned to see Alice rushing toward her, her cheeks flushed red and her halo of curls flying every which way.

"It's wonderful, isn't it?" She grabbed Gigi's hand and gave it a squeeze. "I couldn't believe it when I found out Declan was planning this. It's incredible. This is going to mean the world to Joe and Stacy."

Alice waved to someone, and Gigi turned to look in that direction. It was Stacy . . . in an old-fashioned barmaid's uniform, complete with full skirt and off-the-shoulder blouse.

Alice squeezed Gigi's arm. "Stacy has been working here! Isn't that great? I had no idea. I'm afraid I jumped to the wrong conclusion."

"So did I," Gigi admitted.

"And everything with her and Joe is okay again. Nearly losing him after that fall made her realize what he means to her." Alice smiled benignly in Stacy's direction, but Stacy was busy handing around a tray of drinks.

A blast of cold air blew across the room, and Gigi glanced toward the door. Sienna and Oliver were closing it behind them. Oliver was holding a baby carrier that was completely swathed in a pink and white knitted blanket.

"Oh, it's Sienna with the baby!" Alice exclaimed. "I haven't seen the little angel since the hospital."

Gigi and Alice wended their way through the crowd toward the front of the room. Oliver had placed the carrier on a chair and was hanging up his and Sienna's coats. Sienna began to unwrap the blanket, and Gigi and Alice waited with bated breath until the little sleeping beauty was revealed. She had soft curls and long, dark lashes that rested against her plump, pink cheeks. Gigi thought she was the most beautiful baby she'd ever seen.

"And how is little Miss Camille today?"

"She's wonderful," Sienna cooed as she undid the baby's tiny pink jacket. "A little gassy, though."

"Fennel tea," Alice said knowledgeably. "It worked a charm for my Stacy. My grandmother used it, and so did my mother."

"Really?" Sienna paused in removing Camille's coat.

Alice nodded, and her curls bobbed briskly. "Boil a

spoonful of fennel seeds in some water, add a little sugar and let it cool. It will have her right as rain in no time." Alice chucked Camille under the chin, and the baby sighed and turned her head but didn't wake.

"I'll have to try that."

Oliver returned from the coat check with two ticket stubs which he tucked into his pocket. "I hear we've got some celebrating to do." He smiled at Gigi.

Gigi grinned back. "I guess we do."

"What's this?" Alice looked from Gigi to Oliver and back again.

"I've just signed a contract with Branston Foods."

"Gigi's Gourmet De-Lite is going big time," Sienna said.

Alice clapped her hands. "Wonderful news! Just wonderful."

Gigi beamed at them all.

Sienna grinned as well. "Oliver has some good news, too."

Oliver looked down at his shoes briefly. "Yes, I do. I've snared a couple of new clients so everything is going to be all right."

"That's great," they all chorused.

"As a matter of fact, Jack Winchel is one of them. He's being investigated for some SEC irregularities."

"No more gambling," Sienna said, shaking her finger at her husband in mock-sternness.

"Absolutely no more gambling," Oliver said. "It was terribly boring and not very lucrative."

"I found out something interesting," Sienna said. "A former colleague in New York heard it and passed the information along to me. With Vanessa Huff still in jail for theft, they decided to replace her with that girl, Tammy, who Gigi met at Derek's funeral."

"I'm happy about that." Gigi felt a warm glow. She had liked Tammy and was glad to hear that she was going to be getting ahead.

"Is there a quiet place where we can sit with the baby?" Camille had begun to stir, and Sienna stroked her cheek soothingly.

Gigi craned her neck. "Your best bet seems to be over there." She pointed toward the other end of the room where the crowd was thinner.

Sienna and Oliver moved off, with Alice clucking along behind them, and Gigi was momentarily alone. Before she could move, Declan was at her elbow.

"I'm so sorry. I meant to come over and greet you as soon as you came in, but there was a crisis in the kitchen."

"Oh no."

He waved a hand. "Nothing that couldn't be solved. But I hate to see a pretty lady standing alone."

Gigi didn't know what to say, but she did know that her face was getting as red as the flames in the fireplace. "Everything looks wonderful," she said to change the subject.

Declan gave a satisfied smile. "I'm very pleased. We're going to raise a lot of money for Stacy and Joe."

"It really is amazing of you to go to all this trouble."

Declan shot her a wicked grin. "It's marketing, remember? I had to find some way to ingratiate myself with your little community. The fact that it's helping two really nice people is icing on the cake."

Gigi felt a movement at her side and turned to see Mertz standing there. Very close, so close that they were almost touching. He looked down at Gigi. Their eyes met, and the look in his said everything.

"I've brought you a glass of that wine you like." Mertz

handed her a goblet half full of a ruby red liquid and looked up to glare at Declan.

Declan shrugged, raised an eyebrow and gave Gigi a crooked grin that said *You win some, you lose some.*

Gigi felt a momentary pang of regret, but then she looked at Mertz, who was smiling at her, and it passed, replaced by a warm glow of satisfaction.

....

Recipes

....

"Magic" Omelet

This is an easy way to have breakfast cooking while you're in the shower!

2 eggs
2 tablespoons chopped onion
2 tablespoons chopped red or green pepper
    (or combination)
2 mushrooms, sliced
2 tablespoons low-fat cheese, grated
    (cheddar, Swiss or your favorite)
1 heavy-duty gallon-size ziplock bag

Bring a medium pot of water to a boil. Crack the eggs into the ziplock bag and add the remaining ingredients (or your favorite omelet fixings). Close the bag securely and "squish" the ingredients together, breaking up the eggs. Carefully place the bag in boiling water and boil for 13 minutes. Remove the bag from the water, roll the omelet from the bag onto a plate, top with salt and pepper to taste and enjoy!

1 serving, 190 calories

For a festive brunch, set out quantities of omelet ingredients. Have each guest label their bag with their name in permanent marker and choose their ingredients. Place all bags in a large pot of boiling water for 13 minutes, then serve.

Smoky Chipotle Chili

This is a rich-tasting, smoky chili with the addition of a "secret" ingredient—chocolate! The chocolate adds depth, and the dried chipotle chili (a smoked jalapeno) adds the smokiness. It is on the thick side, so if you prefer your chili to be closer to a soup, add water. To make it "de-liteful," I've used ground turkey. Feel free to substitute lean ground beef if you prefer. I like a combination of beans—feel free to substitute your favorites.

1 medium onion, chopped
2 garlic cloves, pressed
1 tablespoon extra-virgin olive oil
1.25 pounds lean ground turkey
2 ½ tablespoons chili powder
2 teaspoons unsweetened cocoa powder
2 teaspoons dried oregano

2 teaspoons ground cumin
1 teaspoon salt or to taste
1 28-ounce can diced tomatoes
1 15-ounce can black beans, drained and rinsed
1 15-ounce can red kidney beans, drained and rinsed
1 15-ounce can pinto beans, drained and rinsed
1 dried chipotle chili

Sauté the onions and garlic in the extra-virgin olive oil over medium heat until the onion softens. Add the turkey and cook, stirring occasionally, until browned. Add the remaining ingredients (bury chipotle chili in the pot) and simmer for 30 minutes.

Top individual servings with low-fat sour cream and low-fat grated cheese, if desired.

Makes 10 servings, 235 calories per serving, not including toppings.

Tilapia à la Provençal

1 tablespoon extra-virgin olive oil
2 garlic cloves, crushed
1 small onion, diced
1 14.5-ounce can diced tomatoes
¼ cup white wine or vermouth
½ teaspoon herbes de Provence
Salt and pepper to taste
2 tilapia fillets (or other mild white fish), approximately
    6 ounces each

In a medium sauté pan, heat the olive oil over medium heat. Add the garlic and diced onions and sauté 3 to 4 minutes until translucent.

Add the tomatoes and sauté briefly. Add the wine or vermouth and bring to a boil for 30 to 60 seconds to burn off the alcohol. Stir in the herbes de Provence and salt and pepper to taste. Simmer on low for 5 minutes.

Place the fish on top of the tomato mixture and spoon some tomatoes over the fillets. Cover and simmer gently until the fish is opaque and cooked through, approximately 5 to 7 minutes depending on the thickness.

Serve over rice or orzo (rice-shaped pasta).

2 servings, 294 calories per serving (not including rice)